I0738694

FORK IN THE CRICK

Rebecca Zook's Amish Romance

Book Two

Granville Wyche Burgess

Copyright © 2018 by Granville Wyche Burgess

All rights reserved. No part of this book may be used or reproduced in any manner whatsoever without written permission except in the case of brief quotations embodied in critical articles or reviews.

This is a work of fiction. Names, characters, places and incidents either are the product of the author's imagination or are used fictitiously, and any resemblance to actual persons, living or dead, business establishments, events or locales is entirely coincidental.

ISBN 978-0-9913274-9-2

Front cover illustration and book design by Fiona Jayde

Chickadee Prince Logo by Garrett Gilchrist

Visit us at www.ChickadeePrince. com

First Printing

GRANVILLE WYCHE BURGESS

FORK IN THE CRICK

Rebecca Zook's Amish Romance

Book Two

GRANVILLE WYCHE BURGESS received an Emmy nomination for his writing on the soap opera, *Capitol*. He has also received awards from the CBS/Foundation for the Dramatist Guild, the National Endowment for the Humanities, and the Pennsylvania Council on the Arts.

He has also written for the television series, *Tales From The Darkside*, and for PBS. His musical, *Conrack*, based on the Pat Conroy memoir, *The Water Is Wide*, had a sold-out run at Ford's Theatre and was attended by President George H.W. Bush and the first lady, Barbara Bush. Mr. Burgess' plays and musicals have been performed throughout the United States. He is CEO of Quill Entertainment, a charitable company whose mission is "Teaching America's Heritage Through Story and Song."

He lives in Connecticut with his Amish-Mennonite wife, Reba.

Fork in the Crick is his second published novel.

ALSO BY GRANVILLE WYCHE BURGESS:

STONE IN THE CRICK; REBECCA ZOOK'S AMISH ROMANCE, BOOK ONE

DUSKY SALLY

THE FREAK: A PLAY ABOUT EDGAR CAYCE

PLAY IT AS IT LIES

FORK IN THE CRICK

Rebecca Zook's Amish Romance
Book Two

Chickadee Prince Books
Brooklyn, New York

To Reba, my Amish romance

CHAPTER 1

All was so still early in the morning, and so calm. Rebecca Zook drew a deep breath, filling her lungs with the clean, crisp air. She looked down at her hands, folded gently over the Amish quilt she herself had made. Gently she spread them back and forth over the squares of dark purple and lush green, relishing the feel of soft cotton. She raised her eyes to watch the sun rise over the faraway hills. It would be another beautiful day on her farm in Honey Brook, Pennsylvania, a day like thousands before it and thousands more after, no doubt. Except this day would be different. This was the day Rebecca had promised herself she would decide.

This thought disturbed the quiet inside her and she rose to look out the window of her upstairs bedroom. The hay fields were already mowed and piles of hay were stacked high in the barn. The tobacco, too, was hanging in the tobacco shed. Soon brokers would come to negotiate a price with her father, Elam. Only the corn remained in the fields, standing stock-still in the windless morning. It, too, would be harvested soon. Harvest time. That's when she had told Jacob she would decide. "Before all the crops are in." Only a final crop remained. It wouldn't be fair to wait any longer.

Rebecca took her plain blue dress down from its hook, stepped into it, and pulled a cape over the top. She combed her long, brown hair, carefully twisted it, securing it in a knot, then placed the white covering on her head and tied it in back. Below her, she could hear her mother, Mabel, and her aunt, Hanna, stirring in the kitchen, making coffee. She listened for a moment to the soothing murmur of their voices. How many times had she stood in this exact spot and listened in this exact way? The sameness of Amish life could be so satisfying. And yet this sameness was also what had been troubling Rebecca of late.

She had felt stuck in her life, like the large stone in the crick that ran through their farm before tumbling into the river — which everyone also called the crick — at the edge of their property. But a month ago, after a torrential downpour — *hoch wasser*, "high water," Hanna had called it — Rebecca had noticed that the stone had moved. She had been so excited, taking it as a sign that her life was beginning to move in new directions, too. But there was one thing holding her back: her decision.

"Morning, Mam," she called out, entering the kitchen.

"Morning, Rebecca. Here's some coffee." Her mother poured her a cup.

"Becca, today's wash day. You got anything needs cleaning?" asked Hanna.

Rebecca smiled to herself. Sameness: If it's Monday, it's washday. "I've already put it in the wash house, Hanna."

"You won't believe what I saw on a wash line yesterday," Hanna began, sipping her coffee. "Underwear so skinny you could hardly see it."

"We're not interested, Hanna," Mabel said,

"Well, I'm interested in telling you," Hanna replied. "And it was pink! These English, they got no shame. You think women really wear such a thing, Becca?"

"I don't know, Hanna."

"Might as well wear nothing, if they're just going to wear two pieces of string."

"Hanna, could we change the subject?" Mabel asked her sister.

"Sure. Let's talk about men's underwear!" Hanna shot back. Rebecca laughed out loud.

"Hanna!" Mabel shouted.

"I was just teasing you, Mabel. I'm not interested in men's underwear."

"Thank the Lord," Mabel muttered.

Rebecca smiled at the familiar fussing between the two sisters. Hanna often provoked Mabel with her unexpected thoughts and actions. She had been thrown from a horse when a little girl, had landed on her head, and the injury had caused her brain to not develop normally. She was perfectly healthy otherwise and worked as hard as anyone about the farm. She was uninhibited and a little naïve. As far as Rebecca was concerned, it only made her more delightful.

"Speaking of men's underwear, when are you and Jacob gonna get married?" Hanna suddenly asked Rebecca. Rebecca laughed again, despite the subject matter.

"Yes," Mabel followed. "November is coming soon. Madie Lapp and Amos Yoder are getting married, you know."

Yes, Rebecca knew. How could she not; Madie mentioned it every time she saw her. She was only twenty, two years younger than Rebecca. *Twenty!* Rebecca thought. She and Amos might be married sixty years, even longer. Rebecca found it hard to imagine living with the same man for all that time. Sometimes marriages didn't work out, the husband and wife eventually living apart, but never divorcing. No, if she were to marry Jacob, it would be forever.

"Jacob and I are going to talk about it soon," Rebecca answered as vaguely as she could, then quickly grabbed the egg basket and scooted out the door.

"He's a *gut* man, he'll make a *gut* husband!" Mabel called after her.

Yes, he is a gut man. He's kind, considerate, a hard-worker, from a good family, has a gut farm.... She ran through the list of Jacob's attributes in her head. "You'd be a crazy not to marry him," Madie had said to her. *But maybe I'd be crazy to marry him.* She sighed. How would she ever be sure? She shook her head to clear her mind. *God, help me to know.*

As she moved toward the hen house, Rebecca glanced at the small cottage down the hill near the crick. No sign of life. *The English! So lazy! Guess he's still asleep.* She slowed her steps, then smiled at herself. *I'm like some silly schoolgirl, just hoping I'll catch a glimpse of him.* She hurried on her way, trying to dismiss from her thoughts the man in the cottage.

She might as well have tried to stop thinking at all. It seemed thoughts of Gregory Pinckney were all that filled her head some days. Had it only been four months since he had arrived at their farm seeking lodging for himself and his horse, Bojangles? Only two months since Gregory had driven Rebecca, her mother, and Hanna to New York City to see a quilt wall hanging Rebecca had made that was being displayed in a gallery? Only one month since that magical horseback ride on Bo, when her hair had come loose from her covering and Gregory had let it down and kissed her? Rebecca shivered a little, despite the warm morning. She thought of Madie's name for what she had felt when Gregory had kissed her. The "stirring." Yes, she had definitely been stirred.

Yet they had hardly seen each other this past month. She had been very busy talking with Mrs. Ansbacher, planning to take over the quilt shop she was selling to Rebecca. And Gregory had been spending a lot of time at Heminger Stables, helping Mrs. Heminger cope with the loss of her husband, Ivan, and telephoning Ivan's daughter, Wanda, who was away at Penn State. Gregory said Wanda was thinking of coming back home to be with her mother. Rebecca hoped that would mean he wouldn't have to spend so much time there. So what? Even if he were around much, it wasn't as if they could spend a lot of time together. He couldn't court her; he was English and she was Amish. In fact, the few times they were together felt somehow odd. What were they supposed to do, fall into each other's arms every time they met?

Rebecca laughed at the idea. She didn't even know how Gregory felt about her. They hadn't discussed their feelings. She could guess, but in matters of love, were you supposed to guess? And how did she feel about Gregory? Certainly different from the way she felt about Jacob. But was it love? She knew what it was like to love her family and to love God, but she didn't think she knew what it meant to love a man. How was she supposed to find out? And if she did find out, would it mean living for sixty-plus years with the same man? So many questions!

She ducked inside the hen house, glad to focus on something else. "Shoo!" She swatted a hen from her nest and picked up a small brown egg. It felt warm in her hand. She put it in her basket and quickly gathered the other three eggs in the nest, then moved to the next one. Slowly and patiently she filled her basket to the cluck-clucking of the mother hens. Rebecca liked chickens, the noises they made, the way they skittered about. There was something soothing about a chicken, something natural, something common, really, but common in a good way, common like grass was common. They weren't wondrous, like, say, a whale — though Rebecca had only seen pictures of whales. They weren't marvelous, like a night sky full of stars. They were just ... there. A solid presence. Rebecca liked to think of God like that. Just there, always there. She didn't need to think about His power and strength and all the miracles He could perform. She just liked to think about His presence. "Be present with me" began one of her favorite prayers, "and I'll be present with you."

She took the eggs back to the house. Along the way she saw Elam and her brother, Henry, milking the cows, and she waved. Soon they would come in and the family would sit down to a big breakfast of bacon, eggs, potato cakes, and milk. She noticed her brother and father had a few more cows to milk. If she hurried, she might have time to make her decision. She deposited the eggs on the kitchen counter, glad to hear her mother and aunt in the washhouse starting on the clothes, and then hurried towards the barn.

As soon as she entered the large white barn, the air turned thick with the smell of hay. The bottom floor of the barn was cement. A plow rested in one corner, a baling machine in another; an old wagon wheel leaned against a wall, with an old barrel beside it. Various farm implements were scattered about. Against a far wall, a ladder snaked up through a hole to the second floor. Rebecca gathered her dress in one hand and climbed the ladder. She emerged onto the second floor to find bales of hay stacked high on half the floor; the other was half-cleared, with a basketball hoop nailed to the far wall. When he had time, Henry liked to shoot baskets. The heavy hayloft door was closed, and Rebecca caught her breath, remembering the time Henry had been playing basketball by himself and it hadn't been. It was a thirty-foot drop to the ground beneath. She looked up. Massive wooden beams crisscrossed over her. Above the beams, tucked high in the huge barn, a tiny platform protruded in front of a small circular window looking out over the countryside.

She climbed another ladder nailed in the wall. It was dusty. Once, before they had built the shed, her family had hung tobacco in these high reaches, but now no one ever went there. Except Rebecca. The platform was her special place, where she retreated whenever she wanted to be far away from everything on earth and as close to God as possible. Henry had built it for her. It was small, with barely enough room for two people crowded together. But Rebecca only needed room for one. The wall ladder brought her to a large beam, which she stepped onto. Then, holding onto a small crossbeam above her, she climbed up two pieces of wood nailed into the wall and hoisted herself onto the platform.

She could see far, far down into the barn below, but it was the window that interested Rebecca. She peered out. What a view! Miles and miles of farmland stretching to the far horizon. Acres and acres of corn interrupted by fields lying fallow, then soybeans or depleted tobacco fields, then more corn. Distant silos looked like large white thumbs sticking up from the ground. White houses, white barns, white buildings — everything white. And everything in order, everything laid out in straight lines. On one farm, the women had already put the wash on the line.

On others, windmills turned slowly in the still morning air. Rebecca could see the crick snaking its way through the fields. She noticed the fork in the crick, the right meandering gently into the distance, the left eventually rushing over a high dam before continuing on. And everywhere the sky, going on and on, as far as she could see.

Dear God, denki for this beautiful world. Denki for my family and community.

You know, God, I have a decision to make. You know it weighs heavy on my heart. It's Thy will, not mine, that I must follow, but, God, I am having a hard time knowing what Your will is.

Rebecca paused and took a deep breath. She tried to be as still as possible so she could discern any leadings God might be offering her.

I'm going to close my eyes and sit quietly for a while and when I open them, I hope I will see a sign from You. If I don't see one, I understand. But if you can give me a sign, I'd be grateful.

Amen.

Rebecca sat quietly. She could imagine the view out the tiny circular window, the cows being milked, the clothes being washed, the bacon being fried. She focused her thoughts on the beautiful land all around her, land her ancestors had farmed for two hundred years. A sacred land, blessed by God. Slowly she opened her eyes, then gasped. She had been given a sign.

CHAPTER 2

Sluurp! Sluurp! Sluurp! Gregory lay in the soft grass on the riverbank listening to his horse, Bojangles, vacuuming water into his mouth. It was an early October morning, the sun hardly up yet. *Guess I should call it a "crickbank!"* he mused, smiling. "Crick" was what the Amish called the small stream that ran through the Zook property and also the larger river that bordered it. Honey Brook was its official name, but the Amish just called it the "crick." *Confusing!* But there was a great deal about the Amish that was confusing to an "Englisher."

Soon Gregory would be leaving the crick to ride to Doc Jenkins' veterinary office, so he thought it best to let Bo have his fill. He reflected about how he had first met the good doctor in the barn at Heminger Stables when Gregory had found two horses dead and Bojangles dying. Doc Jenkins had saved Bo's life and then had helped Gregory solve the mystery of what had happened. Ivan Heminger had poisoned the horses in an attempt to falsely collect the insurance. Gregory had found the motive: papers showing Ivan owed half a million dollars. But he'd never found out who was Ivan's creditor. Now Ivan was dead, killed by his own poison. Poison he had intended for Gregory.

Gregory sat up. Had he really been almost murdered? And what had stopped Ivan? Or who? And why? The police said they thought Ivan had committed suicide and had closed the case. But things were far from resolved in Gregory's mind. Why would Ivan try to kill himself and then drive to the hospital to try to save himself? Ivan had called Gregory his son. His son! Gregory was the child of a swindler and a murderer? How could that be? Especially when Gregory had spent his whole life in South Carolina and Ivan had spent his in Lancaster County, Pennsylvania?

Gregory knew the answer to the last question, or at least part of the answer. He was adopted. That's why he had come to Lancaster County in the first place, to try to find his birth mother. And had he almost found her? Ivan had drugged Gregory in order to make killing him easier, but Gregory was positive he'd heard a woman's voice that night calling him "son." Well, maybe not positive, but someone had placed his head on a pillow and pulled a quilt over him. His birth mother? But what was she doing in the shack the night Ivan tried to kill Gregory?

He stood up, the innumerable questions agitating his spirit, as they always did. He hated that. After four months living among the Amish, he had finally begun to relax. He'd come to a new understanding of time, not as something he had to "spend" in order to do something or get something, but as something more like the river at his feet, constantly flowing at its own pace, always getting where it was going, but never rushing to get there. Now all these unanswered questions kept popping into his head any time of night or day, stirring him up. That is why he had resolved to find out once and for all if Ivan really was his father. And if he was, to find out who was the mother who had given him birth.

"Let's go, boy," he called out to Bo, then clutched the reins and swung into the saddle. Bo felt fine beneath him: a strong palomino, newly shod, fully recovered from his brush with death. "You don't even think about it, do you, boy?" Gregory asked. "Wish I could be like that." He swung Bo's head around and they took off across the countryside. Riding here wasn't like in South Carolina, where he could ride forever and hardly see anyone. Here, there were farms all around. But he knew if he rode over the land of Cedar Ridge Farm, he could go a long way towards Doc Jenkins' place without having to circumnavigate fields of crops. So he trotted Bo towards a distant fence. When he got there, he dismounted, opened the gate, walked Bo through, then re-mounted.

Before he took off, however, he turned and looked back at the Zook farm. The family would be going about their business, Elam and Henry milking, Hanna and Mabel doing the wash, and Rebecca… *Where would she be now?* Gregory wondered. *Probably still gathering eggs.* He could picture her hair tied in a bun under her covering. He smiled, remembering the time he had let her hair down. How beautiful it had been, falling almost to her waist, luscious and brown. And her beautiful face, with its blue-green eyes, one of which had a tiny freckle in it. Gregory loved to look in Rebecca's eyes and think *not everybody gets this close to notice that freckle.* He felt privileged. More, he felt blessed. "Blessed." That was a word that had come more and more into Gregory's vocabulary since he'd come to live on the Zook farm. He felt blessed to live among these simple people of profound faith, blessed to have found the courage to break free from his former life, and, mostly, blessed to have met Rebecca Zook. And to have fallen in love with her.

Thinking of Rebecca, Gregory impulsively blew a kiss in the direction of the Zook barn, then turned and galloped over the still-green grass of Cedar Ridge Farm. With the wind blowing him full in the face and Bo's strong legs easily eating up yards of earth, all troublesome thoughts soon vanished from his brain.

Passing high on a ridge, he looked down at the Heminger stables and house below. Wanda Heminger had said in his last phone conversation that she was leaving Penn State to come home. Gregory had tried to persuade her to stay in school, since she was due to graduate this year, but Wanda said she needed to take care of her mother. Gregory suspected she was just homesick. He couldn't blame her. Her horse, Dandelion, had been one of the horses Ivan had killed trying to get the insurance. Her own father had killed her horse! Then he had died under mysterious circumstances the police were calling a suicide. How could she concentrate on her studies with all that emotional turmoil roiling inside her? *Poor Wanda! I must try to help her any way I can.*

Leaving Cedar Ridge Farm, Gregory had to travel along a state road for a while. He saw the usual assortment of Amish buggies with their red brake lights and the caution triangle glued to the back. No matter how often he saw them, Gregory continued to be amazed that these people still rode buggies in twenty-first century America. He had to admit, the Amish were firm in their determination not to be seduced by the conveniences of the world, committed to staying separate and distinct. Keeping apart was the glue that kept them together. Gregory had come to admire the Amish and their ways. Sometimes he even wondered what it would be like to "become Amish." He had no idea if that were even possible. But whenever he thought of Rebecca, he found himself hoping that it was.

After a while, Gregory turned down the lane that led to Doc Jenkins' veterinary hospital. It wasn't really a hospital, just a house with an operating room and lots of cages for various animals. Out back was a small fenced-in pasture for larger animals. As expected, Doc Jenkins was already at work, tending to a mule in the pasture. Gregory pulled up Bo and tied him to the fence.

"Well, hello, Gregory!" Doc said. "You given up automobiles?"

"I like to ride whenever I can."

"How Amish of you!" Doc said with a laugh.

"I'm feeling more Amish every day." Gregory smiled.

"Not me. I like my television sports too much. And I don't know what I'd do without my computer. Don't you miss it?"

"It's a curious thing, Doc, but I don't. I don't miss newspapers, I don't miss television, and I certainly don't miss Facebook!"

"Oh, I don't mess with any of that social media stuff," Doc replied. "Waste of time. But I confess I'm in love with Google. Imagine, you can answer any question you have right away. It's a help for my business; I can look up all sorts of things and find out what other vets are doing about certain problems."

"You have to stay 'of the world,' but I'm not so sure I do."

"What do you do, anyway, Gregory? I never asked you." He returned to his examination of one of the mule's feet.

"I was trying to become a lawyer, but I failed the bar three times. That's when I realized my heart wasn't in it."

"So you came to Lancaster to seek your fortune?"

"Actually, I came here to seek my birth mother."

"Really? I didn't know you were adopted. What made you think she was here?"

"Her social worker in South Carolina remembered that her name was Mae Yoder. She had told this worker she was Amish and was from Lancaster County. The worker also gave me the baby quilt my mother had left with me. I still have it. If I find my mother and show it to her, that will be the proof."

"Isn't that something! How are you going to go about finding her?"

"When I first got here, I looked up all the Mae Yoders I could find in this area, but, as you could imagine, most of them were married and Yoder wasn't their maiden name. So now I'm going to try another approach. I'm going to determine if I am Ivan's son."

"You think you're Ivan's son?" Surprised, Doc released the mule's foot.

"I'm not sure I want to be, but, yes, I think I am."

"You said your mother had left an Amish quilt with you. Ivan wasn't Amish."

"But that doesn't mean he couldn't have fathered me with an Amish woman."

"True. What makes you think he might have fathered you?"

"Ivan called me his son the night he tried to kill me."

"That was fatherly of him!" Gregory laughed. Doc Jenkins had a quirky sense of humor. "So how can you prove it?"

"I don't know. I was hoping you could help me. You've known Ivan over twenty years, is there anything you can recall that might make you think he fathered a child when he was younger?" .

Doc Jenkins slapped the mule and it trotted down to the other side of the pasture. He slipped under the fence and stood beside Gregory. "I don't really know that much about him. To tell you the truth, I didn't think much about him until you called me to try to save Bo."

"Thank you again for that."

"I don't think I did much. It was Rebecca's caring for him that I think made the difference."

"She really loves Bo." Gregory's faced warmed at the memory of how Rebecca had taken care of Bo, feeding him, making sure he took his medicine, staying with him as often as possible.

"But I never heard any scuttlebutt about Ivan. As far as I know, Wanda is his only child. Wait a minute!" Doc Jenkins suddenly shouted. "Wanda!"

"What about her?"

"If Ivan is your father, then you and she must share the same DNA."

"You're right! Wanda would be my half-sister!" Gregory paused. "How would I find out if she and I share the same DNA?"

"The computer!"

"Huh?"

"I told you, Google knows everything!" Doc Jenkins ran towards his back door as Gregory followed. He yanked open the door and walked quickly down the hallway and turned into his office. When Gregory arrived, he was already seated at his desk with the Internet opened before him.

"Here's something called 'The DNA Testing Center of America.' Sounds perfect." He typed some words and the computer instantly opened the web page.

Gregory leaned in closer, as Doc clicked the mouse on "How It Works."

"Let's see.... It says here you can purchase ancestry-related information and raw genetic data for $99. You got $99?"

"I do." Gregory scanned the computer screen. "I have to send in a saliva sample. That's easy for me, but that must mean I have to get a saliva sample from Wanda."

"Afraid it does."

"How will I do that?"

"Get her to kiss you!" Doc laughed.

Gregory squirmed. He had thought more than once what it would feel like to

kiss Wanda. What full-blooded male wouldn't, with her shining blond hair and her

beautiful figure? "Let's think of another way," he said.

"Oh, I'll leave that to you, Gregory. At least now you know how you can find out if Ivan really is your father."

"But that won't tell me who my mother is."

"Nope," Doc Jenkins said. "For that, I guess you'll have to go around collecting saliva samples from all the potential Mae Yoders in

Lancaster County! That's a lot of kissing!"

"Very funny, Doc."

"Well, I've got to get back to work. I can't spend my whole morning talking about kissing."

"Thanks. I knew you could help me."

"Just don't come to me when it's saliva-collecting time!" Doc laughed again and led the way back outside to Bo. Gregory mounted his horse.

"Let me know the results, if you don't mind, Gregory. I'm not sure I'd want to

find out if Ivan is my father, but I understand why you need to. Good luck!"

"I'll let you know."

With that, Gregory turned and trotted Bo back down the lane and headed home. His visit to Doc Jenkins had been a success. Now he had a focus for trying to answer some of the questions that kept taunting him: prove that he and Wanda had the same father. All he needed was some of her saliva. How in the world would he accomplish that?

CHAPTER 3

Vinny Bandini waved off the valet and drove into the parking lot behind Angelo's restaurant in downtown Newark. He didn't like anyone touching his Maserati. He also didn't like this part of Newark — too run down — but his host liked it. *Host.* That was a funny word for a guy who demanded you meet him for dinner "or else."

It was Ivan Heminger's fault that Vinny found himself summoned to this meeting. Ivan had owed Joey Mancuso half a million dollars and Vinny had been the man designated to collect it. Then Ivan had killed himself. Or at least that's what the police had decided. Vinny didn't think Ivan had done it, but that didn't matter now. What mattered was that Mancuso was still owed the $500,000 and that Vinny had been the man who was supposed to have collected it. In Mancuso's mind, the two were connected. That's why Vinny found himself parking his Maserati behind Mancuso's favorite restaurant on this mild October evening.

He sat for a minute before getting out of his car and going inside. He'd been working for Mancuso for more than thirteen years, ever since his senior year in high school. He winced at the memory of how he and Mancuso had met. Vinny and his buddy, Stefano, had found a foolproof way of making a few bucks at the track, rigging a few races here and there. Nothing big. They didn't think anyone would even know, much less care. But Joey Mancuso cared. When it came to money, he always cared. So Vinny and Stefano had found themselves visited by a couple of goons one night. Vinny thought he might not survive the beating, but then he heard a raspy voice say, "That's enough, fellas. I need him to keep playing football." The voice belonged to Joey Mancuso, though Vinny didn't know it at the time.

Football saved my life, Vinny thought with a wry smile. That was funny, because Vinny had been only a so-so football player. He'd played linebacker, but he was too big to be agile enough for that crucial position. Several schools thought he had potential, however, and he had scholarship offers from Rutgers, Pittsburg, and Penn State. He was leaning towards Rutgers when one of the goons visited him again and made it clear that a certain person wanted him to attend Penn State. The way he 'd said "wanted" made it clear that Vinny had better want it, too.

Vinny had spent his time at Penn State sitting on the bench of the Nittany Lions. Every Friday he would meet with a guy everyone called

"Smudge" because of a birthmark on his forehead and tell him everything he knew about injuries to key players, if someone was sick, if someone broke up with his girlfriend, anything and everything that had to do with Penn State's players. For this he was paid $200 a week. That was real money for a college student. The way Vinny had spread it around made him one of the most popular students on campus.

But he'd wanted to play football, not sit on the bench, so Vinny had casually mentioned to Smudge that he was thinking about transferring. Smudge told him that transfers needed approval. "Paterno will be fine with it," Vinny had said. "It'll open up a scholarship for somebody who can actually help the team."

"Paterno's got nothing to do with it," Smudge had replied. "I'll get back to you." A few days later he'd given Vinny his answer. "Nothing doing."

"Why not?"

"The man in charge don't approve of the transfer, that's all."

"And if I do it anyway?"

"You'll be sorry."

"Who is this 'man in charge' anyway?"

"If he wants you to know, you'll know."

So he'd stayed at Penn State. As it turned out, he was glad he had, because spring of his senior year he'd met a freshman named Carla Mancuso. They had married that summer. At the wedding, Carla had introduced Vinny to her uncle, Joey. "How ya' doin'?" a man with a raspy voice had said. And Vinny had finally met the man in charge.

They'd had a good life together, Vinny and Carla… and Joey. Vinny had worked as a repo man, taking cars from owners who were not making the required payments. Then he'd moved higher up in the organization, to the collections side of the business. That's when he had met Ivan Heminger, whose failure to pay up — or, rather, Vinny's failure to collect — was why Vinny now found himself walking to the entrance to Angelo's for a dinner with Uncle Joey, as Mancuso had insisted he call him.

"Evening, Vinny," the maître d' greeted him as he walked in the door.

"Hiya, Marco," Vinny responded. "Got a meeting with the old man."

"I know. Right this way." Marco led Vinny through the main dining room, already bustling with customers and waiters. Despite the paper tablecloths and otherwise nondescript décor, the nearby bar was full of people waiting their turn to eat. The food at Angelo's was *delizioso.*

Marco and Vinny passed through a second, smaller dining room reserved for better-dressed customers: no shorts or jeans, coats for gentlemen, dresses or fine slacks for ladies. Finally, Marco opened the door to the third dining room, which could be accessed from the back of the building as well. This was Mancuso's private dining room. "Wait here," Marco said, and closed the door after himself.

The room had no windows. Two tables were dressed with the finest Italian linen tablecloths, silver tableware, crystal wine glasses, and priceless antique plates. A wine cooler in the corner held some 250 of Mancuso's favorite wines. A humidor was stocked with the finest Cuban cigars. A customer in the second dining room had once complained that he smelled smoke. Angelo had apologized, saying that was impossible, there were laws against smoking in restaurants. Of course, the customer never again was allowed to eat in the second dining room.

Vinny lowered his six-foot, two hundred and twenty-five-pound frame into one of the chairs. He pulled a hand through his dark, somewhat oily, hair, and settled his olive eyes on a far wall, looking at nothing in particular, trying to calm himself for the meeting to come. He checked his watch. Seven twenty-five. Five minutes early, which was good, because Mancuso didn't like people to be late. *I'm married to his niece,* he reassured himself. *Family. How bad could it be?* But, if anything his years in the organization had taught him, it was that family was family, and business was business. It was one of Mancuso's favorite lines, and he was sure he'd hear it again tonight.

The door opened and Joey Mancuso walked in. He was a small man, some sixty-five years of age, whose hair was beginning to turn a little gray at the temples. His tan face was lined with wrinkles from too many hours in the sun. He had small, piercing brown eyes and an angular nose that was too big for his face. When he smiled, which wasn't often, two rows of smoke-stained crooked teeth showed between very thin lips. Vinny immediately rose, noticing the henchman who closed the door behind Mancuso and who would prevent anyone from entering or leaving.

"How ya doin', Uncle Joey," he said. "Good to see you."

"Doin' fine, Vinny, fine," Mancuso rasped out. "Penn State's having a great season, so I ain't got no complaints. Siddown, let's have some wine." As soon as the words were out of his mouth, Marco appeared with a bottle of red wine, which he showed to Mancuso. "Two-thousand and two? Why not?" He turned to Vinny. "Hope you don't mind if we drink a little cheap tonight."

Vinny, who hadn't had wine that old since the last time Mancuso had hosted an event, said, "Whatever your pleasure, Uncle Joey."

Marco poured, then retreated from the room. Mancuso held up his glass. "*Salute.*"

"*Salute.*" Vinny took a sip and enjoyed the smooth taste of fine wine sliding down his throat. Knowing what lay ahead, he immediately took another sip.

"Hope you don't mind, but I ordered for us. Speed things up a bit. You probably know why I invited you here."

Vinny decided to play dumb. "Not really."

"Not really? Well, it ain't to talk about your love life." Vinny laughed a tiny laugh, unsure whether his uncle was joking or not. "How is Carla, by the way?"

"She's great, really good, *fantastica.* She sends her love."

"Sweet girl, my Carla. You take good care of her, y'hear?"

"I will," Vinny said. And he would, because he knew what would happen if he didn't.

"'Cause I can always find her another husband, you know what I mean?" Mancuso continued. Thinking any answer was superfluous, Vinny gulped down more wine.

Two waiters entered carrying food, which they placed in front of the diners. "Some veal, *salata,* garlic asparagus on the side, that all right with you, Vinny?" Vinny mused how curious it was that men like his Uncle Joey always asked permission for things when they had no intention of ever listening to what you said. He nodded in response. "*Bene,* I think you'll like it."

Mancuso opened his napkin, placed it in his lap, and took a bite of veal. He chewed slowly, savoring it. "*Perfecta.*" He took another bite. Vinny did the same, waiting for Mancuso to say what he had brought him there to say. "So, Vinny, about the money," he began at last.

"Money?"

"Don't be a *stupido*, Vinny. The money you owe me."

"I don't owe you any money, Uncle Joey," Vinny protested.

"Well, your man Ivan does, which comes to the same thing."

"Ivan is not 'my man,'" Vinny began, but Mancuso held up his hand and he stopped talking.

Mancuso took a bite of salad, but this time Vinny didn't follow suit. He was losing his appetite fast. "Half a million dollars I'm out, Vinny. That ain't peanuts. And another thing: someone like Ivan is worth a lot of money to me. He'd have paid off his gambling losses ten times in ten different ways. Now he's dead. I don't like people being dead in my business unless I want 'em dead. So, I'm thinking, I gotta at least get back what Ivan owed me. Now, you got any plans on how I'm getting back my half a mil?"

"I honestly don't. I didn't know until this minute that I owed it to you."

"Your stupidity ain't my problem. I suggest you start thinking hard about how you're gonna get it to me, you hear me, Vinny? Tell you what, I'm gonna give you a deadline, maybe help you think a little harder." He took a sip of wine. "*Bello, molto bello.* Let's see, now… How about January first? Yeah, that's a good date, nice and simple. You give me $500,000 by January first, and everything's fine. You got any problem with that, Vinny?"

Vinny took a moment. Yeah, he had lots of problems with that, but none that Joey would care about. It was a little over three months; he ought to be able to come up with something in three months. Maybe he could get it reduced. "I was just wondering, Uncle Joey. You know how I got Ivan to make sure his daughter's horse, Dandelion, didn't win in that race. I'm sure you made a bundle on that. How about deducting that from what I owe you?"

Mancuso put his glass down firmly on the table, his eyes flashing with anger. "You don't do the accounting, Vinny, I do. *Capisch?*"

He held his stony eyes on Vinny until he smiled weakly. "Of course, I understand, Uncle. Sorry." Vinny took a moment to wipe his lips and the perspiration underneath his nose.

They finished the meal in near silence, Mancuso concentrating on his food, and Vinny concentrating on not offending his uncle any further. When he'd finished, Mancuso rose, and Vinny did the same. "No dessert tonight, Vinny, if you don't mind." He patted his stomach, rounded from excessive drinking. "Gotta watch the weight, *capisch?*"

Vinny flashed his friendliest smile. "*Si, capisco,*"

Mancuso stretched out his hand and Vinny took it. He held Vinny's hand for a minute. "I really like you, Vinny, and I'm glad you're family. But family is family and business is business, you know what I mean?" He didn't wait for an answer, but patted Vinny's cheek affectionately.

"*Si,* I know you know what I mean, Uncle Joey.

"*Bene.*" Mancuso turned and walked out of the room, leaving Vinny staring down at the mostly uneaten food on his plate. He poured what was left of the wine into his glass and took a long drink. It was a good wine. He drained the glass. Very good. And if he wanted to taste anything that good again, he'd better come up with a plan about how to get half a million dollars by the first of January.

CHAPTER 4

The tiny bell tinkled when Rebecca opened the door to Mrs. Ansbacher's quilt shop. As expected, Mrs. Ansbacher was already at work, making sure the quilts were stacked nicely or hung straight on their rods.

"Morning, dear," Mrs. Ansbacher called cheerily. "How are you today?"

Rebecca, feeling less anxious now that she had made her decision, answered, "Fine!"

"I've looked over your figures from yesterday," Mrs. Ansbacher said. "We did quite well. Looks like you'll be buying a good business."

"I know." Mrs. Ansbacher had offered to sell her shop to Rebecca, but the thought of actually taking over the shop made Rebecca nervous. She'd never run a business before. What if she wasn't any good at it? How much time would it take out of her life? Would she be overwhelmed with all she had to do? She didn't want to become like some of the English she knew, crazed by filling every nook and cranny of their lives with "things to do." Rebecca had never had a "to do" list and she didn't want to start one now. Still, she loved making quilts and being surrounded by them, so she had accepted Mrs. Ansbacher's offer to sell her the shop.

"I thought this would be a good day to start talking about how I'll actually sell you the shop," Mrs. Ansbacher continued. "Have you talked it over with your folks?"

"Yes. Dat thinks it's a good idea. You know how we are trying to deed the farm to the Lancaster Farmland Trust?"

"Yes. Such a wonderful idea to make sure it always remains a farm. It's scary how many Amish farms are being sold to developers. It makes me sick to see all

these cookie-cutter houses where there used to be beautiful fields. How does it work, exactly?"

"It's called a Charitable Remainder Trust," Rebecca explained. "I don't really understand it, it was Gregory's idea, and he's the one who is working with Dat to make it happen."

"It's so lucky for your family that he came along right when you needed him."

Rebecca thought it was more than "luck." She was sure God's will had brought Gregory into her life, but she had no idea what God's will was now that he was here. Yet, as with His help with her decision earlier this morning, she knew that, if she had an open heart and mind, she would be able to discern what God wanted her to do. "Yes, we are very lucky that Gregory moved into our cottage," she replied.

"Is he a lawyer?"

"He went to law school, but he hasn't passed the bar." Because she was unsure exactly what their relationship was, Rebecca didn't like talking about Gregory with other people, so she re-focused the conversation. "Anyway, Dat is turning over the farming to Henry so Dat can open a leather shop, so he's quite happy I'm opening my own shop. 'Two peas in a pod' he calls us."

"He doesn't mind a woman deciding to run a business, not a farm?" Mrs. Ansbacher asked. "That's lucky for you. How about your mom?"

"Mam is a different story. She wants me to marry and live on a farm, follow the Amish traditions." *She also knows who she wants me to marry.*

"Which is hard for an artist to do." Mrs. Ansbacher looked at Rebecca. She knew how uncertain Rebecca was about calling herself an artist, so she tried to remind her of her gift whenever she got the chance.

It was true, Rebecca didn't like thinking of herself as an artist. She knew how outside the Amish tradition such thinking was. The Amish never liked to draw attention to themselves. They were supposed to be free of pride. But how could you make a work of art and not be proud of it? Sometimes Rebecca thought she should just stop making her wall hangings altogether. But she realized that would be stifling a true part of herself. Was that really what God wanted?

"You don't have to buy the shop, Rebecca. Not if you think it is going to cause problems at home. Or even in your church." Mrs. Ansbacher wasn't Amish, but she knew the strong hold the church had over its people.

For once, Rebecca didn't hesitate. She knew what she wanted to do, and she had prayed about it enough to know that she thought it was God's will. "I'm buying the shop," she said confidently.

"Good," replied Mrs. Ansbacher. "Then let's sit down and go over the paperwork." She led Rebecca to a pair of chairs around a small table, where a notepad and pen lay waiting. "I thought you might need to take some notes. Now, here's how I think it needs to happen. I have a company that is the official owner of the shop. You'll have to form your own company and my company will sell it to yours."

"Form a company?" Rebecca asked anxiously. "How do I do that?"

"We'll get to that in a minute. First, write it down."

Rebecca carefully wrote "Form company" in her delicate handwriting. "Now, to form this company — it's called an LLC, or Limited Liability Company — you need to have Articles of Incorporation."

"Articles of Incorp — !" Rebecca was about to protest, but stopped. She wrote it down.

"And by-laws."

"What are those?"

"Just rules for how you're going to run your company. How many officers there will be, and so forth."

"Mrs. Ansbacher! I didn't know how complicated this was going to be. Maybe I'd better think about it some more."

"It's not that complicated, Rebecca, but you will need some help. I could help you, but I'm not the best person. What you need is someone who knows something about the law. Do you know of anyone?" Mrs. Ansbacher asked with a sly smile.

Rebecca's eyes lit up. "Gregory!" she exclaimed, then blushed when she realized how excited she had sounded. "I mean, if he would do it."

"I think he probably would," Mrs. Ansbacher said gently. She had noticed how happy Rebecca had seemed when she'd returned from New York. She had noticed how that happiness grew as the summer progressed. And she possessed an older woman's intuition about the source of that happiness. Having Gregory help Rebecca was a wonderful idea, and she was secretly proud of how she had made it come about.

Just then the door opened and Lydie King, preacher Omar's wife, entered. She was a small woman, with a tiny oval face that seemed, to Rebecca, constricted by some secret sorrow. Lydie had the fit frame of most Amish women. For all the food they consumed and all the sugar they liked to have with that food, Amish women were hardly ever fat, due to the hard work they did every day. Amish men, too.

Mrs. Ansbacher and Rebecca rose. "Hello, Lydie," called out Mrs. Ansbacher.

"Hi, Mrs. King," said Rebecca.

"*Gut* morning," Lydie replied. "I've come to pick up my covering for church this Sunday."

"I've got it right here, Mrs. King." Rebecca returned to the counter and pulled out the covering she had made from the white fabric Lydie had picked out earlier.

"Thank you, Rebecca, it's beautiful. You sure know your way around a needle. How much do I owe you?"

"Ten dollars, please," Rebecca answered.

"Are you ready for us all to come over Sunday for church?" Lydie asked Rebecca, handing her some money.

"Yes. We've cleaned out the barn and we're all set in the kitchen," Rebecca said.

"Will Gregory be there?" Lydie asked.

Rebecca was surprised by the question. "I suppose so. Why do you ask?"

"No reason. He came to church that one time but he hasn't been back."

It was true. Gregory had gone to church with them one Sunday. Rebecca would never forget. Not only had Jacob been there, but also Johnny Schmucker, her boyfriend from long ago until her Mam had told her she didn't like Rebecca dating Johnny. That Sunday, Johnny had told her he was giving up trying to become a professional baseball player and was returning to Lancaster County to take up farming. He'd also told her he wanted to marry her, if she didn't choose Jacob. What a day that had been! Three men, all of them romantically interested in Rebecca, all in the same place. Rebecca knew Jacob would be at church this Sunday and maybe Johnny, too. What if Gregory wanted to come? Would she feel the same discomfort all over again?

"I think he's waiting for us to invite him again," Rebecca said, "And Mam thinks it might make members uncomfortable to keep having an Englisher at our service."

"I certainly don't mind," Lydie said, "And I don't think Omar does, either. Why don't you invite him?"

Rebecca couldn't understand why Lydie seemed so interested in having Gregory come to church. "I'll see what Mam thinks," she said. "I'll wrap your hat."

"Oh, that's all right, I'll just lay it on the buggy seat," said Lydie. "It's not far to home. See you Sunday. 'Bye, Elizabeth," she said to Mrs. Ansbacher.

"Good-bye, Lydie," Mrs. Ansbacher answered.

When Lydie had left, she continued, a twinkle in her eye "Well, you'll have all sorts of things to ask Gregory about now!"

Rebecca had been wanting to have a conversation with Gregory for a long time, but she hadn't expected it to be about corporations and church. "We still haven't talked about a price, Mrs. Ansbacher," she said.

"I've been thinking about that, too, Rebecca. I don't need much, I've got enough for retirement, and I know you don't have much money, so here's what I propose. You pay me $20,000 for the shop. That includes the inventory, customer lists, accounts receivable, and so forth. But don't worry, I don't need the money all at once. I suggest you pay it off slowly from the profits of the shop. We'll leave the time open-ended. Take as long as you need to pay me. You can tell your Gregory to draw up an agreement with those terms. All right?"

Before Rebecca could answer, the phone rang. Mrs. Ansbacher answered. "Hello...? Why, hello, Mr. Goldfarb! Just a minute, our artist is right here." She cupped her hand over the phone. "It's your agent!"

Rebecca picked up the phone. "Hello, Mr. Goldfarb."

"How are you, Rebecca?"

"I'm fine."

"I hope you've been making more of those quilt wall hangings with the horse theme."

"I've been awfully busy, Mr. Goldfarb."

"Well, you're about to get busier. I've just gotten commissions for ten more quilts."

Rebecca's mouth rounded in surprise. "What?"

"That's right. You remember the one you sold to Ted Snow. Well, Ted allowed me to keep it displayed in my gallery for a while, and some of my clients just fell in love with your style."

"But Mr. Goldfarb, making ten quilts… It takes me about a month to make one. And I was just talking to Mrs. Ansbacher about…" She sank into a chair near the phone. Perhaps this wasn't the time to tell him she was about to become the owner of a quilt shop.

"About what?" Mr. Goldfarb asked.

"Oh, nothing."

"My clients can probably wait a while, but I don't want to wait too long. The more you get your work into the homes of others, the more orders we'll get."

Rebecca was dazed. "More orders?"

"Are you all right, dear?" Mrs. Ansbacher whispered. Rebecca nodded, but she felt anything but all right.

"Well, we won't worry about that now," Mr. Goldfarb said enthusiastically. "I've got an idea. Why don't you hire some other women to help you make the quilts? You can design them and they can do the stitching. You could make it more like a regular business."

Rebecca almost moaned. A business? Making quilts? Something she had always done for the sheer joy of it? "I suppose..." she managed.

Mr. Goldfarb took a deep breath. He remembered whom he was dealing with: a young Amish woman unschooled in the ways of the world. He would have to guide her gently. Whereas other clients might have shouted with excitement about selling so much of their art, Rebecca was obviously feeling overwhelmed. "Rebecca, you don't have to start today, or even tomorrow. Just think about it for a while. If there's one thing I've learned, it's that you can't force art. Artists have to work at their own pace, and they have to work when they feel the inspiration. But remember one thing: you *are* an artist. Don't ever forget that. That's why people are responding to your work."

An artist. That word again. She didn't know if she liked being an artist. Her work? Was that what she produced, "work"?

"Rebecca are you still there?" Mr. Goldfarb asked.

"Oh, yes, I'm sorry." Rebecca drew a breath. "Thank you, Mr. Goldfarb. I will think about it."

"Good. Give me a call when you're ready. If I don't hear from you after a while, I'll call you again. Is that all right?"

"Yes, that will be fine."

"Good. Have a wonderful rest of your day, Rebecca. I'll speak to you soon. Good-bye."

"Good-bye, Mr. Goldfarb." Rebecca heard the click from his phone and hung up her receiver. For a long minute she stared at her hand on the phone.

"Here you go, dear." Rebecca looked up to see the glass of water Mrs. Ansbacher was handing her. She took it gratefully and swallowed a long drink.

"Thank you."

"Well," Mrs. Ansbacher said. "I can't tell if it's good news or bad. It certainly seemed to shock you."

"Mr. Goldfarb told me he has commissions for ten quilt wall hangings."

"Why, that's wonder — " Mrs. Ansbacher caught herself, remembering how Rebecca had received the news. "That's quite a tall order, isn't it?" Rebecca nodded dumbly. "And on top of our discussion about buying the shop, I'll bet you're feeling a little overwhelmed." Rebecca just stared into space. "Tell you what, why don't you take the rest of the day off."

"Oh, Mrs. Ansbacher, I don't need to do that," she protested.

"It's all right, dear. It's early in the week, we usually don't have many customers. I've got some thinking about my own life to do, and I'd prefer to do it alone."

"If you think it will be okay?"

"I do."

Rebecca stood up. She did need some time to think about everything. "Thank you, Mrs. Ansbacher. I'll be in tomorrow, same time."

"I look forward to seeing you, Rebecca. As always." Rebecca moved towards the door. "And Rebecca — " She turned to see Mrs. Ansbacher pointing to the quilt hanging on the back wall. "Remember, you did that. And it's beautiful. I give it to you as the first of your ten quilts."

"But Mrs. Ansbacher, I gave it to you!"

"I know you did, dear, and I love it. But you can always make me another one when you have time. I'm in no hurry. It would make me feel good to know I am contributing to your career."

"Thank you," Rebecca mumbled, opened the door, and went outside. For a minute she leaned against the door. *Career?* She didn't think she wanted a career. That's what the English had, and she wasn't English, she was Amish. "I'm Amish!" she said out loud.

"Of course you are," a passer-by said to her. Rebecca looked up, startled. It was Sarah Stoltzfus from a neighboring farm. "Whoever said you weren't?" Sarah smiled at Rebecca and continued on her way.

Rebecca gathered herself and set off in the opposite direction. She had started the morning making what she'd thought was the hardest decision of her life. And now she had even harder ones to make. As she walked slowly along, she sighed and shook her head. *God certainly works in mysterious ways* was all she could think.

CHAPTER 5

Gregory picked up the large pot from his back yard and looked down at the tea bags floating in the brown liquid. He had put them there a couple of hours earlier to let the sun heat them. Sun tea, his favorite way to brew it. He remembered how his mother had shown him how to do it when he was a little boy. Not his real mother, but the woman who had adopted him twenty-five years ago in South Carolina. Now he had a plan for finding out who is real mother was.

He carried the pot into his cottage and set it on the kitchen counter. It wasn't a kitchen like he was used to. For one thing, it had a sink but no running water. Gregory got his water from a pump in the yard. For another, it had no electricity. Gregory used kerosene lanterns at night. It did have a refrigerator and a stove, both of which ran off the propane tank outside. Gregory was surprised to learn that these appliances were allowed, but Rebecca had explained to him that the Amish couldn't hook up to public gas lines, but it was all right if they used their own. *They have so many rules, and so many exceptions to the rules,* he thought. *That's kind of the way it is in the English world, too.* "Whoa!" he said out loud. "Now I'm calling myself 'English!'"

He chuckled, reached in, grabbed a tea bag, squeezed the remaining tea into the pot, put the used bag aside and grabbed another one. When all the bags had been squeezed, he reached into the cabinet and took down a five-pound bag of sugar that he had bought especially for the occasion. He poured a generous amount into the pot, and then stirred it with a wooden spoon. When he thought most of the sugar had dissolved, he placed a thermos in the sink and filled it up. "Sweet sun tea," he announced, and then took a sip from the spoon. "Not bad."

He placed the thermos into a small shoulder bag and added the most important items: two large plastic glasses. Then he went out the door, walked to where Bo stood munching grass, grabbed the reins, swung into the saddle, and headed off to Cedar Ridge Farm and what he hoped would be the beginning of his date with destiny — his own.

Ten minutes later Gregory dismounted outside the main barn at Heminger Stables. He noticed Wanda's red Corvette parked in the driveway. He'd heard she had returned home from Penn State and it was true. Gregory was grateful. He hadn't wanted to have to travel all the way to State College to get what he needed from Wanda.

He walked onto the front porch with his shoulder bag and saw the table and two chairs. The last time Gregory had been on this porch, Ivan had given him a beer laced with drugs to make him woozy before leading him to the shack to finish him off. *Finish me off?* It still seemed incredible to Gregory. *My own father? If he is my father — or was.* Well, that was what he was here to find out. He rang the doorbell. "Who is it?" a voice called out.

"It's Gregory Pinckney, Mrs. Heminger. Is Wanda here?"

"Gregory!" Wanda cried. He heard footsteps, then the door opened, and Wanda rushed into his arms. "I'm so happy to see you!"

"Hi, Wanda," he said. She still held him tightly, which made Gregory a little uncomfortable. Was this his half-sister, or a beautiful woman he wasn't related to? "How are you?" he said, pulling away from her.

"Okay," she said, half-heartedly.

"It's so good to see you," he said. And he meant it. Gregory was very fond of Wanda. He remembered how spirited she was, how full of life, and wondered how much her father's death might have dampened that spirit. If it had, maybe he could lift it back up. But first things first. "Can we sit down?"

"Sure." She led the way to the table, where they sat, Gregory placing his shoulder bag on the floor.

"I made some sweet sun tea. Want some?" He pulled the thermos and the two glasses from the bag.

"No, thanks. I just had a snack."

"Maybe later." Masking his disappointment, Gregory left the thermos and glasses on the table. "Wanda, you're looking good!" he said. And she did, in her custom-fit jeans and bright, yellow blouse, her thick, blonde hair spilling over her shoulders.

"Thanks. I don't feel so hot."

"Are you sick?"

"No, just kinda blah, you know."

"Yeah." He nodded his head sympathetically. "I'm so sorry about your father." Gregory paused to reflect on the irony that it might be his father, too, but he felt none of the emotion Wanda was feeling.

"Thanks. Sometimes I can't believe it's true. I keep expecting him to be in the den watching TV, or in his office in the barn, or watching me ride."

Gregory didn't know what to say. He'd never lost anyone close to him. So he said the one true thing he did know. "I can't imagine how you feel."

"Mama's worse. She hardly ever leaves the house. Vinny's the only one who can get her to go out."

"Vinny?"

"A friend of Daddy's. You've never met him?"

"I don't believe so."

"He's been a sweetheart. He came by a lot when it first happened. While I was at State, he'd bring Mama ice cream. I think he once even got her to go to the movies. He was really happy when I told him I was coming back, said he'd drop by as soon as he can."

"I'm glad you've got a friend." Gregory opened the thermos to pour himself a drink. "You sure you don't want any? I made it just for you."

"No, thanks, Gregory. I don't really like ice tea."

Disappointed again, Gregory poured himself a glass and drank. *Guess I'll have to think of another strategy.* Getting Wanda's saliva was a long shot anyway. The DNA center said it had to be a cheek swab, but he couldn't figure out how to get one from Wanda. He was hoping that he could swab the rim of a glass and that would suffice. But if she wasn't going to drink anything… "Are you guys okay money-wise? I don't mean to pry."

"That's all right. It's funny, Daddy didn't have much money in the bank. I guess he put it all in the farm. But the lawyers think his life insurance policy will pay up soon. That'll last for a while. I guess I'll have to get a job sooner or later."

"I hope you can finish your college education first. "

"I guess," Wanda said vaguely. Gregory thought Wanda might not be that interested in academics, but if she didn't have a degree, what would she do? He took another sip of his tea and looked at her. She was staring into space.

"Let's go see Bo!" he said suddenly.

"You rode him?" Wanda asked excitedly.

"Sure did."

"I'd love to!"

Gregory put the top on the thermos and stored it and the glasses in the bag. He knew how much Wanda loved horses, and now there wasn't a single horse on the farm. *Might as well bring her a little joy.*

They left the porch and walked across the circular drive to the side of the barn. "Bo!" Wanda cried, running to him and stroking his cheek. "How are you, beautiful Bo?" Bo neighed, shook his head vigorously, then nuzzled her. He had a good feel for people who genuinely loved horses.

"He's good as new," Gregory said, forgetting for an instant that it might be hurtful to remind Wanda that Bo had survived Ivan's treachery while her horse, Dandelion, had died from the poisoning. Then he had a wonderful idea. "Hey, Wanda, would you like to go riding?"

"I don't have a horse."

"You've got this one." He ducked under Bo's neck, put his head beside Bo's, and pretended to be the horse talking. "Oh, please, Wanda, take me for a ride. Please?"

Wanda laughed. "You mean it?" Gregory-as-Bo nodded enthusiastically. "Seriously, Gregory, do you really think I should ride Bo?"

"Not only 'should,'" Gregory said in his normal voice, "You must."

"I don't have the right shoes."

"Kick 'em off!"

Wanda giggled as she let fly both shoes towards the side of the barn. Gregory held out his hand, she took it, put one foot in the stirrup, and swung her leg over Bo's back. Gregory handed her the reins and slapped Bo on the flank. "Hyah!" he shouted and Bo and Wanda took off across the field.

Wanda was an excellent horsewoman. Maybe she could do something with horses, Gregory mused, watching them. She had this beautiful farm, state-of-the-art stables, and not one horse. He felt a twinge of sorrow. Well, he didn't have the money to buy her one. Maybe when her insurance money came in.

He retreated to the shadow of the barn. The day was becoming hot. He unscrewed the cap and drank from the thermos. The cold tea tasted good. He'd have to try again. Maybe take her for a beer. Then what, pocket the beer bottle? He felt a little bad, scheming to get Wanda's saliva. But what could he do? Say, "Excuse me, Wanda, but would mind if I swabbed your cheek?" He shook his head at the absurdity of it all.

After a few minutes, Wanda and Bo rode back to the barn. She jumped down and gave Gregory a big hug. "Thank you so much! That was wonderful!" Her blue eyes shone her face glistened with perspiration. "I think I'll take that tea now, please."

Gregory had a moment of panic. *Did I drink it all?* He quickly unscrewed the cap, noticed with relief the tea swirling in the bottom of the thermos, and poured Wanda a glass. "Sorry, since you didn't want any, I almost drank it all."

"Thanks." She took a long swallow, brought the glass down for a moment, then drank some more until all the tea was gone. "You're right, that's delicious."

"Mama's secret recipe," Gregory said, taking her glass and putting it very carefully into his shoulder bag.

"Your adopted mother. You came up here to find your real mother, didn't you? Gregory, please let me know if I can help you in any way."

Gregory almost laughed out loud. *You just did!* "I will, Wanda, when I figure out exactly how to go about it."

Wanda wandered over and patted Bojangles. "And, thank you, you handsome thing!" She turned to Gregory. "Do you think I might ride Bo from time to time, if you're not riding him?"

"Wanda, I'd love it. What's more, Bo would, too!" He slung the bag over his shoulder and took the reins in his hand. "Well, we'd better be getting back." He mounted his horse and smiled down at her. "I'm glad you came home, Wanda. It feels right for you to be here now. I promise to come back soon."

"Thank you, Gregory. You have really brightened my day."

With a final smile, Gregory tapped his heels into Bo's sides and rode away. He'd accomplished his task and had made a lonely woman feel good in the process. "We done!" he called down to his palomino pal as they sped along.

A half-hour later Gregory was brushing down Bo in his makeshift stall inside the stable where the Zooks kept their mules. He had taken the glass with Wanda's precious saliva on the rim, placed it in a plastic bag, and put it in the refrigerator. Tomorrow he would take it to the post office and mail it to the DNA agency. Now it was time to settle his horse, turn him out to pasture, and maybe take a plunge into the crick to cool off.

"Gregory?" The sound of Rebecca's voice made his heart skip.

"Over here, with Bo," he called back. He watched her come down the length of the stable. He loved how she moved so effortlessly, almost skimming over the earth, her long dress brushing the ground.

"Hi," she said, when she'd reached the stall. She smiled sweetly at Gregory. "Mind if I help?"

Gregory handed her the brush, knowing how much she loved to brush Bo. It was that desire that had first started them talking four months ago. As she began brushing his mane, Bo stomped his foot with pleasure.

"Been out for a ride?" she asked.

"I rode over to Wanda's."

Wanda's name always brought Rebecca a twinge of… what was it? Jealousy? Envy? Worry? She tried to push the feeling away, with limited success. "Is she home?"

"She decided not to continue at Penn State, at least for this semester. She seems lonely. I took her some sweet tea."

"Sweet tea? Why?"

Gregory realized he wasn't ready to tell Rebecca about his plans yet. "Just to be friendly." At least that was part of the reason. "I let her ride Bo."

Now Rebecca really was jealous. She had never been allowed to ride horses when she was growing up. "Animals are for work, not play," her father had sternly told her. That's why it had been such a thrill to have ridden Bo, holding onto Gregory, on that magical day when they had first kissed. How long ago that seemed now. Why had their relationship not progressed?

Rebecca knew the answer. They couldn't really tell anyone about their feelings for each other. Gregory was English. What's more, Rebecca was still affianced to Jacob. So their relationship had entered a kind of limbo the last month. It didn't go backwards, which was good, but it didn't go forward either. It left them both a little unsure of how to proceed, and maybe even a little unsure of what they really felt for each other. At least, it left Rebecca feeling that way.

She brushed Bo harder. She hadn't come here to think about their relationship. "Gregory? May I ask you something?"

Anything! "Sure," he said.

"You know how Mrs. Ansbacher wants to sell me her quilt shop?"

"Yes. That's such a good idea."

"Yes. But the thing is, Gregory, I don't really know how to do it. Mrs. Ansbacher talked to me the other day about it. She told me I would have to form a company, draw up Articles of Incorporation, I think she called them, and file some forms with the state."

"That's all true, Rebecca. But it's not that complicated."

"Well, it seems that way to me. And the thing is…." Rebecca paused. She had thought exactly how she would ask Gregory, but now the words just wouldn't come. "You see…"

"Yes?" Gregory asked, helpfully.

Grow up, Rebecca! Just say it! She took a deep breath and blurted it all out. "I was wondering if you would help me. I know you went to law school, but maybe they didn't teach you that, and maybe if they did, you don't want to do it, or you don't have time, and that's okay, I really understand, I'm sure I can find somebody else — "

"Rebecca!" Gregory interrupted. "Slow down and give me a chance to speak." He smiled at her. "I can't think of anything else I would rather do with my time than help you set up your business. It would be an honor."

"Really?" Rebecca was so relieved she impulsively took a step towards Gregory to hug him, but stopped herself. "You sure?"

"Sure as rain!" Gregory said. "Absolutely positive." He felt almost giddy at the prospect of helping Rebecca. It would give them time together, legitimate time. He'd be acting as her lawyer, so no one could raise an eyebrow over that. But he'd be so much more than a lawyer to her.

"*Gut!*" Rebecca said happily. She handed the brush back to Gregory. "I don't know how we'll start, but I'll leave that up to you." She smiled. "Up to my lawyer. What do they call lawyers sometimes?"

"Legal counsel," Gregory answered.

"Yes, my legal counsel. That's a good word for it, because I'm going to need a lot of counseling."

"I'll go to the library and figure out exactly what you have to do," Gregory said. "Then I'll get back to you."

"Thank you."

"No, thank you!"

For a minute they stood still, an awkward silence descending between them. Neither of them wanted the moment to end. Bo suddenly neighed, breaking the spell. "I guess I'd better let him out," Gregory said.

"And I'd better go help Mam and Hanna with supper," Rebecca said. She lingered for a moment, then turned and walked away.

When she was gone, Gregory slapped the side of the stall with excitement. "Bo, we're going to start a business! And maybe it'll end up being a partnership — and I don't mean a business one!"

CHAPTER 6

Vinny watched the dark bay horse move around the corral in back of the Lancaster Downs racetrack. He liked the look of him: heavily-muscled upper legs, good spring in his stride. The horse looked smaller than the usual seventeen hands, but since it was a short track, that shouldn't be a problem. He wished the horse were black, his favorite color. He always felt he could win if the horse were black. He knew superstition should play no part at a racetrack, but he couldn't help himself. Sometimes he'd bet on a black horse even if the odds were thirty-to-one.

Vinny had come to the track to think about his problem. Somehow he had to get half a million dollars to his uncle, and he had to do it in three months. He carried a roll of cash in his pocket. *Maybe I'll just stay here all week and bet every race!* He wasn't going to do that — that was stupid — but what was he going to do?

He pulled the Daily Racing Form from his pocket and looked it over. The horse, Wise Guy, had been doing pretty well. He liked his trainer, Shorty Jones. His jockey, Miquel Dominquez, had been winning of late — seventh in the top ten jockeys for the season. That was important. The top ten riders won ninety per cent of the time. Favorite horses won thirty-three per cent of the time. At least Wise Guy wasn't a favorite. They don't pay anything if they win. He felt like really gambling today. And he sure liked the name.

Vinny hardly ever really gambled, if gambling meant taking a chance. He used insider information to place his bets: which jockey was having problems at home, which horse had come up lame but the trainer had used drugs to mask the injury. More than insider information, Vinny liked to know the race was fixed before he bet. Like when he had forced Ivan to make sure Wanda's horse, Dandelion, didn't win, place, or show in that race last June. That had been Mancuso's idea. But Mancuso didn't have any ideas about how Vinny was going to get the five hundred thousand dollars. At least he wasn't offering any. *You'd think he'd be on my side. I'm married to his niece!*

He thought about his wife, Carla. They'd been married for six years, ever since Vinny turned twenty-four. They'd been mostly happy. Vinny couldn't imagine being with the same woman for the rest of his life, but Carla was fine for now. She might have to be fine forever, depending on Mancuso. He might not have a choice about staying married to Carla, not if he wanted to stay alive. But today was no time to be thinking about that future. He had another future to take care of first.

"Nice horse, eh?" Vinny looked to his right. A small man in jeans and a tan cowboy shirt looked back at him through wire-rimmed glasses.

"Yeah, I like him," Vinny said. "You know anything about him?"

"Got a good bloodline. Sired by Castaway, whose line goes all the way back to Intrepid. Good out of the gate. We got a dry track today, he should do all right. He's not much for mud."

"Do all right or win?"

"I don't think he'll win. He just doesn't have that fire in his belly. He might show."

"You seem to know a lot about him."

"I should. I'm his owner. James Ross."

Vinny took the outstretched hand. "Vinny," he said. He didn't like giving people his last name if he didn't have to. If he did, he usually made one up. "Nice to meet you."

"You come here a lot, I've seen you," Ross said.

"I love horses and I love horse racing. I was practically born in a stable." Vinny returned to his thoughts about betting. "Maybe I'll put a little something on Wise Guy, but what are you going to do about him never winning?"

"I was actually thinking of selling him. You interested?"

"No, I don't buy horses. I wouldn't know where to keep him, even if I did. All the vet bills, trainer fees. No, thanks. I'll keep my ears open, though. How much you want for him?"

"He's no spring chicken," said Ross. "Or maybe I should say 'spring horse.'" Vinny forced himself to laugh appreciatively. "I'm thinking maybe $10-15 grand."

"Sounds reasonable." The bell sounded — five minutes to place bets. "Better get going. Good luck with Wise Guy."

"Thanks."

Ross moved away to watch the stable boy walk Wise Guy around the corral. Vinny walked to the betting booth, consulting his racing form again. He liked to bet the Trifecta, picking the first, second, and third horses in the exact order, but only if he was sure of the outcome. Today, since he really hadn't come to the track to bet but only to get away and do some thinking, he decided just to bet the odds. Wise Guy had ten to one odds. He liked the horse, but his owner hadn't been too keen on him, so Vinny decided to pick Triumphant to win, Skirmish to Place, and She's A Prince to show, putting $200 on each horse. Then he went to the bar, ordered a double bourbon on the rocks, and headed out to the grandstand to watch the race.

It was a beautiful sunny day, a perfect day for racing, but Vinny was in no mood to enjoy the weather. He thought about going back to rigging races, which is what he had been doing as a teenager when Mancuso had first manhandled him for cutting in on his territory. *No point in getting beat up again.* There was always the drug business, but to make as much as half a million by January first, he'd have to get in big, and he didn't have the cash for that. Why did Ivan have to go and kill himself! Leaving him holding his debt. If he killed himself. Vinny didn't think Ivan was that kind of man. Then again, what would he do if he couldn't pay off a large I.O.U. to a man like Mancuso? *I won't kill myself,* he promised.

"And they're off!" The announcer's voice brought Vinny out of his reverie. "Spartan is off to an early lead.... Optimum taking his usual spot on the rail.... Life Support making a move on the outside.... As they enter the first turn, it's Spartan still in first, Life Support trailing by two lengths, then Skirmish, Optimum, She's A Prince, Triumphant, and Wise Guy bringing up the rear! Twenty-one and one in the opening quarter mile...."

Well, Ross had his horse figured out. Come on, Triumphant!

"As they enter the backstretch, She's a Prince is making a move on the outside, pulling into fourth.... Triumphant seems to be getting a second wind.... Life Support is beginning to fall back.... And here comes Wise Guy!" Vinny strained to see. Sure enough, Ross' horse was passing a few other horses on the far side of the track. *Come on, Triumphant! Let's go, Skirmish!*

"Entering the far turn we've got Spartan still holding steady in first, then Skirmish, Optimum.... Wise Guy is pulling even with Optimum.... Now he's passed him!... Triumphant is threading his way through the pack...."

Vinny pounded the plastic seat in front of him. *Come on, come on!*

"It's Spartan in first, Skirmish second, Triumphant third... and Wise Guy gaining on the outside...." *Triumphant! Triumphant!* "Looks like we've got ourselves a horse race, ladies and gentlemen...! And they're in the homestretch! Look out, here comes Wise Guy...!"

Wise Guy? You said he couldn't run!

"Spartan's got him by two lengths, Skirmish is neck-and-neck with Wise Guy, Triumphant is falling back!" *Falling back?* The announcer's voice was rising with excitement. "It's Spartan by a length.

The finish line is in sight.… Wise Guy is pulling even, they're neck-and-neck.… Spartan's jockey goes to the whip…. Still even… Look at those horses straining...!" *What happened to Skirmish?* "Here they come! Here they come! And … it's … Wise Guy by a nose, Spartan second, and Optimum sneaking past Skirmish to take third place!"

Wise Guy!!! Vinny crumpled his racing form and threw it on the ground in disgust. *He won, the horse won!* He kicked at the form. *No fire in the belly, right!* For a minute, he thought about looking for James Ross and confronting him about his horse. *Ah, forget about it!* He tore up his betting tickets and went into the bar.

"Double bourbon, Mac," Vinny said to the bartender when he sat down. When Mac served it, Vinny took a long drink. *Six hundred bucks down the tube. That's nothing when I'm looking at half a mil.* He sipped his bourbon, enjoying the warm tingle as it slid down his throat to his stomach.

He wished Carla was there. Always helped to have a nice broad on your arm. That Wanda wasn't too bad-looking herself. He swirled his drink around his glass, watching the brown liquid squeeze between the ice cubes, feeling his anger abating. Maybe he ought to invite her to the track sometime, as long as Carla didn't find out. Of course Joey would know, he knew everything. But he'd just explain she was Ivan's daughter, and he was "protecting our investment." Vinny suddenly sat straight up. Wait a minute, wait a minute! The best way to protect their investment was to get his hands on that investment! "Mac, gimme another!" he shouted to the bartender. Was to own that investment! And the best way to own that investment was to… Vinny leapt off the bar stool and ran out the door. "Hey, Vinny!" Mac called. "Your drink!"

Half an hour later Vinny pulled his Maserati into the circular drive at Cedar Ridge Farm. Wanda's red Corvette was parked nearby. He grabbed the flowers he'd bought on the way and walked onto the front porch. "Anybody home?" he shouted through the screen door.

Wanda appeared at the doorway. "Vinny!" she exclaimed, opening the door.

"Hiya, babe," he said. "For you." He held out the flowers.

"Roses! That's so sweet! Come in, come in." She held open the door and Vinny entered, then she passed him and led him into the living room, where her mother was looking through a glamour magazine. "Mom, look who's here!"

"Hello, Mrs. Heminger. How ya' doing?"

"Hello, Vinny. About as well as could be expected," Liz said.

"Yeah. I'm sure you're lonely. You, too, babe," he said, looking at Wanda.

"I miss Daddy so much," she said, her voice cracking a little.

"Sure you do," Vinny said sympathetically.

"I'll put these in some water," Wanda said, moving off towards the kitchen.

"Have a seat, Vinny," Liz said.

He sat down on the sofa, facing her chair. "I still can't believe Ivan's not with us. And to die that way…"

"At least the insurance company didn't give us any problem about paying up. It's not like he took out a policy then killed himself. Not that he killed himself, no way," Liz said firmly.

"I don't think he did, either, but what other explanation is there?"

"Gregory was there, but he claims he doesn't remember anything. Says Ivan drugged him and was going to kill him. Have you ever heard of anything so ridiculous?"

"Makes no sense. I think the cops were too light on Gregory, if you ask me."

"Me, too."

"So, your money come in?" Vinny asked, as casually as he could. "I mean, how are you paying for food and stuff?"

"Any day now, they say. Ivan split the insurance money half-and-half with Wanda and me. That's good 'cause she'll need it to pay for school."

"Gotta get that education," Vinny said, with as much enthusiasm as he could muster. He was developing other ideas about how Wanda might spend that money. "And what about the inheritance, if you don't mind me asking?"

"Oh, no, Vinny, I don't mind. You've been real nice, coming by to see us and all, after the death. The inheritance is going to take some months, I believe, but the lawyer says they'll be no problem, I'll inherit everything."

"Good." Depending on how much life insurance Ivan had, and how much Wanda's half would be, he might not have to be concerned about the inheritance, though it never hurt to have as many irons in the fire as possible. If he could stay on the good side of Liz, there'd be no reason to worry about access to her money, assuming things worked out the way he hoped.

"Aren't they pretty?" Wanda said, entering and placing the flowers on a table. "I just love the smell of roses."

"Me, too." Vinny rose. "Well, I just wanted to see how you both were doing. Take care, Mrs. Heminger."

"Come any time, Vinny," Liz said.

"Thanks, I'll do that."

"I'll walk out with you," Wanda said.

"I'd like that," Vinny answered, with his most charming smile.

He and Wanda went out the front door and down the porch steps towards his car. "Your mom looks pretty good," he said.

"She's doing all right. A lot better than I am."

"That why you came back from Penn State?"

"I was just so lonely. I didn't have the energy for anything."

They reached the car. "Wanda," Vinny began, "I've been thinking… Since you're here, and since you're lonely, what would you think about going out with me?"

Wanda looked surprised. "Going out?"

"Well, yeah. I took you to that party last summer, and you had a good time, I think."

"I had a great time!"

"Me, too. And, well, there're not many parties around anymore, but maybe we could think of something else to do."

"You mean, like a date, Vinny?" She looked at him with her large blue eyes.

He looked back at her with his small olive ones. "Sure, call it a date, if you want. We could go to the movies, or just ride around." He gave her his sincerest look. "I'd just like to spend some time with you, Wanda. What do you say?"

"I say yes!" She laughed, and Vinny did, too.

"Great!"

"That would take care of my nights," Wanda said pensively. "Now if I could just figure out how to fill the daytime hours." She turned towards the barn. "It's so quiet here without any horses. I've never been on Cedar Ridge Farm when there weren't any horses. I wish I had a horse," she sighed.

Suddenly an idea hit Vinny like a left hook to the head. A horse! A horse! That's what would make Wanda happy. And whatever would make Wanda happy would make Vinny more than happy. "I wish you had a horse, too, Wanda," Vinny said. And he vowed to make her wish come true!

CHAPTER 7

The slow, very slow, melody of the *Das Loblied* spilled out of the open doors in the Zook barn. Rebecca sat next to her good friend, Madie Lapp, the other women on backless benches on one side of the barn, the men and boys seated on the other, their voices blending in the sing-song rise and fall of the familiar words. No one needed to look at the *Ausbund,* the hymnal. Tradition was strong in the Amish faith, and *Das Loblied* had been at the core of Amish worship since the first hymns created by Anabaptists were published in 1564.

> *O Gott Vater, wir loben dich und deine Gute preisen wir,*
> *Die du, O Herr, so gnaediglich*
> *An uns neu hast bewiesen.*

Even though Rebecca spoke only Pennsylvania Deutsch, she understood the High German words of the hymn completely.

> "O God Father, we praise You
> And Your goodness exalt,
> Which You, O Lord, so graciously
> Have manifested to us anew."

Rebecca closed her eyes and listened to the warbling voice of the song leader, the *Vorsinger*, stretching out the words in chant-like rhythm, the congregation responding, the *Vorsinger* again, then the congregation, the voices slowly stretching the words on and on and on. Rebecca had once heard that the early Anabaptist martyrs had sung their hymns slowly on purpose so that passers-by could not understand the words. If she hadn't known them by heart, she, too, could not possibly have understood them.

The martyrs. Rebecca loved that about her faith, how the early believers had been so strong in their faith that they would give up their lives rather than forsake their religious beliefs. They rejected the Catholic Church's authority and believed that the true church was composed of only those who separated themselves from the corrupt world and obediently followed the teachings of Jesus. As in many Amish households, the Zooks had a copy of *Martyrs Mirror,* a thick book with over a thousand pages filled with the stories of those who had built the foundation of the Amish church, a foundation that supported Rebecca's faith to that very day. Her favorite was Dirk Willems.

"It is your Christian duty to return good for evil." Rebecca could still remember her father's words when he'd first read her Dirk's story. Dirk had escaped from prison. When the guard pursuing him fell through the ice, Dirk had gone back and rescued him. But the guard turned him in and he was burned at the stake. "How could he be so brave?" she'd asked her father. "I don't think I could do it."

"You can do anything with God on your side," her father had solemnly answered.

Yes, I can, Rebecca thought, as she continued singing. What she had decided to do was not as significant as dying for your faith, but it was an important decision nonetheless. She stole a glance across the barn to where Jacob was seated. She was scared. But she knew what she was doing what God wanted her to do. Because when she'd prayed and opened her eyes that morning, God had given her a sign. The memory excited her again. He had been far away on Bojangles, on a little rise, and he'd waved his arm towards… what? The farm? Her? It didn't matter. She'd seen Gregory.

Knowing what God wanted her to do was the easy part, however. Now came the hard part. Telling Jacob. And then telling her family. Especially her mother. She could hear her now. "Rebecca, you're twenty-two, this could be your last chance." Well, just because it might be her last chance, didn't mean she should take it. Dirk Willems had a chance to keep on running, but he didn't take it. He did the Christian thing. And telling Jacob is the Christian thing. He wouldn't want a wife who didn't love him. And even if he did, Rebecca didn't want to marry someone she didn't love.

Rebecca let out such a deep sigh that Madie asked, "Are you all right?" She nodded. She wasn't really all right, and she'd soon probably be feeling a lot worse, but eventually she'd be fine. She was sure of it.

She looked toward the front of the barn. Omar King stepped forward and began the opening sermon. Then there would be a silent, kneeling prayer, a scripture reading, then the main sermon, then various men would stand and affirm what was said in the sermon, or maybe express different opinions about it. The Amish church was a communal church. All were encouraged to be part of the service. Except the women. Rebecca still didn't understand why women weren't allowed to speak. Well, she understood it — tradition — but she didn't think it was right. There were plenty of things in God's world she didn't understand, of course. That's where faith came in. Faith, and acceptance.

"H-h-here I am, Lord," Omar intoned, with his usual stutter. It might seem unusual to have a preacher who stuttered, but Amish ministers weren't preachers as a profession. They were chosen by lot. "Abraham answered the L-L-Lord," Omar continued. Rebecca settled in for the sermon. It was one of the favorite themes of Amish worship: Abraham's obedience to God. He was even willing to kill his own son, Isaac, just because God said he must. *I couldn't do it*, she said to herself, even before Omar began the story. *I couldn't kill my own child. How could Abraham raise that knife?* She shuddered. And then she prayed. *Forgive me, Lord, for my unbelief. And please, don't ever ask me for such a sacrifice.*

It was a selfish prayer, Rebecca knew, and she immediately felt bad for having prayed it. Why was she having such thoughts? Was it because she knew she might be being disobedient for choosing not to marry Jacob? No one had ordered her to marry him. She was a grown-up woman, free to make her own choice. But she worried that members of the church might think her wrong for not obeying tradition by refusing to marry a good and godly man like Jacob, just because she didn't love him.

Be still my mind! Feeling she must direct her mind away from churchly matters, even though it was a kind of disobedience, she forced herself to think about the one person she loved to think about.

What was Gregory doing now, she pondered. Maybe she should have taken Lydie's hint and invited him to church? She wondered what he thought about Abraham and Isaac. Would he be able to do it? Sometimes men are stronger than women. No, she didn't think he could do it. What if it were their child*? Slow down, Rebecca!* She was getting way ahead of herself!

Some hundred yards away, the object of Rebecca's thoughts was sitting outside his cottage in the warm morning sun, listening to the service. Gregory couldn't understand a word of it, but he loved listening to the singing. Now he could faintly hear Omar's voice coming through the open barn door. He thought of Rebecca, sitting inside. She would be wearing the pale purple dress with black cape and apron she wore every Sunday, her hair tucked under her covering. He wanted to see her hair let down again! It was so beautiful. But how could he? She was engaged to Jacob. "Gosh darn it!" he shouted impulsively.

He realized he might have been heard inside the barn. Feeling a little silly, he got out of his chair and retreated to the other side of the cottage. *I'll just lie in the grass until church is over.* Then maybe he could think of some excuse to see Rebecca. He lay down and felt the warm sunshine cover his body like a soft blanket.

Three hours later Rebecca and the other women spilled out of the barn and began to lay out the food on the long table Henry and Elam had brought down from the main house. It was a simple meal, since the host family was in charge of making all the food. Homemade bread, pickles, red beets, coffee, and *schnitz* pie.

Madie was her usual chatty self, as she and Rebecca worked. "I'm getting so excited, Rebecca. Just think, in another six weeks I'll be Mrs. Amos Yoder!"

"I'm very happy for you, Madie," Rebecca said, using a bread knife to slice a large loaf.

"I can't decide whether my dress should be sky blue or navy blue. What do you think?"

"It's your wedding, Madie. But I love the color of the sky."

"Me, too. I'll come by your shop and we can pick out the fabric. I've got to hurry, I don't have that much time to make my dress. We'll be published Sunday after next. Has your dat decided the date and time of your wedding? I hope it's not the same as ours. I want you to be one of my *newehockers.*"

Such a funny name, "newehocker," thought Rebecca. *"Sidesitter."* Being "published" was when the deacon announced in church the names of the girls and who they planned to marry. All those things would not be happening for her For a minute, she felt a twinge of regret. She could see how utterly happy Madie was. Was she a fool for giving up a chance at that happiness?

"Don't forget to try my *schnitz* pie, Becca. You, too, Madie." Rebecca looked up to see Hanna smiling her crooked smile. "It'll put some meat on those skinny bones."

"I might have a small piece, Ms. Zook, but I've got to watch my weight so I can fit into my dress," Madie said.

"Just make it bigger!" Hanna said.

Rebecca laughed. Of all the Amish she knew, her aunt Hanna had the sweetest tooth. She was always eating candy, she loved to dump sugar on just about everything, and she'd been known to consume nothing but cookies for breakfast and claim she was eating just fine.

Just then she saw Jacob out of the corner of her eye. He had taken his plate of food and wandered toward a tree near the crick. He was alone. This was her chance to talk to him. A chance she didn't want to take. A chance she had to.

"Excuse me," she said to Hanna and Madie. She put down the bread knife, wiped her hands gently on her apron, and set off.

"Goin' to see your fancy, eh?" Hanna called after her, laughing. *You won't be laughing when you know why I'm going*, Rebecca thought sadly.

"Hello, Jacob," she said, when she had reached him standing under a shade tree.

"Hello, Rebecca," he answered. He smiled at her beneath his neatly-combed black hair, his brown eyes meeting her gaze steadily.

Such a nice man. No, don't think like that, that doesn't help! "How's the food?" Rebecca asked.

"Very *gut*. What did you make?"

"I made the red beets."

"Delicious. You make the best beets of anybody I know."

Stop being so polite! Rebecca looked up at the sky. *Say it now, Rebecca, just say it!* "It's awfully hot for October, isn't it?" *You're talking about the weather?* she scolded herself.

"It is. I heard some of the youngsters talk about going swimming in the crick. Would you go?"

He was asking her to go swimming? This wasn't going well! "I might," she said. The Amish didn't wear bathing suits. The girls waded in the water with their dresses on, and the men went in wearing their trousers. Rebecca would have liked to wade in and float right away!

"Jacob," Rebecca began, "I need to talk to you."

"Sure." He placed the food on the ground. "Do you want to sit?"

"I don't think so." He looked at her. *God, please give me the words. The right words, the words that won't hurt him too much.*

"Jacob, remember how I said I would tell you whether I would marry you — I mean, whether we'd be getting married — I mean, you know, whether we'd be published this year after the crops were in, and…" *Just say it, Rebecca! Just say the words!* "Jacob, I think you are a really *gut* man, a very kind man, and I'm so flattered that you want me to be your wife, but, Jacob, I just cannot marry you." Rebecca looked at Jacob. *You must look at him!* she told herself. *He deserves your complete attention and your complete honesty.*

Rebecca saw the shock in Jacob's eyes. His mouth opened wider, his eyebrows rose. He didn't breath for a long minute, and neither did Rebecca. *Look how I've hurt him!*

"I see," he said softly. He looked at her. She forced herself to meet his gaze. "I can see that you mean it. That you have no doubt." He stared at her a long time, then said, "I'm sorry, Rebecca."

"Jacob, I am, too! I'm so very sorry! I wanted to be in love with you, I tried so hard, I really did, I tried to make myself think we could be married and live a happy life, but when I looked deep into my heart, when I made myself stare with penetrating eyes into the very bottom of my soul, I just couldn't make myself believe it. You really are a wonderful person, and you deserve a wonderful woman who will make you very, very happy. I just don't think I am that woman. Please forgive me, Jacob, please!"

"There's nothing to forgive, Rebecca. You are being honest with me. And with yourself. That's all God wants from us. Complete honesty." He took a moment to look at her, as if for the last time. "Good-bye, Rebecca." He bent down, picked up his plate, and walked slowly off, never looking back.

"Oh, God!" Rebecca whispered loudly. She ran down the bank to the edge of the crick, then slammed to a stop.

There it was! The stone! The stone that had been lodged just off the bridge that crossed the crick in the middle of her farm. The stone she had imagined her life to be, when she had felt stuck in her Amish life, the stone in the crick she had prayed so hard would move. "Why did you move?" she cried in anguish at the stone. "Why did my life have to change so much?"

And then she cried for real. She stood on the bank of the crick and heaved great sobs of sorrow at what she had done. *God's will can hurt so much sometimes.*

CHAPTER 8

Gregory heard water splashing. It sounded like the surf on the beach in South Carolina. He and Rebecca were in the ocean, splashing each other like children. She was wearing a bathing suit. The Amish didn't wear bathing suits, he thought. Rebecca took a big swing with her arm and cascaded water at him. She was laughing, laughing. Then it seemed like there were more of her, laughter was coming from everywhere. How could this be? The laughter grew louder and louder....

Gregory opened his eyes and sat up. He looked around. He was sitting in the grass behind his cottage. He heard the laughter again, this time mixed with men's voices. It was coming from the other side of the cottage. He'd been dreaming. He smiled. It had been a wonderful dream. He and Rebecca had been happy together, there in the surf in South Carolina. She had been dressed as an Englisher. Gregory had a sudden thought. Maybe he didn't have to become Amish. Maybe she would become English.

He got up and walked around to the front of the cottage, where the laughter was louder. He looked down to where the small crick that ran through the farm fed into the larger crick. He could see young people standing around.

Gregory walked towards the crowd on the crickbank. As he got closer, he could see that several of the Amish boys and girls had waded into the water, a few of them splashing water at each other, the girls giggling, the boys shouting. He moved beside a tree, partially hiding himself, scanning the crowd. Where was Rebecca?

Then he saw her. She was standing apart from the others, staring at them. She was holding her arms around her body, as if hugging herself. He'd never seen her stand like that. She didn't look happy. He had a strong urge to run to her to see what was the matter. But he knew he couldn't.

Rebecca didn't move and neither did Gregory. Other Amish continued wading into the crick. None of them swam. It would have been hard for the women to swim in their dresses. The men would have been encumbered by their pants and vests. He bet they didn't even know how to swim. Where would they learn? They wouldn't go to a swimming pool. They'd have to learn in the crick. Imagine not knowing how to swim! What if one of them slipped and fell in? He watched them intently for a moment, then decided the crick wasn't that deep; they could probably stand up even in the deepest part.

Suddenly, a yellow canoe came floating down the river. The man paddling steered it towards the bank. Gregory watched him get out. He was Amish, dressed in pants, suspenders, and a white shirt, no coat. He had a thick head of blond hair, and seemed to have bigger biceps than most Amish men. He looked to be about Gregory's age, twenty-five, maybe a little younger.

Many of the men came down to the crick to examine the canoe. Gregory could hear their voices. "Beautiful.... Must have cost quite a lot.... Why would you buy a canoe...?" Gregory thought the same thing. He had never considered that an Amish person would own a canoe.

Then Gregory got a clear look at the man. *Johnny!* He knew he'd seen that face before. That time he went to church. Gregory's eyes narrowed. He'd heard that Johnny had been an old boyfriend of Rebecca's.

Johnny got out of his canoe and pulled in onto the bank. One or two of the men approached him and began talking in earnest. Gregory couldn't hear what they were saying, but Johnny's smile left his face. He nodded his head at one of the men, then turned and looked in Rebecca's direction. Her back was to Johnny. Gregory watched him go to Rebecca and tap her on the shoulder. She turned, and Gregory could see how surprised she was to see Johnny.

Gregory thought about moving down the smaller crick so he could hear better, but he didn't want to be seen. They'd think he was snooping on them. Then he saw something that amazed him. Johnny led Rebecca down to the canoe, helped her in, got in himself and pushed off into the crick. Several of the men and women waved at them. Johnny grabbed the paddle and began stroking on one side, then the other, the yellow canoe moving slowly down the larger crick.

Before he knew what he was doing, Gregory started running after the canoe. He didn't run to the crickbank. He didn't have to. He knew where the crick ran; he had explored it several times in his four months on the Zook farm. He took off across the pasture. Fortunately, there were trees growing beside the crick, affording Gregory protection in case Johnny or Rebecca chanced to look in his direction. But they didn't. They were deep in conversation, Johnny gesturing animatedly, one time thrusting the paddle into the air, making Rebecca laugh.

The crick turned away from the pasture. Gregory tried to follow, but the bank became steep and overgrown with high grass. He stumbled and fell. When he looked up, he could see the canoe moving quickly away from him. He jumped up, ignoring a small cut on his forearm, and ran along the crick. They were too far ahead to see him. And they weren't looking anywhere but at each other. *Why was she with him? Why was she with him?* The question kept pounding into his brain.

The canoe came to a fork in the crick. Gregory could see that Johnny was steering the canoe towards the left fork, towards Gregory's side. He could still follow them if they took that fork. But Rebecca pointed to the right, urgently. So Johnny switched the paddle to the other side of the canoe, and they moved down the right fork and, eventually, out of Gregory's sight.

Gregory stopped. He was breathing hard from running. He waded into the water. It flowed around his calves, cooling him. Impulsively, he sat down, the water rising to his waist. He was hot and tired, but mostly he was… empty. He felt empty. Like Rebecca had gone off with someone and now she was gone forever. He knew it wasn't true, that she'd be back at the farm eventually. But that's the way he felt. *Bereft.*

He sat for a long while, staring at the water. Several tiny fish swam nearby. Some leaves floated past, reminding him that autumn was here. *Jacob.* He'd been worrying she'd marry Jacob. But she went off with Johnny*!*

He knew he wouldn't have a chance to talk to Rebecca today. It was Sunday, a day of rest for the Amish. She would be spending it with her family. *Once she gets back from her canoe trip*, he thought bitterly. Then he had an idea. He wasn't going to sit there and mope. He had people he could visit, too. And he turned and splashed his way out of the crick and back to his cottage.

A half hour later he was tying Bo up to a fencepost near the Heminger stable. He saw Wanda's Corvette and was headed towards the house when he noticed the stable door open. He reversed his steps, entered, and climbed the stairs to the second floor. Light spilled from an open doorway. Gregory glanced inside. Wanda was seated at Ivan's desk, looking at something.

He paused, remembering the last time he had been in this office. He'd been searching for clues as to why Ivan would have wanted to kill the racehorses in his stables, including Wanda's horse, Dandelion, and Bojangles. And he'd found the motivation: a slip of paper that seemed to indicate Ivan owed $500,000 to someone. Gregory never found out who. Ivan took that information with him to the grave. And whoever it was hadn't showed up to collect the debt. Yet.

"Knock, knock," Gregory said.

"Oh, Gregory!" Wanda said. "Hi. Come in."

He walked towards the desk. Wanda was wearing her usual ~~pair of~~ jeans and a dark blue Ralph Lauren polo shirt. "Whatcha doing?" he asked.

"Looking through some old photographs I found in Daddy's files." She held one up to him. It was Wanda at about age twelve, sitting on a horse, holding a blue ribbon. She looked very happy and very beautiful. "My first blue ribbon."

"You won a bunch of them. I saw them all framed in that room down the hall."

"You were in here before?"

Gregory realized that no one, not even Ivan, knew that he had once snooped around the entire barn. He didn't want to lie, and there was no reason Wanda should be suspicious. "Yes," he answered simply, hoping that would be sufficient answer. "Is that Dandelion?"

"No, that was my first horse. Daisy. She died, too, but not because..." Wanda stopped. *Not because my father killed him,* Gregory finished the thought for her in his head. "I wish I had another horse, but we don't have any money."

"Didn't your father have life insurance? Maybe through his law firm?"

"He did. A million dollars. Half for me and half for Mother."

"Well, that's great — I mean...." Gregory paused. "I mean I'm sorry you have to collect it, Wanda, but I'm glad you and your mother will have something to live on. That will pay for school, and it might even pay for a horse."

"Maybe. When we get it. At least it's not 'if' we get it. We were worried the insurance company wouldn't pay because the police ruled it was a suicide."

"But he'd had the policy longer than three years, right, so it was all right. That's what the law usually states."

"Yes. I guess we'll get a check someday, we just don't know when."

"Wanda, you don't have to answer if you don't want to, but..." Gregory hesitated. It was a hard question, but he needed to ask it. "Do you think your father killed himself?"

"No, I don't! That's just not like Daddy. But how did he get that poison in his system? You were with him, Gregory, do you know?"

Gregory had told his story to the police, but he had asked them not to tell Wanda and Mrs. Heminger unless they had to. There was no point in saying to Wanda, "Your father tried to poison me and somehow got the poison in himself." He had a strong suspicion that the answer to what went on that night lay with discovering who put his head on a pillow and covered him with a quilt, who it was he thought he'd heard call him "son."

"Wanda, I want to talk to you about the future, all right?" Gregory took a breath. "I've been trying to decide what I want to do with my life. And I've decided I want it to be something to do with horses."

"That's great. I know you love them as much as I do."

"I do. And that's the point. You love horses, and I love horses. So maybe we should do something together about horses."

"You and me and horses...? But, what?"

"That's the problem, I don't know. I thought if we talked about it, maybe we could come up with an idea."

Wanda got up from her chair. "Horses..." She walked around the room, thinking. "Do you know how to take care of them?"

"I don't think I could be a blacksmith, if that's what you mean."

"Even if you could, what would I do? The only thing I know how to do is ride."

"But you do it beautifully." Gregory thought for a minute. "That's it!" he said excitedly. "You could teach people to ride."

"I'd love that!" Wanda exclaimed. "I'd love to teach. I could teach them to jump, too, I'm really good at that. I'd be a great teacher, Gregory."

"I know you would, Wanda. But there's one problem."

Wanda stopped pacing, realizing. "We don't have a horse," she said. Gregory nodded. Then she brightened. "But we could buy one, as soon as the insurance money comes in."

"I guess so. But you sure you want to spend your money on buying a horse? You've got school and other expenses."

"Maybe we could use some of Mother's money. She'll be getting a lot more when she gets her inheritance."

"I don't know about that, Wanda. I'd like it to be our money. But I don't have much."

"Let's not let that stand in our way now, Gregory. Think: how else could we make money besides teaching? If we can show Mother how we'll make money, she might want to invest in our business."

"We could sell stuff," Gregory said. "We could have a tack shop."

"Yeah, maybe. We could sell saddles, bridles, everything."

"Elam is opening a leather shop. He could supply us."

"Fantastic!" Wanda cried. "This is turning into a really good idea."

Gregory thought so, too. It would be a kind of payback for all the kindness the Zook family had shown him. And he could still live on their farm and do the business with Wanda.

"I've got another great idea!" Wanda said. "When I was a little girl, I loved everything to do with horses. I used to buy little plastic horses. And then I'd buy the barns, the water troughs, I'd put up fences and make pastures. I spent hours playing with my horses on my farm. We could sell all those things!"

"Yes, I see, I see..." Gregory pondered. He didn't really like plastic things, but the Amish seemed to love plastic. Many of their homes had plastic birds sitting on plastic branches. They had plastic flowers on the tables, even plastic clocks. These people of the earth never hesitated to buy things not of the earth. It was a paradox that had often puzzled Gregory. He admired the Amish. But that didn't mean he had to be exactly like them. "Wanda," he said. "I'd want the horses to be either wooden or a nice ceramic. And I definitely want the barns and fences to be wooden. Let's stay away from plastic."

"Agreed. You can do all the legal stuff, can't you, Gregory, setting up the partnership?"

Gregory remembered his promise to help Rebecca with her business. And now Wanda. *For a man who didn't pass the bar, he sure had a lot of legal business on his plate!* "I'd be glad to, Wanda," he said.

"Gregory, I think it'd be great to work with you, but let's not go too fast, okay? A lot has happened to me, and I need to think about this. All right?"

"Of course, Wanda. I need to think about it, too. But it does feel kinda right, doesn't it?"

"It really does."

"I'd better be going."

"I'll walk you out."

They walked outside to where Bo was tied up. Suddenly, both stopped dead in their tracks and shouted simultaneously, "Bojangles!" Bo snapped his head around to look at them. But they hadn't been calling him. It had just hit them: "We do have a horse!" Wanda said, and they both began to laugh at the stupidity of not remembering Bo.

But Gregory stopped laughing. He remembered how upset Rebecca had been when he'd begun stabling Bo at Cedar Ridge Farm. She'd missed him so much, and now he was going to take him away from her again.

"Wanda," he said slowly, "We could always use Bo, I guess, but I hope we don't have to. I'd like him to stay at the Zook farm. He likes it there, and I don't really want him to be in lessons all the time. Is that selfish of me?"

"No, Gregory, I understand," she replied. "We've agreed to go slow, and it'll take a long time to set this up if we do decide to go ahead. If we're ready to go, and we don't have the insurance money yet, then we can talk about using Bo for lessons."

"Thanks." He mounted Bo and swung him around to face Wanda.

"No, thank you, Gregory," she replied. "I've been obsessing about the past. It's nice to have something in the future to think about instead. I'm so glad you came over to talk about this partnership." She smiled gratefully at him.

"Me, too," Gregory said,

He turned Bo around and rode off. He felt really good, not just because he may have thought of something to do with his life, but also because his idea seemed to have made a real difference to Wanda. Best of all, he had completely forgotten about Johnny, Rebecca, and the yellow canoe.

CHAPTER 9

Rebecca slowly opened her eyes, lying in bed in her neat and tidy room. Once again, she drank in the peace around her, the calm stillness. She turned her head to the right and looked out her window. Cloudy. The sun would not rise in majestic glory this morning. *How appropriate.* It would probably be a cloudy day for her.

She lay for a moment, thinking about yesterday's conversation with Jacob. How she had hated what she'd had to tell him! Watching Jacob slowly move off, she'd felt worse than she had in years. Of course, why would he have wanted to stay, with everybody splashing about and having fun? When Amos Yoder had come up to Jacob, Rebecca had turned away. She could imagine what Jacob had told him. Soon the whole crowd would know.

Then the strangest thing had happened. Johnny Schmucker had tapped her on the shoulder. "Hi, Becky," he'd said. He was the only person she let call her that.

"Johnny!" she'd gasped. Even though she knew he'd decided to give up trying to become a professional baseball player and had returned to the family farm, she hadn't seen him since he'd been back. And now her old boyfriend was standing before her, on this of all days.

Johnny had gotten right to the point. "They told me you'd broken up with Jacob. I'm sorry, Becky. I know it must have been hard to tell him." She could only nod her head. "Hey, Becky," he'd suddenly said. "Let's get out of here."

"Out of here?"

"In my canoe."

Johnny had a canoe? She didn't know anybody who had a canoe. But, then, she didn't know anybody like Johnny. "I bought one, see?" He'd pointed towards the canoe.

"I don't know...."

"It'll do you good, Becky," he'd urged. "You don't want to stay here with everybody, do you?" He hadn't waited for an answer. "And I'm betting you don't want to go home and face your parents, at least right away."

Rebecca couldn't deny the truth of that. "I've never been in a canoe."

"It's fun! It'll be relaxing on the crick. Let me paddle you down and back. We won't be gone long."

Rebecca had relented. It was true, she had really wanted to get away from the group and she hadn't wanted to go home or talk to anyone in her family. And Johnny was always fun. He was high-spirited, full of confidence and good humor — exactly what she'd needed at that low point in her life.

The trip down the crick had indeed been relaxing, the current slow and steady. Johnny had hardly needed to paddle as they'd drifted past trees with limbs that draped web-like over the water, the sun glinting through the branches, bouncing its golden light off the wave-less water. Rebecca could look down through the clear water and see the swarms of minnows darting this way and that above the small stones scattered like seeds over an aquatic countryside.

Johnny had kept silent for a while, letting the calm of the crick ease its way into Rebecca. Finally, he'd spoken. "Feeling better?"

"Yes. Thank you for making me come."

"I hope I didn't have to make you too much. I hope my charm and good looks had a little to do with your decision," he joked.

Rebecca had smiled. Johnny's carefree humor had been a tonic for her sadness. "Just a little."

"Good. You know, Becky, I am sorry about you and Jacob. But, in all honesty, I'm glad, too. Because since you're no longer engaged, maybe you'll reconsider my offer to let me be part of your life, now that I've given up baseball. I'm going to inherit the farm from my folks. It's a *gut* farm."

Before answering, Rebecca had stuck her hand in the water and watched it slice through the crick like a small motorboat. *Why can't I move through life like that? So effortlessly.* Sensing her hesitation, Johnny had continued. "I don't expect you to answer today, or even any time soon. I just hope you'll consider letting me go to a singing with you, or walk you home after church, you know, simple things."

Simple things. If only life were that simple. "I hear you, Johnny. And I'm glad you don't' expect me to talk about it today — Wait, watch where you're going!" she'd suddenly shouted

"I'm taking the left fork."

"You can't! Mam told me never to take that fork. It leads to a high dam next to the quarry. It's dangerous. Haven't you ever been there?"

"No, I've never been down the crick in a canoe."

"Me, neither." Rebecca suddenly pointed, "Look, see how the water is rushing against itself! It's a rip tide!"

Johnny had laughed. "The crick doesn't have tides, Rebecca."

"That's what my mam calls it. Just please don't go to the left."

"Fine." With a few quick strokes of his paddle, Johnny had headed them down the right fork.

"Thank you."

"Anything dangerous down this way?"

"No. It's quite peaceful. Just what I need. Johnny, if you don't mind, could we just drift along in silence for a while?"

"Sure."

And that's what they had done. Rebecca had enjoyed gazing at cows munching grass in the pastures near the shore, following the zigzag of butterflies dipping and diving above the water, drinking in the cool, crisp October air. And when Johnny had rammed the canoe back on the bank near her farm an hour later, she'd realized that Johnny had rescued her from the anguished aftermath of her dreadful decision, at least for a while.

But not any longer, she thought, as she got up from her bed and put on her dress, cape, apron, and shoes. Looking out the window, she saw Henry and her father already at work in the fields. *That means Mam and Hanna are alone.* Gathering her strength, she descended the stairs.

"Morning, Mam," she said, entering the kitchen.

"Morning," her mother responded, pouring out Rebecca's cup of coffee.

"Wash day, Becca. You got anything needs washing?" Hanna asked. She loved washing clothes and was sorry the Amish washed only once a week.

"Only what I've already put in the basket, Hanna."

"It might rain, Hanna," Mabel said. "Maybe you should hold off."

"It won't rain," Hanna replied.

"It is cloudy, Hanna," Rebecca chimed in.

"No rain," Hanna said firmly.

"How do you know?" Mabel asked.

"I got six senses."

"You mean a 'sixth sense'?" Rebecca asked.

"Yep. I might have a seventh and a eighth sense, too," Hanna said proudly. "That's why I always can tell if it's going to rain."

"You'll be sorry if you're wrong," Mabel said. "Having to bring in all those wet clothes."

"I'll just get you to help me!" Hanna said, laughing.

"No, you won't," Mabel assured her. "I've got my own chores to do."

"You don't work hard enough, Mabel. Everybody knows that."

"How dare you say such a thing!"

"I'm a daring person," Hanna said, and Rebecca laughed.

"You're also an impossible one," Mabel countered. She took her coffee cup to the table and sat down. Hanna sat with her, and Rebecca leaned against the countertop. For a moment, all three women sipped in silence. *Now is the time. But how do I do it?*

Hanna paved the way. "Saw you talking to Jacob yesterday, Becca. He didn't look too happy when you were finished."

"He wasn't."

"Why not?" Mabel asked.

Rebecca screwed up her courage, once again praying, *God, please give me the right words.* "Mam, I told Jacob I wasn't going to marry him."

"What?" Mabel put down her coffee so forcefully it spilled on the table. "You called off your wedding?"

"Yes, Mam."

"What is wrong with you, Rebecca?" Mabel began, her anger growing. "Jacob is a *gut* man, from a *gut* family, with a *gut* farming business. Why would you do such a thing?"

"I don't love him," Rebecca answered.

"Love's got nothing to do with it. I didn't love your father when I married him, but I do now."

"I can't count on that happening to me, Mam," Rebecca pleaded. "I can't take that chance."

"Chance? Chance?" her mother almost shouted. "This is probably your last chance and you'll end up an old maid. *Du bist ferhoodled!*"

Her mother was right, she did feel mixed up. But, mixed up or not, she had made her decision and she was sticking to it. "I'm sorry, Mam. I know I may have hurt you with this decision."

"Hurt? No, I'm not hurt, daughter. I'm embarrassed, is what I am. What will his parents think? And the church? How can I show my face at church after this? You ought to be ashamed of yourself."

Rebecca didn't answer. What could she say? She didn't feel ashamed. She actually felt proud of herself for doing what she knew was the right thing, for Jacob and for her. And maybe one day her mother would come to feel that it had been the right thing, too.

"Leave her alone, Mabel," Hanna said. "Let it go. What's done is done. *Sie's un gute maidel.*" Rebecca looked at her aunt, grateful for the support.

"I didn't say she wasn't *gut* girl, but even *gut* girls can make bad choices. Have you told your father?"

"I'm going out there now."

"He'll be on your side, like always," Mabel said, a little bitterly.

It was true. Rebecca shared the special relationship daughters often have with their fathers. Her dat was always kind to her, always supported her, always loved her. She knew her mam loved her, too, and she loved Mabel, but love was often more complicated between mothers and daughters.

Hanna put an arm around Rebecca. "Don't you worry none, Becca. You'll find yourself another man. And if you don't, why, we can be old maids together." She leaned down to whisper in her ear. "Sometimes it's better without the men."

Rebecca put her arm around Hanna, rested her head on her shoulder, and gave her a thankful squeeze. Then she put her cup in the sink and left the kitchen, not looking at her mother. Time for healing would have to come later.

When she reached her father, Elam was coming out of the barn after milking. "Finished your chores already?"

"No, Dat, but I wanted to talk to you before breakfast."

"'Bout you and Jacob?"

"You know?"

"Hard to keep something like that a secret for long — though I'm proud of myself for keeping it from your mother. I wanted you to be the one to tell her. How'd she respond?"

"She wasn't happy, Dat."

"No, I 'spect not. But God will help her get over it."

Rebecca smiled. That was one thing she loved about her father, his way of accepting the simple truths of living. He was a superb example of the deep Amish belief that the will of God ruled everything. Bumper crop? Will of God. Bugs ate your tobacco? Will of God. Marriage not going forward? Will of God.

"I do have some good news, though, Dat. Gregory is coming to the shop today to talk to Mrs. Ansbacher and me about selling me her business. I think I'm getting closer to actually owning my own quilt shop."

"That's wonderful, Rebecca. Now you let me know if you need any money, you hear?"

"I will. But Mrs. Ansbacher is giving me really favorable terms."

"At least you're buying a business, not doing what I'm going to be doing."

"I wish it was going faster with the Lancaster Farmland Trust so you could start your leather shop, Dat."

"I didn't know it would be so hard to give away the development rights to our farm."

"How does it work?"

"Well, I'm giving up the right to sell my farm for development so they've got to figure out how much those rights are worth. To do that, they've got to make an appraisal of the property."

"Who, the Lancaster Farmland Trust?"

"Yes. Those are pretty good folks. They've preserved over four hundred and seventy-five farms in Lancaster County alone."

"That's so wonderful! That many farms will be Amish forever?"

"I'm not sure they're all Amish, but a good many of 'em are. They'll be farms forever. And guess what Gregory just told me."

"What?"

"Once the appraisal's in, the Trust will give me a cash payment for a portion of it. They pay as much as $1500 an acre."

"Dat, that's — !" She paused, trying to do the math.

"Many thousand dollars, I know," Elam said with a smile. "Don't tell your mam, though. I don't want her to think we're rich!"

Rebecca laughed. "I won't."

"Thank goodness Gregory's helping me with the paperwork. Turns out he's a right handy man to have around, wouldn't you say?"

Rebecca blushed and turned aside to hide it. "Right handy to have around" was one way of putting it. Gregory might be "around," however, but she hardly ever got to spend time with him. What would they do together, anyway? Sometimes, to be nice, her mam had told her to invite Gregory to eat with them, but that had been hard, sitting near him but not really being able to talk about anything important. Like how they felt about each other. They had kissed on that long walk they took after church one Sunday. He had said he loved her, and she had told him she loved him. But then it seemed they had both realized the impossibility of their situation. They couldn't declare their love. She was engaged to Jacob. And Gregory was English. Was she ready to leave the Amish church to marry him? Was he ready to become Amish? These were important questions, but when could they talk about them? She couldn't just sneak out to his cottage to meet him some night. And he hadn't invited her to do so, in any case. If anything, he seemed to have pulled back in his feelings for her. Why hadn't he tried to kiss her when she had gone to the barn to ask him about being her legal counsel? *Out of respect for my situation with Jacob?* Maybe when he heard about her and Jacob, he'd ask her for a walk or something. They had to find a way to be together without arousing suspicion!

Composed now, she turned back to her father. "Yes, Dat. Gregory's been really helpful to us."

"Well, shall we go into breakfast? I'll try to soften your mother up a little."

"Oh, Dat, thank you." And impulsively she snaked her arm through his and they set off for the house and her first meal with her family as the no-longer-engaged Rebecca Zook.

An hour later Rebecca entered the quilt shop. She was surprised to find Mrs. Ansbacher sitting in a chair, gazing out the window, instead of working. "Good morning," she said.

"Oh, hello, Rebecca," Mrs. Ansbacher answered.

"What are you doing?"

"Thinking about all the years I've spent in this shop. I've walked around the shop, touching some of my favorite quilts like they're my children, and now I'm sitting here remembering all the people I've met here and all the quilts, and fabric, and needles, and yarn, and patches — everything."

Rebecca noticed the touch of sadness in her voice. "There's no hurry to sell me the shop."

"No, dear, that's nice of you, but there's no sense in hanging on."

"Mrs. Ansbacher, might I ask: What are you going to do with yourself?"

"Oh, don't worry about me. I'm going to travel, for one thing. You'll see, being tied to a shop can be limiting. I've always wanted to go to Pinecraft in the winter, like everybody else. This year I think I'll do it!"

Rebecca had never been to Pinecraft, either. It was a place in Sarasota, Florida where lots of Amish and Mennonites spent the winter. Madie had been once and had told her how much fun it was. There was a community hall where performers would come and sing. There were fish fries. Everybody played shuffleboard, and the men played bocce. A river that flowed through Pinecraft that was home to herons, ducks, even alligators. Rebecca didn't know what a heron looked like, much less an alligator. She hoped she'd go to Pinecraft herself some day.

"That is a wonderful idea, Mrs. Ansbacher! You'll really enjoy it, I'm sure. And you'll miss all the snow we always have."

"I'm really looking forward to it. Just as I'm looking forward to not having to come to work every day."

The doorbell rang as Gregory entered the shop. "Hi, is this a good time?"

"Yes, it is," replied Mrs. Ansbacher. "Let's sit over here."

She led the way to a corner of the shop where three chairs were gathered about a small table. They sat down and Gregory opened a manila folder he'd brought with him. "This shouldn't take long," he said. "I just want to go over what you've agreed to in this purchase agreement." He handed Rebecca and Mrs. Ansbacher each a sheet of paper. "Now, the figure at the top is the total cost of the business."

Rebecca looked at the paper. $600,000. Seeing the figure there in black and white caused a small frown on her face. *That's so much money!*

Mrs. Ansbacher looked up from her sheet of paper. "Now don't you worry, dear," she said to Rebecca. "It looks like a lot of money, but you aren't paying it all at once."

"No, you're not," Gregory said. "Mrs. Ansbacher has agreed that you can pay her $1000 a month for the first five years, and you won't owe her the full amount until ten years from now." He leaned over and pointed to the relevant figures on Rebecca's piece of paper.

"What if I can't pay it?" she asked.

"I'm sure you'll have most of it paid off by then," Gregory answered. "And a bank would be happy to give you a loan for the rest."

"And I would be happy to extend the time," Mrs. Ansbacher put in. "Buying my business is not meant to be a burden, Rebecca. It's something I want you to feel good about."

"They are very generous terms," Gregory added.

"I know they are," Rebecca said. "It's just a little scary, that's all."

"You'll be making plenty of money each month, Rebecca," Mrs. Ansbacher said. "I bet you'll end up paying me back before ten years, especially if you begin selling your own quilts. People are beginning to pay a lot of money for Amish quilts."

Rebecca kept silent for a moment. Did she really want to begin worrying about money, and loans, and how much to charge for quilts? The Rebecca Zook Company? That is what Gregory had called her when he sent in those incorporation papers to the state? *Me, a company?* She looked up and saw Gregory and Mrs. Ansbacher patiently waiting for her to say something. *Time to grow up, Rebecca. Time to take charge of your life.* "Do I have to sign something?" she asked Gregory.

Gregory produced more pages. "I typed this up on the computer at the library." He handed the pages to Mrs. Ansbacher. "Why don't you have your lawyer look this over, then you and Rebecca can sign it whenever it suits you both."

"Thank you, Gregory," Mrs. Ansbacher said, taking the pages. "I'll take it to him right away."

"Sounds like you're anxious to get out of this shop," Gregory said.

"I'll miss it a lot," Mrs. Ansbacher said. "I'll especially miss working with you," she said to Rebecca. "But I just believe, when you've decided something, it's best not to dilly-dally but to do it and move on. Now don't forget, Rebecca, you call me any time to ask about anything. I know you've worked here a long time, but running everything yourself is different. And you don't have a Rebecca to help you."

That's right! Rebecca suddenly realized she would be running the shop all by herself. And she hadn't even begun to work on the nine quilts she still had to complete for Mr. Goldfarb.

Mrs. Ansbacher saw the look on Rebecca's face. "Now don't you worry, dear. There are plenty of Amish women who would love to work here. You just get settled in and then you can think about hiring someone." She got up. "All right if I leave you here by yourself for a little while, Rebecca?"

"Of course."

"It shouldn't take long at my lawyer's."

"I'll be going, too," Gregory said. "Congratulations to you both!"

"Thank you, Gregory," Rebecca said. *I wish he wouldn't go. I wish he'd stay and tell me everything's going to be all right.*

Gregory held the door for Mrs. Ansbacher. When she'd exited, he turned, gave Rebecca a warm smile, and followed her out.

The door clicked with a finality Rebecca had never noticed before. For a moment she just stood there, her mind racing. *What am I doing? Buying a quilt shop! What if it fails, what if I go into debt, what if nobody comes to buy anything?*

She moved behind the counter, her eyes continuing to stare at the closed door. Slowly, she began to look around her. That pile of quilts there. She would own them soon. That bin of patches, they'd all belong to her. Those rolls of fabric, hers.

She dropped her head in silent prayer. *Dear God, please be with me. Give me the strength I need to do the work I need to do. And always keep me focused on what I want to do: help others make beautiful quilts to add to the splendor of the wonderful world you have made for us all.*

Rebecca opened her eyes. There was complete silence in the shop. With a deep breath, she gathered herself and went to work.

CHAPTER 10

Vinny checked the rearview mirror. The truck pulling the horse trailer was right behind him. He smiled. Inside the trailer was something he knew Wanda would love. It had cost him $20,000 — he couldn't get Ross to go any lower. He'd seen Vinny was too anxious to buy it. *Gotta watch myself, I'm getting sloppy. Don't be a chooch!* But he wasn't a dummy for buying the horse, that he was sure of. That was a smart investment, it would pay off big-time.

He slowed to make the turn down the long driveway to Cedar Ridge Farm. In the mirror, he saw the truck swing wide, then follow him. When he reached the circular drive, he parked his Maserati, got out, and directed the driver of the truck to back it towards the stable. He had just given him the signal to cut the engine when Wanda came out from the house.

"What are you doing, Vinny?" she called from the porch. She was wearing jeans and a bright red blouse that nicely accented her blond hair.

"Found something I think you might like," he shouted back.

"A horse trailer?" Wanda asked, descending the stairs.

"That I had to rent. What I found is what's inside."

"You found a horse?"

"In a manner of speaking. Let's take a look. Hey, Louie," he called to the driver, "Gimme a hand."

Louie got out of the truck and came to the back of the trailer. Vinny slid open the door bolt. "Close your eyes, babe."

"Why?"

"It's a surprise. But it's too big to wrap, so you gotta close your eyes."

"Vinny, I'm so excited!" she said, closing her eyes.

Vinny slid out the ramp from under the trailer. "Get him," he said to Louie. Louie went inside the trailer, took the bridle, and brought Wise Guy down the ramp. "Over there," Vinny motioned to Louie, then went to Wanda and turned her to face the horse. "Okay, babe, you can open your eyes now."

Wanda opened her eyes. "Oh! What is it?"

"A horse," Vinny teased.

"I know it's a horse, wise guy."

"How'd you know his name?"

"His na — . Vinny," she protested, "make sense!"

"This horse is named Wise Guy."

"What do you mean, you found him?"

"Well, first I found him for sale, and then I 'found' the money to buy him. The second was a little harder than the first."

"You bought a horse?" She nodded. "Oh, I get it. You bought a horse and you want to know if you can board it here."

"That's half-right. I bought a horse and I want to know if *you* can board it here."

"Me?"

"Yeah. I figure you probably want to board your own horse in your own stable."

"My own horse...?" Wanda asked, understanding spreading across her face. "You bought a horse for me?"

"Bingo!"

"Vinny!!!" Wanda shouted, jumping into his arms and squeezing him in a huge embrace. Vinny felt her voluptuous body pressed against his own. He smelled the perfume in her hair. He relished the big, wet kiss she planted on his cheek. *This is gonna be great!* "You are too wonderful!" Wanda gushed. "I can't believe you bought me a horse!"

"Believe it," he answered. "Better yet..." He pulled Wanda towards the horse, introducing them. "Wanda, this is Wise Guy, Wise Guy, this is your new owner. Now, Wanda, we are going to prove something the world has never known. Move your head closer and look carefully, now."

Wanda got closer to Wise Guy and Vinny reached up and spread the horse's lips apart so his teeth showed. "Babe, you and I have just proved that you *can* look a gift horse in the mouth!"

"You silly man!" Wanda laughed and playfully slapped him.

Louie had stood patiently holding the reins. "Okay if I go now, Vinny?"

"You bet, Louie. Thanks." Louie gave Vinny the reins, got back in the truck, and slowly pulled the trailer away.

Vinny offered Wanda the reins. "Give him a walk."

"Vinny, can I really let you buy me a horse? I know how much they cost."

"You're worth it. Here." He put the reins in her hand and she slowly walked Wise Guy around the circular drive. Seeing the radiant look on her face, Vinny felt such joy at her happiness that, for a minute, he almost forgot his ulterior motive in buying the horse.

Wanda returned and stood in front of him. "Thank you, Vinny. You are an incredibly kind and generous man." She kissed him full on the mouth. Then Vinny really did forget why he'd bought her the horse, wanting, if only for the length of the kiss, for it to be true that he really was a kind and generous man.

The neighing of a horse made them separate. Only it wasn't Wise Guy who had made the noise. Looking around, they saw Gregory sitting on Bojangles a little way off. "Hope I'm not interrupting anything," he said, smiling.

Wanda blushed. Vinny didn't appreciate the interruption. "Who are you?" he asked, impatiently.

"Oh, hi, Gregory," Wanda said. "You won't believe what just happened. Vinny gave me a horse!"

"Really?" he asked, surprised.

"She deserves it," Vinny said firmly. "And, like I said, who are you?"

"Oh, I'm sorry," Wanda said. "Gregory, this is my friend, Vinny. Vinny, this is Gregory. He lives on the next-door farm."

Gregory dismounted and came over to shake Vinny's hand. "How do you do?"

"Gregory…." Vinny said. "Are you the guy who was mixed up in Ivan's death?"

"Kinda. Did you know Ivan?"

"Yeah."

"Vinny was a friend of Daddy's," Wanda explained. "I met him at the racetrack one day."

"Did Ivan do legal work for you?" Gregory asked.

"No."

Gregory realized Vinny was not going to offer personal information unless he had to. He decided to wait for further investigation into how Vinny knew Ivan. "I came over to talk a little more about our business," he said to Wanda.

"Business?" Vinny asked.

"Gregory and I are thinking of setting up a partnership. We'd have a tack shop, and I'd teach, and — Gregory!" she suddenly shouted. "Wise Guy solves everything!"

"Wise Guy?"

"My horse!" Wanda exclaimed. "The one Vinny just gave me. We needed a horse so I could give riding lessons," she explained to Vinny. "Your gift is perfect!"

Riding lessons so Wanda could set up a business was not the reason Vinny had spent a lot of money on a horse. "She's giving lessons, what are you going to do?" he asked Gregory.

"We haven't really worked out all the details."

"What's wrong with your horse?"

Gregory noticed the slightly aggressive tone in Vinny's voice. "I really didn't want to board him here — "

"And now we don't have to," Wanda chimed in. "Gregory, I've been thinking," she continued. "We should open our shop right here on the farm. We can convert that old shack into a really nice store."

"Good idea."

"Store?" Vinny asked.

Wanda explained. "We're going to have a store where we can sell all kinds of things. Bridles and saddles and brushes — everything you need for a horse. And toys — little horses, barns, fences, all hand-made."

"Quality stuff," Gregory added.

"We'll have to fix that shack up," Wanda said. "Probably put in new walls, use that space for something else, paint everything."

"That's gonna cost," Vinny said.

"But I'll have my half of Daddy's life insurance," Wanda said.

And I won't, Vinny thought. *Not if you spend it on this business.*

"Wanda, we can talk about this some other time," Gregory said, re-mounting Bojangles. Gregory and Vinny looked at one another, sizing each other up. "Probably see you around, Vinny," Gregory said.

"Probably," Vinny said.

"Congratulations on your new horse, Wanda. That's quite the gift." With a nod, he turned Bojangles and rode off.

"He's right, Vinny," Wanda said. "I mean, a horse. It's kinda too much."

"I got a deal on him," Vinny said. "But, hey, if it makes you feel any better, you can do something nice for me when your business starts booming. By the way, Wanda, did you tell Gregory how much money you're putting into this business?"

"I just told him Daddy's insurance gives me half a million dollars."

Half a million! Just what I need. Unless she starts spending it on fixing up shacks and buying inventory. "And how much is he putting in?"

"We didn't talk about it."

"Don't you think you should?"

"You don't think this business is a good idea, Vinny?"

"Depends. How much do you know about this Gregory guy anyway?"

"Not that much, I guess. He's from South Carolina, I think, and he's staying at the Zooks' farm, and, I don't know, that's about it."

"Let me check him out. There's all kinds of scam artists out there, babe, you gotta be careful. If I was you, I'd go slow with this business."

Wanda considered for a moment. "Well, all right, Vinny. I don't think Gregory is scamming me, but if you want, maybe you could advise me about my end of the business deal."

"Nothing I'd like better, babe. Now, how's about you take Wise Guy for a ride?"

Wanda happily ran to her horse and mounted. Vinny came to stand beside her. "Really glad you like your gift, babe."

"I love it! We're going to be so happy together." She clicked her heels and rode away.

We sure are, Vinny thought. *You, the horse, and me!*

CHAPTER 11

Gregory looked at the envelope in his hand. The return address said it all: the DNA Testing Center of America. He had swabbed the inside of his mouth, put it and Wanda's saliva sample in the DNA kit the Center had sent him, and mailed it in. The instructions said the sample had to come from the inside of the mouth. Since Gregory could hardly have asked Wanda if he could do that — "Excuse me, Wanda, would you mind if I used this cotton swab on the inside of your cheek?" — he had made do with what he could get from the tea glass and had sent in his and Wanda's samples with his check for $150. And now he had the answer in his hand — or at least, *an* answer.

He turned the envelope over and back again. If it said Wanda was his half-sister, then he would know Ivan was his father. Did he really want to know that his own father tried to kill him? That he had the blood of a murderer running in his veins?

He put the envelope on his desk and went to the door of his cottage. It was the middle of the afternoon. No one was in sight. He looked towards the house. How would Rebecca feel about knowing Ivan was his father? Would that change her feelings towards him? *It's been so long since we've been able to talk!*

He walked down to the pump and splashed water on his face, just to have something to do. He looked about. Fall was definitely here. The sugar maple tree that hung over the crick was fiery-red with leaves. The beech trees that dotted the woods behind him winked their yellow leaves through the evergreen branches. And in the crick, yellow, red, and orange leaves floated lazily by on their way to the larger crick.

Gregory drew in a breath. The air was cool and crisp. If he was going to have a future with Rebecca, then he had to know who he was, and she did, too.

He returned to his desk, took up the envelope. *God, whatever the results, please help me to deal with them.* He smiled a little. He'd noticed he'd been praying more often of late. Not long prayers, and not in church. Just little whispered prayers from time to time about his life. Another change brought about by living among the Amish. He opened the envelope and read:

Dear Mr. Pinckney:

Here are the results from your DNA testing. We tested all 16 STR markers on each sample, obtaining a full genetic profile for each individual. By looking at the numbers of markers shared, the rareness of the markers, and the pattern in which the markers appear, we generated a sibling index. If the two individuals are full siblings, the full siblings index will be higher than the half siblings index. If the individuals are half siblings, the half sibling index will be greater than the full.

As you can see by the chart below, the two individuals are half siblings.

The sibling test may not always provide conclusive results. We recommend a paternity test wherever possible.

If you would like to discuss the results in more detail, please contact us at 1-888-714-2222.

Thank you.

The DNA Testing Center of America

Gregory let out a long breath. *Wanda and I are half siblings!* He stared at the letter without really seeing it. *Wow….*

He tucked the letter back inside the envelope and walked outside. He looked toward the west. *Over that ridge is my half-sister. Should I tell her? How would she react? How would her mother react? How would the whole community react?* He stared at the ground. He didn't know what he was getting into when he set out to find his birth mother.

Gregory started walking slowly, not really knowing where he was going, still pondering his problem. Instinctively, his steps brought him into the barn. Bo was in his stall, eating. The sight of him comforted Gregory. "Bo, ol' boy, you won't believe what's happened. We've got a new half-sister. Now, let me ask you something. If you had a half-brother you didn't know about, would you want to know?" He looked at Bo. Bo stopped eating and looked steadily at Gregory, his large brown eyes still and focused. After a minute, Gregory continued. "I guess you're right. Okay, then, let's go tell her."

Twenty minutes later Gregory tied Bo to a post outside the Heminger stable and walked onto the front porch. He knocked. "Come in," Liz shouted. Gregory opened the door and entered. Hearing a TV, he made his way to the den, where he found Liz sitting on the sofa, watching a soap opera.

"Oh, hi, Gregory. Just a minute." Liz clicked the mute button on the remote. "Did you know this is the only soap left on daytime? Such a shame. You looking for Wanda?"

"Yes, ma'am, I am."

"She's not here. She and Vinny are off somewhere."

"Know where?"

"Wanda never tells me, they just go off."

Normally, Gregory would have left and come back some other time, but he felt a new urgency. "Mind if I have a seat, Mrs. Heminger?"

"Of course. Would you like some coffee?"

"No, thanks." Gregory took a moment to settle in. "Who is Vinny, Mrs. Heminger?"

"How do you mean?"

"Well, where did he come from?"

"He's a friend of Ivan's. I met him at the racetrack at the beginning of last summer. And since Ivan died, he's come around, asking if there's anything he can do. Tell you the truth, I'm glad he's taking Wanda out. She seems to be happier."

My half-sister is happier. Why can't I leave it at that? "It sure was nice of him to buy Wanda a horse."

"Can you believe it?" Liz exclaimed. "I was shocked."

"It is a little surprising. He must really like your daughter." *Or really want something from her.* "I wonder where your husband met him."

"Don't know. Vinny went to Penn State, I do know that. He's thinking about taking Wanda up to a football game this fall."

"She'll like that. What's his last name?"

"You know, I don't even know that. Maybe Wanda does."

"So you like Vinny, then?"

"Of course, why do you ask?"

"No real reason. I mean, if he's coming around a lot, and he's given your daughter a horse, and they're going out, looks like he's pretty interested in her. Just wondered what you'd feel about having him in the family."

"I'd feel fine. I like Vinny. He's been super nice to Wanda and me. If Wanda wants to marry him, she should do what makes her happy."

Gregory decided he'd have no ally in Liz regarding Vinny's trustworthiness. "How about you, how are you doing, Mrs. Heminger?"

"All right. I'm getting used to my new life. And now that the insurance check has come in, I can start doing things again."

"Oh, it came in? That's great. Did you tell Wanda?"

"Of course."

"Did she say anything about it, about how she was planning to use it?"

"Not really."

"You know, she and I are thinking of going into business together?"

"Wanda did mention that once."

Once? Gregory waited to see if she'd mentioned it again, but when Liz said nothing more, he concluded she hadn't. He thought that was odd. "Mrs. Heminger, how did you and Ivan meet, if you don't mind my asking?"

"I was his secretary at the law firm."

"Oh, so you didn't know him as a young man?"

"Not really. I believe his parents were from Lancaster. Grandparents, too. The family had been here long enough to have found a place in Lancaster society. They originally lived in a big house in town, but that got sold a long time ago. When Ivan got his inheritance, he bought Cedar Ridge Farm. That's where he lived when I met him." She paused. "It's a shame, we never even got to celebrate our twenty-fifth wedding anniversary."

Gregory didn't speak, letting Liz have her private moment about her husband. *Should I tell that her husband was my father…? Wanda first.* "Well, I won't take any more of your time. Tell Wanda to give me a call — " Gregory stopped. He was going to give Liz his cell phone number, but then he remembered that he'd put it in a drawer and never used it. Another way he had become more Amish without even realizing it. "Tell Wanda I've got some news and I'll be in touch." He stood up. "I'm glad the money came in and you can start re-building your life, Mrs. Heminger."

"Me, too," Liz said, picking up the remote and turning her attention back to the television. "I just wish they hadn't taken off all my soaps." She punched the remote and the sound came back on. Tossing off a quick "Goodbye, Gregory," she returned to watching.

Riding home, Gregory's mind was restless. Did he really want to get involved in this? If Vinny was making Wanda happy, what did he care? But something about Vinny made Gregory uneasy. Was he the reason Wanda seemed not to be as enthusiastic about their business partnership? He didn't want his half-sister to get hurt. "Help me out here, Bo!" he said out loud. Bo just kept cantering home. Gregory laughed at himself. *Talking to a horse! I've got no horse sense!* And he laughed even harder at his terrible pun.

When he reached the farm, he saw Hanna coming from the garden, her arms full of squash, so he slowed Bo, jumped off, and walked toward her. *"Pald sell gall avec fum micht!"* Hanna shouted at him.

"What's that mean?" Gregory asked.

"It means, I don't want you near me with that animal!"

"Oh, that's right, Hanna, I forgot. You had an accident on a horse, didn't you?"

"Fell off one when I was little. Landed on my head."

"I remember. When I first met you, you made me feel your head to see if you were 'soft in the head.'"

"That's what folks sometimes said. I never could find any soft spots. But I don't like horses."

"Now, Hanna, don't say that. You'll hurt Bo's feelings."

"Horses don't have feelings."

"'Course they do." Behind his back, Gregory pointed to the ground with his index finger. Years ago, for fun, he had taught Bo to move his head in certain directions, rewarding him with sugar cubes when he did it right. True to form, Bo lowered his head. "See there, Bo's hanging his head down. He's sad."

"Really?" Hanna took a step toward Bo. Bo raised his head.

"Maybe if you pet him, he'll forgive you."

"I don't want to. I'm scared."

"Bo's gentle as a lamb, Hanna. Here." He took her hand and gently brought it up to rub Bo's long face.

"He'll bite me!"

"I promise he won't. If he does, I'll take you into town right now and buy you a tub of ice cream." Gregory knew she would risk practically anything to have ice cream.

"How about you buy me some for just rubbing his face?" Hanna countered.

Gregory laughed. "All right, deal. But you have to do it without my help." He took his hand away.

Hanna slowly brought her hand to Bo's face and tentatively rubbed it. *"Scheney gall, scheney gall.* Don't bite me."

"What are you saying to him?"

"Pretty horsey."

"I think he likes you, Hanna."

"Well, I don't like him. He's *drechich.*"

"What's that mean?"

"Dirty."

"Well, you'd be *drekick* too, if you slept in a stable." Hanna laughed. "What's so funny?"

"The way you say '*drechich.*'"

"Teach me how to say it right, then."

"It's '*drechich*,'" Hanna said.

"'*Drekick,* '" Gregory tried.

"No, you're not saying the 'ich' right." You make it sound like "kick."

"Well, teach me, then. I want to learn your language."

"Why?"

Gregory knew why. He wanted to be able to talk to Rebecca in her own language. For months he'd been hearing her talk with her family, but he had no idea what they were saying. He liked the way Pennsylvania Dutch sounded, the rise and fall of the melodious words, and the guttural T's and the S's that didn't sound like any S sound in English. It was all part of this feeling that had been growing in him like a spring flower, the feeling of wanting to become more Amish. And he knew why. But he couldn't tell Hanna why. "I just want to be able to understand you. Please, Hanna?"

"I don't have time to teach you how to talk Deutsch," she said firmly. "Got too much work to do. Get Becca to teach you. She usedta say she wanted to be a teacher. She'll learn you *gut.*"

Gregory stopped still. His mind raced with excitement. *Rebecca teaching me Deutsch! Every day we'd have lessons! I'd be with her every day, and no one would care, no one would think anything of it!* "Hanna, you're a beautiful woman!"

"I'm not beautiful."

"Oh, yes, you are!" Gregory felt like hugging her, but knew he couldn't. Instead, he turned to Bo. "Isn't she, Bo?" He grabbed Bo under his face and nodded his head up and down. "See there, Bo agrees!"

"Gregory, *du bich kindich.*"

"I don't know what you said, Hanna," Gregory said, swinging himself up into the saddle, "But some day I will! Thank you!" And he turned Bo, gave his flanks a soft kick, shouted "Hyah!" and off they sped over the fields. Gregory was so pumped up with this new idea that he forgot about Vinny, Ivan, Wanda, about everything but Rebecca. "She's gonna teach me!" he shouted into the air.

Hanna watched him go. "*Kindich* man," she said, shaking her head. "Crazy man."

CHAPTER 12

"Hiya, Vinny, what's cookin'?" The maître d greeted Vinny as he slipped into the racetrack bar, Wanda on his arm. "Hiya doin', Ms. Heminger?"

"Hiya, Billy," Vinny replied.

"Hello, Billy." Wanda smiled her gorgeous smile at him.

"Do all right today?" Billy asked.

"We did great!" Wanda replied. "Vinny really knows how to pick winners."

Billy winked at Vinny. "That he does, Ms. Heminger, that he does. Got your table right here," he said, leading the way to a table in the corner overlooking the track.

On the way, a couple of the regulars shouted greetings to Vinny, and he quickly shook a few proffered hands. The bar was full, noisy with the after-racing crowd, but it was quiet at the corner table. "Having your usual?" Billy asked as he pulled out a chair for Wanda. Vinny nodded. "How about you, Ms. Heminger?"

"I'll have a Bud light, please."

Vinny grimaced. "Don't drink that — " He stopped himself. His usual characterization of the "King of Beers" wouldn't do today. Since he'd been going out with Wanda, he'd cleaned up his language. He'd bought himself a new suit, one less shiny, stopped wearing silk shirts, and toned down his overall image, all in an effort to seem like a "normal guy" to Wanda. "Why don't you have a real drink? Billy, bring her a Manhattan. Something sweet for my sweet."

"Vinny, you're so cute," she said.

"Yes ma'am, Ms. Heminger," Billy said with a smirk, "That's what we're always saying: That Vinny is sure cute!"

"Just bring the drinks," Vinny ordered, not amused, and Billy sauntered away towards the bar.

"What's in a Manhattan?"

"Whiskey, sweet vermouth, and bitters. And a cherry. If Billy knows what's good for him, he'll put in two cherries."

"I love cherries!"

"I know you do, babe, that's why I got 'em. Did you have fun today?"

"Yes. I can't believe you won all those races, Vinny. You really know how to pick 'em."

"You bring me luck, babe, that's all."

"No, I think you really know horses. Did you have a horse when you were younger?"

"Not a chance. Too much moolah. But I confess, I did hang around a few stables." *And a few guys who knew the ins and outs of betting, like Uncle Joey.* Vinny had to admit that Joey taught him a lot. And now he wanted some payback. "Where the heck are our drinks," Vinny said, looking around. He didn't like thinking about Mancuso.

"I'll just freshen up while we wait, okay?"

"Sure thing." Wanda pushed back her chair, rose, and walked towards the restrooms. Vinny watched her go, admiring the easy sway of her buttocks in her tight jeans. Courting Wanda hadn't exactly been hard. In fact, returning to Carla after a night out with Wanda had been … well, not exactly awkward, but different. He wondered if Carla had noticed the difference. After a lifetime of women, he'd learned they often knew more than you thought they did.

Women. How was he going to pull this off, being married to one woman and pretending to be married to another? Well, he'd have to pull it off, that's all. Mancuso had made that perfectly clear earlier today.

"Vinny, Vinny!" Mancuso had said when Vinny had entered his office. "Come here!" He'd embraced Vinny, then held him at arm's length. "You're looking good. Siddown."

Vinny had taken a seat in the large, brown leather chair. His shirt was soaked. He'd been stuck in traffic on the Ben Franklin Bridge on his way to Mancuso's home in Newark. Driving an hour and a half to Jersey wasn't Vinny's favorite thing to do, but he knew he couldn't go through with his plan without Mancuso's approval. He also knew it was such a bold plan that Mancuso might just laugh in his face. Vinny figured the odds of approval or laughter were about fifty-fifty.

"So how's it going?" Mancuso had asked.

Vinny knew this wasn't just a pleasantry. Mancuso didn't waste time on pleasantries. And he knew what his uncle had been asking about. "It's going good, Uncle Joey, real good. I'll definitely be able to repay Ivan's debt to you."

"That's good news, Vinny." Mancuso had smiled his you'd-better-repay-me smile. "It's been more than a month since Ivan's unfortunate passing. You learn anything more about what happened? They say he over-dosed on drugs or something."

"I don't believe it."

"You think somebody offed him?"

"Maybe."

"Then maybe this someone is someone you ought to pay a visit to. If you could get something on him, he might fork over some dough, lower your responsibility."

"He don't got any." Gregory was Vinny's chief suspect, and, as far as he'd been able to find out, Gregory just lived at the Zook farm without a job. "I got a better idea."

"I'm all ears."

Vinny had taken a deep breath. *Might as well tell him. Never keep nothing from Uncle Joey, I learned that a long time ago.* "Ivan's daughter, Wanda, I told you about her." He'd paused, but Mancuso had just stared at him with sphinxlike detachment. "Well, she's gonna get half of her daddy's life insurance policy. And I'm gonna get her to give it to me."

"How're you gonna do that?"

"I'm gonna marry her." Vinny knew this was not news that his uncle was going to exactly embrace.

"Vinny, Vinny," Mancuso had said, "Might I remind you that you are already married to a wonderful woman. Her name's Carla. And she happens to be my niece."

"I know that, Uncle Joey, of course I know that." Vinny had shifted in his seat, leaning forward, trying to be as intimate as possible. "And you're right, Carla is a wonderful woman, and I'd never do anything to hurt her. What I got planned is this: I take Wanda out to Vegas. You got lots of friends in Vegas. I got lots of friends in Vegas. We go out there, I arrange a quickie marriage, and that's it. Only it won't be a legal marriage. I'll just let Wanda think it's legal. Then we'll set up a joint bank account, I'll slide the money over to it, pay you off, and disappear."

Vinny had waited, looking intently at his uncle, who'd sat perfectly still. *Is he gonna buy it? I know it sounds crazy. I'm not even sure it'll work. But it's the only idea I got.* After a long half-minute, Mancuso had smiled. "I like it, Vinny. It's a little unusual — I've never heard of anyone pulling off something like this. But if you wanna give it a try, go ahead."

"Good, Uncle Joey, I'm glad you like it." *Now for the hard part.* "The thing is, I'm having trouble coming up with an explanation for Carla."

"I can see that. You can't exactly say, 'Carla, excuse me, but I gotta take this woman to Vegas and pretend to marry her, hope you don't mind.'" Mancuso had let out a hearty laugh.

Vinny had made sure to laugh, too. "Yeah, you see my problem. I was thinking, maybe you could help me."

"How?"

"I thought maybe you could explain to Carla that it's a business deal. I mean, I'm gonna tell her first, but if you could back me up, that'd probably do the trick."

"Business deal, huh...?" Mancuso had mulled this over for a minute. "Yeah, well, it is a business deal, so that's the truth…. Course, a woman's not gonna like a business deal that involves you leaving town with another woman. But a woman who happens to be my niece, well, she's gonna like it. Or else."

Vinny had finally relaxed when he'd heard that "or else." He knew what Mancuso's "or else" meant, and, in this case, it meant he was free to go ahead with his plan. "Thank you, Uncle Joey. I knew I could count on you."

Mancuso had risen, which Vinny knew was the sign the meeting was over. "You know what, Vinny? I like you. So I tell you what I'm gonna do. When you let me know where you end up once you run away, I'll send Carla to you, and you both can go some place nice, maybe Italy or something, and enjoy yourselves 'til I let you know it's safe to come back. Whaddaya say?"

Vinny had been almost speechless. "Uncle Joey, I…. That is just such a wonderful thing to do, it's so generous of you."

"People do right by me, I do right by them, Vinny. Of course, we both know what the opposite side of that coin is, don't we?" And with a smile, Mancuso had left his office, and Vinny had sped back to the Lancaster Downs Racetrack to put into play the next step in his bold plan to abscond with Wanda's money.

"Here you go, Mr. Bandini." Vinny looked up, his reverie interrupted, to see the waiter putting the drinks on the table.

"You new here or something?" he snapped. "Don't use my last name. Call me 'Vinny,' or 'sir,' or something, but don't ever use my last name."

"What is your last name, Vinny?" Wanda asked, having returned from the restroom. The waiter pulled out her chair, then quickly moved away. "You know, in all this time, I never even asked you."

"Mangini," Vinny lied.

"It's funny, I hardly know anything about you," Wanda continued. "Where you're from, who your parents are. All I know is you went to Penn State and played football."

"Isn't that enough? Plenty of women would love to date a guy who played for Joe Pa."

"That's not why I go out with you, and you know it."

"Then why?"

Wanda turned serious. "Because you're kind and considerate. You've been so nice to Mom and me since Daddy's death. You even gave me a horse, for gosh sakes! And I've loved our dates, the way you take me dancing, that time you took me to the mountains to hear that comedian. You're a good person, Vinny Mangini."

Vinny almost cringed. He hated being called "good," because he knew he wasn't. At least he didn't used to be. But he'd actually enjoyed being nice to Wanda and her mother. He'd taken genuine pleasure in their smiles, their gratitude. Was he actually starting to like Wanda? Then he remembered. *This is business.*

He lifted his vodka on the rocks and Wanda raised her Manhattan. "To my beautiful, wonderful new friend!"

They drank. "Oh, this is good!" Wanda said. She took another sip. "Real good."

"I'm glad you like it. Tell me, have you and Gregory talked any more about your business?"

"Not really. I decided to go slow, like you said."

"That's good, because I've looked into the guy a little. Seems like he couldn't pass the South Carolina bar exam after three tries, so I wouldn't count on him helping you out in any legal way."

"I shouldn't let him draw up the partnership papers? I've already said I would."

"Well, you can let him do it, but I'd take 'em to another lawyer to check 'em out. I can recommend one for you."

"Thank you, Vinny, that'd be good."

"Also, Gregory's been here four months without working, so I'm not sure what kind of capital he's got to put into this business. You discussed financing it yet?"

"No. I sort of volunteered my half of Daddy's insurance money."

"That's what I figured. So far, you teach riding lessons and you finance the whole thing. What's Gregory gonna do, run the tack store? He got any experience as a salesman?"

Wanda could see where Vinny was going. "I don't know," she said uncertainly. "Are you saying not to trust Gregory?"

"I'm just saying to be cautious. It's always good to be cautious in business. By the way, how much is your half of the insurance, babe?"

"Five hundred thousand dollars."

"Five hundred grand, that's perfect!" Vinny exclaimed.

"Perfect for what?"

Stupido! You brought it up real casual, then you go shouting about it! "I meant perfect for you to be able to do what you want with your life now, you know, pay for your college, travel, maybe invest a little in the business if you want, you know what I mean?" *That's the lamest answer I ever heard.* He looked at Wanda. She looked back at him, her eyes scrutinizing his. He had to change the subject fast! "I'm just glad your father took care of you, babe. He was a fine man." He raised his glass. "To Ivan."

Wanda raised her glass and drank silently. Vinny pressed on. "Enough talk about business. Wanda, I got a confession to make. I'm beginning to think of you as more than just a friend. I think you kind of may have figured that out, the way I kissed you the other night."

Wanda smiled at the memory. "It was wonderful, Vinny. I told you that."

"I know you did, and that made me feel real good. I was worried that maybe I was going too fast."

"You're not going too fast, Vinny," Wanda said warmly. "I maybe like you more than just a friend, too."

"I am really glad to hear that. Because.... Well, maybe this is too fast, too, but...." He reached inside his coat and pulled out a brochure. "Take a look at this." He handed it to Wanda. The cover had a picture of a beautiful waterfall set in the woods.

"Bushkill Falls," she read. "They look beautiful."

"They are."

"You've been there?"

"I have." *No need to tell her it was with my wife.* "And I'd like to take you there, too."

"That sounds fun. Is it far?"

"Coupla hours."

"Okay, sure, that'd be great. We could make it there and back in a day easy."

"Or we could come back the next day." Vinny looked at Wanda, steadily and warmly.

"Oh!" she said, realizing what he had in mind. "I see."

"Listen, babe, I've already booked us for this weekend. *Separate* rooms, Wanda, I want to make that clear. I am *not* trying to rush that part of our relationship. But it's a beautiful place, with lots of wonderful walks, and those falls are just.... Aw, heck, Wanda, they're just so romantic." He reached across and put his hand on hers.

"Oh, Vinny!" She blushed. "That is just so sweet, so, so sweet!" She turned her hand over and squeezed his. "Of course I'll go to Bushkill Falls with you. Thank you."

Vinny smiled broadly, and waved his hand in the air. Billy immediately appeared with a bottle of champagne. He opened it, catching the popped cork in his hand, and poured. The golden liquid bubbled into each glass. Vinny raised his and Wanda did the same.

"To us!" he said. They clinked glasses. He swallowed, thinking: *And to our bank account!*

CHAPTER 13

Rebecca looked at the sketchpad in front of her. Blank. It had been blank for thirty minutes. Once again she tried to concentrate. *Come on, just put anything down, anything!* She looked at the list of objects written on a piece of paper beside the sketchpad. Saddles, bridles, reins, hooves, horse blankets, brushes, bits, show halters, girths, spurs, boots. She'd even listed water buckets and ropes. *Can't you make a design out of any of these?*

She held a pencil listlessly in her right hand. After staring at it for a moment, she turned it over and began tapping the pad with the eraser. Tap, tap, tap, tap, tap, tap, tap. The rhythm echoed her agitation. *Why can't I think of anything?*

Making a quilt had never been hard for her. She'd started with the simple nine-square pattern when she was a young girl. Since then she'd moved on to diamonds and simple appliques like butterflies. But always traditional quilts. That's what her mother and Hanna had taught her to make. That's what they still made. But then she'd decided to make that wall hanging with the horse theme. She'd decided to break with tradition. And then Mr. Goldfarb had seen it hanging in Mrs. Ansbacher's quilt shop, talked her into displaying it in his gallery in New York City, Ted Snow had purchased it, and before she knew it, Mr. Goldfarb had wanted to be her agent, and now she had an order for ten horse-themed wall hanging quilts. Nine, really, since Mrs. Ansbacher had loaned her the one Rebecca had made for her, until Rebecca had time to make her a replacement.

Time, that was the problem. She didn't have any. Mrs. Ansbacher had returned with the papers from her lawyer the same day she had taken them to him and she and Rebecca had signed them. And now that it was no longer Mrs. Ansbacher's quilt shop, but Rebecca Zook's quilt shop, Rebecca spent all her time keeping track of inventory, doing the books, taking care of customers, completing orders for coverings and aprons, cleaning up, opening up — the list went on and on. But what never seemed to get checked off the list was "design and make my own quilts." And now it was three-weeks since his phone call and she still hadn't made any quilts for Mr. Goldfarb. *I know he's going to call again soon, I just know it. What will I tell him?*

She laid aside the sketchpad, got up from her chair, and began to walk around the shop. She had come in especially early that morning in hopes that she could draw some designs before she had to open up, and now it was nearly nine o'clock and she'd drawn nothing. She never used to worry about time. She never used to worry about lists of "things to do." She always had enough time to do her chores, prepare meals, help in the garden or the fields when necessary. She even had time to work part-time in the quilt shop. Work was something she did for the pure pleasure of working. Now, because of "time," she worked so she could finish one task and get onto the next one. She worked to finish, not to enjoy. All because of "time." "Why did I do it?" she said out loud in exasperation. "Why did I ever want to own a quilt shop?"

She went to the sink in the bathroom, drew herself a glass of water, and drank it. She looked in the small mirror above the sink. The same blue-green eyes looked back at her. She could see the tiny freckle in her left eye. She could also see the tiny sag in the corner of her eyes, the slightest drawing down of her eyelids. *I never used to be so tired this early in the morning.*

She closed her eyes. Was she wrong to want to be an artist? She never used to call herself one. But then Mrs. Ansbacher, Mr. Goldfarb, even Gregory, all had said she was an artist. That she had talent. And she had listened to them. Pride. The sin of wanting to stand out. "Pride goes before destruction, and a haughty spirit before a fall."

"God, don't let me fall!" she prayed out loud. "Please forgive me for being prideful. I didn't mean to sin. Remember how I prayed for You to show me what to do? It seemed You wanted me to make a different kind of quilt." She remembered the joy she'd felt when she worked in secret in the cottage, knowing her mam wouldn't approve. But then she'd gone to New York and had sold that quilt. "God, I am so confused! Please help me to know what You want me to do. If You want me to make these wall hangings for Mr. Goldfarb, show me how to do it. Make my fingers draw out a design that is pleasing to You. And help me to find the time, God, the time to do all the things I want to do. No — all the things *You* want me to do. Amen."

When she opened her eyes, Rebecca felt better. She always did after she'd prayed. Prayer reminded her that God loved her, that God cared for her, no matter what she did, how she might sin, whom she might hurt, what things she might have done, and what things she might have left undone. She was a child of God, and that was enough.

She went back into the shop, walked to her sketchpad, picked it up, grabbed the pencil, and put everything away underneath the counter.

She actually smiled. She was glad to have her "problem" out of sight. And she felt sure that God would show her what to do and how to do it.

She thought of Gregory. She had made her choice and called off her marriage to Jacob when God had given her the sign she had prayed for. When she'd been in her special place and opened her eyes and had seen Gregory, she'd felt sure that God had been telling her that he was the man for her. But that was almost a month ago and nothing had happened. They hadn't been able to see each other very much, and they were never alone for long. Gregory had been spending a great deal of time at Wanda's. Why? Was he becoming interested in her? Was he falling in love with her? Why hadn't God shown Rebecca how she was to make a relationship with Gregory work? He was English, she was Amish, but she had been sure that God would show her the way. But so far, nothing. Had she misinterpreted what God had been telling her? Had her pride, or her love, or her something clouded her vision? So many questions. And so few answers.

The shop doorbell tinkled. Rebecca looked up to see Lydie King enter. "*Guder daag,* Lydie."

"*Guder daag,* Rebecca. *Wie bischt du?*"

"*Ich bin gut,*" Rebecca answered. "*Kan ich helfa?*"

"*Yah,*" Lydie answered, and then switched to English as the Amish effortlessly do. "I need to buy some thread."

"Of course," Rebecca said. She led the way to the cabinet where spools of thread were stacked. "What color?"

"White."

"How many spools?"

"Three should be enough for now. I want to have plenty on hand for our next quilting bee. I hope you can come."

"I don't know, Lydie. The shop is keeping me extremely busy."

"Don't you have anyone to help you?"

"No. I don't want to hire anyone until I understand my expenses better."

"You must have help, Rebecca. Mrs. Ansbacher had you."

"I know, Lydie, I know," Rebecca said, a hint of exhaustion in her voice. "To tell you the truth, I haven't even had time to think about the problem, much less how to solve it." She took the thread to the counter and wrote out the charge slip.

"I wanted you to know," Lydie said. "I talked to Omar and he said it would be all right to invite Gregory to another church service. I know you are worried that it would make some members uncomfortable to have an Englisher there. But Omar asked around and everyone seemed to feel it was all right once in a while."

"Okay," Rebecca said, without much enthusiasm.

"Don't you want him to come?"

"If he wants to," Rebecca replied. "But the service is in *Hoch Deitsch.* He can't understand it, so maybe he doesn't want to come." Rebecca wasn't even sure she wanted Gregory to come. The last time he'd come, Johnny had been there, and Jacob, too. True, Jacob was no longer her fiancé, but Johnny had told her he wanted to go out with her. If he were there, and Gregory were there, who knew what might happen? Best to keep them apart.

The phone rang. "Excuse me," she said, then answered. "Rebecca's Quilt Shop."

"Hello, Rebecca. It's Stephen Goldfarb."

Her heart sank. "Oh, hello, Mr. Goldfarb. How are you?"

"I'm fine. How are you?

Rebecca tried to muster as much positive energy as she could. "Fine. I suppose you're calling about your quilt order."

"You suppose right. My clients keep asking about them. How's it going?"

"Actually, Mr. Goldfarb, it's not going at all." She paused. Although she couldn't hear the conversation, Lydie noticed the pained expression on Rebecca's face. "I only have one quilt for you so far."

"That's not very many," Mr. Goldfarb replied. Like many New York businessmen, he didn't mince words. "I expected you to be almost finished. I can't promote you if you can't produce," he said bluntly.

"I know." Rebecca turned away from Lydie's gaze. "Maybe I'm not worth promoting."

"You most certainly are. As a matter of fact, I have been talking to a client who might want to commission a large quilt, not just a wall hanging." Rebecca almost shouted, "No!" but held her breath.

"Rebecca, are you there?"

"Yes, Mr. Goldfarb." She drew a deep breath. "You see, I have just bought this quilt shop from Mrs. Ansbacher and running it has taken all my time. I'm sorry."

"I see." There was a long pause. Then he spoke gently but firmly. "You know, Rebecca, you might have to decide if you want to be a business woman or an artist."

Business woman or artist? How did my life ever become about those two choices? Those might be choices for an Englisher, but not for me. Am I becoming too English?

"Do you have any idea when you might be done?" Mr. Goldfarb asked.

"I really don't," Rebecca replied weakly. She felt terrible about letting him down, but what could she do? She couldn't make the day longer than twenty-four hours, and, at that moment, she felt it had to be longer if she were to live up to her obligations. "All I can say is, I will try my hardest to get them to you as soon as possible."

Mr. Goldfarb softened. He could hear the sad weariness in her voice. "All right, Rebecca. I'll put off my clients, somehow. I'll call you in a week to see how you're making out. Will that be all right?"

Rebecca felt she would have made no more progress in a week, but, just to end the painful conversation, she agreed. "That will be fine, Mr. Goldfarb. And thank you for your patience."

"You're worth it, Rebecca. You're a very talented person. Just believe that about yourself and get to work. Goodbye."

"Goodbye." Rebecca heard the phone click and she hung up her receiver. She stood still, her shoulders slumped.

"Everything all right?" Lydie inquired.

"That was my agent, Mr. Goldfarb. He has commissions for my quilt wall hangings. Ten of them. Mrs. Ansbacher gave me the one I made for her. I've got nine to go. I've had nine to go for weeks. And I don't even have the designs sketched out for what I want to make, much less the time to actually make them." Stating the problem in its starkest terms made Rebecca feel like crying.

Lydie looked at Rebecca, standing there with her shoulders slumped, her eyes down. She liked Rebecca, always had. She liked her earnestness, her friendly manner, the way she always helped at church. She could sense the great capacity for love within Rebecca. How strange that, at age, twenty-two, she had not yet found a man with whom to share that love. But maybe that was fortuitous. Maybe Rebecca had been waiting all these years to meet the perfect man for her. Maybe she'd been waiting to meet Lydie's son, a son she herself had met only four months ago.

Gregory. Praise God that he had come into her life, looking for his birth mother. She had figured out that he was her son, and she hadn't needed DNA testing to do it. Gregory had brought the proof of his parentage with him: the baby quilt Lydie had made for him while she'd been waiting to give birth, staying with her family friend in South Carolina. Nine squares with butterflies appliqued inside each square. She'd seen it in this very shop when Rebecca had introduced her to

Gregory. And she'd known immediately that he was her son. It was not only the quilt. It was his resemblance to his father, Ivan Heminger.

The thought of Ivan brought the familiar loathing. How could she not loathe him, when he had raped her when she had been hired to clean the Heminger house? Twenty-five years ago. She'd been sixteen. Ivan had drugged her and then had sex with her. The same drugs he had used on Gregory when he had tried to kill him with a syringe full of poison. Thank God Lydie had been there in Rex's shack to rescue her son. In the fight with Ivan, he had accidentally fallen on his own syringe, and that had been what had killed him. The police had ruled it a suicide. But Lydie knew the truth. She was the only one who did.

Maybe here was a chance to make something good out of all that evil. Maybe God was providing her with an opportunity not only to be with her son forever, but also to guide him to the sublime happiness of marrying the woman he loved. For Lydie was sure Gregory loved Rebecca. She could tell by the way he looked at her in church that first time. And how he had wandered down to watch the young people after church at the Zook farm just two weeks before. Watching from the main house, Lydie had seen how Gregory had gazed fixedly at Rebecca. She'd noticed how he'd run after the canoe with Johnny and Rebecca in it. A mother knew.

And she was sure Rebecca loved Gregory. Whenever she'd visited Mabel and Hanna, she'd seen how Rebecca always kept glancing towards the cottage where Gregory lived, hoping to see him. She'd heard about how Rebecca had taken care of Bojangles, Gregory's horse. She'd even observed the slight gleam in Rebecca's eye when Lydie had proposed asking Gregory to come to church again some Sunday. *Yes, they love each other. But they think there is a problem for their love, since Gregory is English. Except for one important fact: He's not English, he's Amish. I am his mother. I'm Amish, therefore so is he.*

There was another problem, one huge, insurmountable problem. Lydie couldn't tell anyone the truth. That would bring shame to herself, her family, her husband. The Amish community would be outraged. No, she must keep her secret, no one must ever know. Then how were Rebecca and Gregory ever going to marry? Would Rebecca have to leave the church? Would Gregory have to join it? What if he didn't want to become Amish? And, worse, what if they decided they had to move away, to live in peace in another community? What if she lost her son just as soon as she'd found him? Lydie was determined not to let that happen. She would bring Rebecca and Gregory together. After that, it would be God's will.

"Rebecca, let me help you," she said.

"What do you mean?"

"Let me help you make those quilt wall hangings. As a matter of fact, let's get the women at the quilting bee to make them. We could turn them out in no time."

"The quilting bee? Mam wouldn't do it. She doesn't like my designs with horses. She wants me to do traditional quilting. She's not even in favor of me running this shop. I don't see how she would agree to make quilts for me."

"Leave that to me," Lydie said. She knew Elam was glad Rebecca had bought the shop. She knew Hanna did not have the same scruples about quilt making as Mabel. Most importantly, she knew Mabel loved her daughter. Lydie was convinced Mabel would eventually come around. "But we'd have to know what we were making."

"I'm not sure," Rebecca said. She'd never thought of having anyone help her make quilts. Could she really say they were "hers" then? But what did that matter? Wanting to feel they were "hers" was a sign of pride. The Amish had always done things as a community, that was one of their strengths. Besides, they would still be her designs. She would still be the artist. *If I even want to think of myself that way.*

What a relief it would be to have some help! If she knew Lydie and the other Amish women would be there to make the quilts, all she'd have to do is design them. She could find time for that, she was sure. And when they were all done and shipped off to Mr. Goldfarb, then she could think about whether she still wanted to design her unique quilts, whether she still wanted to be an artist. Or, rather, whether God still wanted her to be one. She had been asking for a sign from God. Maybe this offer from Lydie was that sign.

"Let's try it, Lydie, if you're sure you want to. We can try one quilt, and see how it goes. I'll design it and your bee women can quilt it."

"*Gut!*" Lydie said. "We meet this Friday afternoon. Do you think you can have a design by then?"

"I *will* have one!" Rebecca said happily. "Thank you, Lydie."

Lydie thought of her secret. She thought of how important this young woman would be to the future happiness of her son. "I am very glad to do it," she said truthfully.

Rebecca smiled. "Tell you what, Lydie," she said. "As thanks for your generous offer, let me give you this thread free of charge. I know you don't want anything in return, but it would make me feel good to make this gift to the quilting bee. And after all," she continued in a half-whisper, "It's only six dollars!"

The two women laughed. "Fine, thank you, Rebecca."

As Rebecca put the thread in a small paper bag, the doorbell jingled again. Both women looked around and both gave a small, unnoticeable gasp at the new customer. Gregory.

"Oh, hi, Mrs. King," he said, closing the door and coming towards them. "Hello, Rebecca," he said warmly.

"Hello, Gregory," Lydie replied.

"Hi, Gregory," Rebecca said.

She waited for Gregory to state his business. But Gregory didn't have any business involving the quilt shop. He had personal business, a business proposition he couldn't wait to tell Rebecca about, but he hadn't considered how he'd proceed with another customer in the shop. "I, uh, came to ask you something," he said uncomfortably.

Lydie noticed the awkward silence and took her cue. "Well, I'll be running along," she said, gathering up her thread. "Goodbye, Gregory. Goodbye, Rebecca. Don't forget about church," she said pointedly to Rebecca, then turned and went out the door.

"Church?" Gregory asked inquiringly.

Rebecca knew what Lydie meant, but she wasn't ready to act upon her suggestion just yet. "Oh, yes," she said vaguely. "Why are you here, Gregory? I thought you'd be at Wanda's." She tried to keep the hint of jealousy out of her voice, but wasn't sure she'd succeeded.

"I'm on my way," he said. "Decided to drive this time. Want to go by the library first, use their computer."

"Do you miss not having a computer all the time?"

"Absolutely not. But they are useful for research."

"What are you researching?"

Gregory realized he couldn't tell her. What would he say, "I'm trying to find the person my father slept with years ago?" Or, "There's this guy, Vinny, who's been hanging around Wanda, and I don't trust him?" But he didn't want to lie. "Something about Ivan," he said.

"Still trying to figure out why he called you his son?"

Gregory knew why, of course. But this wasn't the time to tell her, much as he wanted to. "Sort of," he answered vaguely. "Anyway," he went on quickly, "I wanted to ask you something."

"Of course." *Is he going to ask me for a walk? Is he going to take me for a ride on Bojangles? Is he...? Is he...?*

Now that he was facing her, Gregory felt a little sheepish about his idea. But he had come this far, so he straightened up, looked her in the eye, and said, "Rebecca I want you to teach me how to speak Pennsylvania Dutch."

"What?" she asked. This was not the question she'd been anticipating.

"Dutch. Your language. Will you teach it to me?"

"Why?"

"I just want to learn it." He couldn't tell her the real reason. *So I'll be more like a man you might marry someday.* So he said, "I don't like not knowing what you and your family are saying. And I'd like to go to an Amish church again, and it'd be nice if I could understand part of what was going on. I know, you're probably too busy. I understand, if you don't want to do it."

"I'll do it."

"It was a dumb idea, I guess," Gregory continued, not hearing her from the embarrassment of thinking he'd done something inappropriate. "I don't know what I was thinking — "

"Gregory, I said I'd do it," she emphasized.

Gregory stopped speaking. "You will?"

"Yes. I'd love to teach you how to *sprech Deutsch.*"

"I take it that means something like 'speak Dutch.'"

"What a fast learner you are!"

For a minute, they just stood still, looking at each other, smiling. No one was in the shop. For the first time in a long while, they were alone together. Gregory had an overwhelming urge to kiss her. Rebecca had an intense hope that he would. He knew this was not the time or the place. But when he was alone with her learning Deutsch? The thought of what might happen then almost made him clap his hands in delight. Finally, he spoke. "*Gut.*"

"*Gut,*" she said back.

He couldn't kiss her, but he had to touch her. He stuck out his hand. She took it. They shook. But he still held her hand.

"Gregory," she said. "You say you want to understand more in church. How about I teach you some of the things that are usually said and you come to church to practice them?"

"Come to one of your church services? I'd really like that, Rebecca."

"I'll let you know when the next one will be when we have our first lesson."

"And when might that be?"

"How about after work tomorrow?"

"Deal!" Gregory said enthusiastically. He noticed they were still holding hands, so he shook hers again and reluctantly let go. "Well, I'd better get to the library."

"Yes, you'd better."

He took a few steps towards the door, then turned. The joy each felt filled the space between them, connecting them with endless possibilities. "Goodbye, Rebecca. Have a nice day."

"*Denki,* Gregory. You, too."

Gregory turned and walked briskly out the door. When it closed behind him, Rebecca closed her eyes. "Dear God," she prayed. "Thank You, thank You so much. How woeful I was when this day began, but now, thanks to Your mercy, my heart is racing like a — "

She stopped, drawing in a quick breath of surprise. She ran behind the counter and took out her sketchpad and pencil. With mounting excitement, she wiped her left hand over the blank page, needlessly smoothing it out while her mind raced. Then she took the pencil between her fingers and began to draw. She drew fast, with bold, confident strokes, her hand flying from one point on the page to another. In a few minutes, she had finished. She held up the sketch and looked at it, a smile spreading across her face that was magnified by the tremendous thrill in her breast. There on the page before her was a horse, a beautiful horse, galloping across the page. A galloping horse, galloping as her heart was now galloping. Towards Gregory. Towards God. Towards both.

CHAPTER 14

Gregory rubbed his eyes. He'd been at this for hours, combing through old newspapers for any mention of the young Ivan Heminger. The trouble was, the Lancaster Intelligencer-Journal hadn't yet put all of its past newspapers online, so instead of searching on the computer, where he would have just had to type in the name "Ivan Heminger" to see whether he had ever been in the newspaper, Gregory had had to do it the old way, on microfilm. That meant threading each film into the reader, cranking the handle on the side, and then watching the pages scroll by. Fortunately, he was only searching for an article or a photo in the society pages, so he could fast-forward through the other pages of the newspaper until he reached them.

Still, it was taking forever. Gregory had decided to start when Ivan would have been age fifteen. He knew that was early, but, from what little he knew of Ivan, he wouldn't have been surprised to learn that he was making himself known at an early age. He had contemplated starting at age sixteen or even seventeen, but what if he'd missed something? He'd never know. *Better safe than sorry.* But now he felt sorry he'd ever started out to search for his birth mother.

No, that's not true. If I hadn't come to Lancaster County, I would never have met Rebecca. He leaned back in the uncomfortable chair and decided to allow himself a few minutes' rest.

That was a good idea he'd had about the lessons. Where should they have them? In his cottage? Would Rebecca think that was too intimate? They could just sit in the barn or sit in the grass. *But I want to be alone where nobody can see us. Then maybe....*

He closed his eyes. The thought of kissing Rebecca made him smile, then shudder with anticipation. He could almost feel her soft lips, her hands pressing firmly into his back, the smell of her hair —

"Excuse me, no sleeping in the library."

Gregory opened his eyes to see the librarian standing over him. He felt a little embarrassed. "I'm sorry, I wasn't sleeping, I was — " He stopped. What was he going to say, I was dreaming of kissing a woman? "I was just taking a rest from looking through all these newspapers."

"What are you looking for?"

Gregory looked at the librarian. She was a small woman, her brown hair tied back in a bun, her simple black dress neatly pressed.

Glasses dangled from a chain around her neck. Did all librarians wear glasses? Did they issue them with the job? "I'm trying to find information about Ivan Heminger."

"The man who died last month? I know Ivan," she said. Gregory looked again. She was indeed about Ivan's age. "What do you want to know about him?"

Once again, Gregory felt constrained in his answer. He couldn't say, "Oh, whom he might have slept with twenty-five years ago, who got pregnant and then went to South Carolina to have the baby." He said carefully, "I'm actually trying to find out who he might have been dating when he was a teenager." She looked at him, acknowledging that it was an odd search, so Gregory went on quickly, "Did you know Ivan well?"

"We were classmates, that's all, I didn't really know him. Let's see, I do seem to remember Ivan dating someone…." She reached for her glasses, put one stem in her mouth and began lightly tapping her teeth. "She was a pretty girl, but Ivan always dated the pretty ones…. Hmmm…. Nancy…. Nancy…." She tried to recall the name. "Nancy Newsome!" she exclaimed at last. "Yes, that's who it was. I remember, he took her to the senior prom." She put her glasses on and looked at the newspaper in the microfilm reader. "You're in the wrong year, two years too early." She looked over the other microfilms in their boxes, labeled with dates. "Here, this is the spring of his senior year, let's see if there's a picture."

The librarian took the film out and expertly threaded it into the machine. Gregory moved aside so she could sit down. As she scrolled through paper after paper, he became more and more excited. *Maybe I'm finally making progress!*

"All right," she finally said, "This is the right time of year, the end of May…." She began to scroll slowly, the blur of endless words coming into focus. And then a picture appeared. "There he is! And there's Nancy!"

Gregory bent to look. Sure enough, there was Ivan, looking very handsome in a tuxedo. Next to him, a beautiful blonde stared at the camera with large, round eyes. The picture wasn't in color, but Gregory was sure her eyes were blue. She wore a shapely white dress, sequins around the collar, that flowed to the floor, the picture-perfect image of a debutante. "Ivan Heminger and Nancy Newsome, voted Most Likely To Succeed by their classmates," he read underneath the picture.

"I told you she was beautiful," the librarian said.

"She sure is. Do you know what happened to her?"

"She got married, but not to Ivan. To a successful lawyer at Wood and Brown. They live out in the country somewhere, I believe."

"What's their name?"

"Jackson. She's Nancy Jackson now."

"Do you think I could find her address?"

"You want to visit her?" the librarian asked, growing a little suspicious. "What's all this about?"

Gregory was tired of pretending. And what did it matter anyway? This librarian wasn't going to care about his search. If anything, she might be sympathetic. "I am searching for my birth mother. I'm an orphan. I think Ivan was my father and I am trying to find my mother."

"And you think Nancy might be her?"

"It's a long shot, I know. If she's not my mother, maybe she'll have a clue about who is. I can't think of anything else to try, can you?"

The librarian took her time. Finally, she said, "No, I can't. Come with me." She led him to the front desk, went behind it and began typing into her computer. Then she wrote something down on a piece of paper and gave it to Gregory. "Looked up their address through the law firm. Here's where she lives. Good luck. I hope Nancy can help you out."

"Thank you so much. You have been really helpful."

He started for the door, then remembered the other reason he had come to the library. Choosing a computer in the back of the room, he sat down and typed in "Vincent Mangini." The computer spat back "no results for this name." Gregory pondered. *That's strange. I know that's the name Wanda told me.* He tried under "Vinny Mangini," but still got no results. Then he typed in "Vinny Mangini/Penn State University." Nothing. Then "Vinny Mangini/Penn State University/football." Again the screen read "no results."

Gregory stared at the machine. Why couldn't he find Vinny? Lots of people weren't on Google, but something should have come up at Penn State. Especially if he played football. With a shrug, he clicked "back to main menu" on the computer, got up, and headed out to talk to Nancy Newsome Jackson. He'd drop by Wanda's afterwards and see if she knew anything else about Vincent Mangini, or whatever his real name was.

Gregory left the Honey Brook library and headed for Route 30 towards Lancaster. It felt strange to be in his pickup. He hardly ever drove these days. He would either ride Bojangles over to Cedar Ridge Farm or walk to town to buy groceries or visit the quilt shop. *How small my world has become*, he thought, nudging his truck into the heavy traffic. No quick trip to McDonald's. No driving to the country club for dinner. No dashing into Charleston for a meeting. The Zook farm, Cedar

Ridge, Honey Brook, that was his life now. Looking around at all the cars coming and going, passing the strip malls and gas stations and fast food restaurants, Gregory prayed: *Thank You, God.* He smiled in surprise. Without realizing it, he had slipped back into a relationship with God, one that felt personal in a way he hadn't felt since he'd been a little boy first going to church and experiencing the soothing mystery of faith.

Eventually, Gregory was able to leave noisy Route 30 and turn south towards New Holland. As he drove along, the congestion of the busy world gradually gave way to farm after farm of rolling hills, interspersed with mown fields of corn or soybeans, sturdy houses, white-gleaming barns, the clean lines and ordered life of the Amish. He could feel his shoulders relax and his grip on the steering wheel loosen. He remembered how he'd felt when, months ago, he had first encountered this land. It was as if he'd gone down a rabbit hole and emerged into a world of incredible, pristine beauty, uncluttered and serene. *My world now*, he thought happily to himself.

And what of the world he had left behind? Gregory thought about his parents, about his father's anger when Gregory had failed to pass the bar exam to become a lawyer, about his socialite mother and her ladies-who-lunch world of designer clothes and afternoon cocktails. Gregory had emailed them from time to time, just so they wouldn't worry, but he'd always done it from a different library. He supposed they could have traced the sources of the email, but he hoped they wouldn't take the trouble, if they knew he was safe and happy. Once he'd arrived in Honey Brook and settled in at the Zook farm, he had needed to completely separate himself from his former life. It wasn't a conscious decision; it had happened naturally.

Consulting the map he had printed from the library computer, Gregory turned down a narrow lane. Overhead, beech and oak trees threw late-afternoon shadows across the pavement. He emerged onto a circular driveway that curved in front of a large, neo-Colonial, two-story house with white columns arising from a large veranda. *The South comes North*, he thought, as he parked his truck. He sat for a moment. He didn't really have a plan. He was just going to talk to Nancy Jackson about her time with Ivan, see if she could provide him with any clues he could use to find his real mother.

He walked under the columns and rang the doorbell. After a moment, a striking woman in her early forties answered the door. Her blond hair was professionally streaked, and she wore a simple but elegant purple blouse and creased black silk pants. "Yes?"

He was momentarily at a loss for words, trying to determine if this woman could possibly be his mother. Would she have made the baby quilt? But it didn't have to have been made by his mother. She could have simply bought it. "Hello, I'm Gregory Pinckney," he said at last.

"Hello. What can I do for you?" she asked politely.

"Did you know Ivan Heminger?"

She was surprised. "Ivan? Why, yes, I did. I was so sad to read that he had killed himself. Is that what this is about?"

"Not really. I'm not the police or anything."

"Frankly, I don't believe it was suicide."

"Why not?"

"Ivan wasn't the type to kill himself. He was always so confident, so full of life. I did hear that he'd begun drinking quite a lot. But if it's not about Ivan's death, what is it about?"

Gregory pursed his lips. *There's no way around it.* "Mrs. Jackson, I am an orphan. And I have reason to believe that Ivan was my father."

"Reason to believe?"

"DNA testing has confirmed it."

Nancy Jackson looked at Gregory carefully. "I'm afraid I don't understand. I know Ivan had a daughter, but I didn't know he had a son. An orphan, you say? Who is the mother?"

"I saw a picture of you and Ivan at the senior prom. I know you were dating him your senior year in high school." Gregory let the rest of his thought hang in the air.

Nancy Jackson wrinkled her brow, and then suddenly burst out, "You think I am your mother? You come here insinuating that I slept with Ivan when I was seventeen? What kind of a woman do you take me for?"

"I don't mean to imply — "

"How dare you knock on my door out of the blue and start making accusations! I am a respectable woman with children of my own!"

"I'm sorry, Mrs. Jackson, I'm only trying to find my mother."

"Well, you can look elsewhere, young man! I'm going to tell my husband about this. He's a lawyer, and he can make your life miserable."

Gregory felt miserable enough already. He was trying to find a polite way to apologize when a voice came from the interior of the home. "Excuse me, Mrs. Jackson, but do you want me to wash the sheets?"

Nancy Jackson turned her head and spoke down the hallway. "That won't be necessary, Sarah."

"Yes, ma'am," Sarah replied. Glancing down the hallway, Gregory saw a young teenager with an apron over her red dress and her hair pulled back under a covering. That, and the distinctive lilt of her accent, told him she was Amish.

"I'll thank you to leave my property this instant," Nancy Jackson said.

"Yes, ma'am," Gregory said, backing away. "I am so sorry. I didn't mean to offend you."

"Well, you did," she replied and went inside, slamming the door after her.

Gregory wasted no time returning to his truck and driving away from the Jackson estate as fast as possible. This time, as he sped back through the surrounding farmland, he had no time for thoughts about the beauty of the passing landscape or the noisy congestion of the highway. He just drove, trying to quiet the agitation inside him. He felt terrible about hurting Nancy Jackson's feelings, and even more terrible about embarrassing himself. Of course no one wanted to be accused of having a child out of wedlock. Did he think she'd take him in her arms and say, "Oh, my long-lost boy?" He grimaced. *Yes, that's exactly what I thought.*

Gregory finally began to notice his surroundings and was surprised to discover he had taken the road to Cedar Ridge Farm. Examining his feelings, he realized that, after his emotional encounter with Nancy Jackson, he had a yearning to see Wanda. He had a yearning to tell her that she was his half-sister, a yearning born of the need to have family on his side in his quest to find his birth mother. *She'll help me, especially when she knows I'm her half-brother. It's definitely time to tell her.*

When he pulled into the driveway, he saw Wanda on the veranda, brushing her hair. She looked up when he got out of the car and came down the stairs to greet him. "Hi," she said, pulling some strands of hair from the brush and tossing them into the wind.

"Hello, Wanda. Your hair looks beautiful."

"Thanks. I'm getting ready to go someplace, but I'm glad you dropped by, because I wanted to talk to you about something before I left."

"I wanted to talk to you about something, too. I've got what I hope is some wonderful news for you. But first, your mom told me the insurance money had come in. I'm happy for you, Wanda. I know you can use it."

"That's kind of what I wanted to talk to you about. Have you drawn up the partnership papers yet?"

"As a matter of fact, I have. I was going to bring them over to you. Do you want me to go get them?"

"No, that's all right." Wanda brushed her hair a few strokes, thinking. "Gregory, what did you put down for how we'll pay for this business? Who's putting up the money and things like that?"

Gregory hadn't really wanted to talk business with Wanda. He'd wanted to tell her what he hoped was the good news that they were related, but he had to go where the conversation was leading him. "I'd left that part blank, since we hadn't really discussed it. We'd talked about using some of your insurance money to start us off."

"I know. But what about your part?"

Money? We have to talk about money, when I've got news that is so much more important? "Well, Wanda, I don't have much money, so I was thinking that you would own more of the business, so you'd get more of the profits. Plus, I could pay you back for my share of the start-up costs from my share of the profits. We can work it lots of ways. The papers I've drawn up are just a start."

"Oh, good. Because, you know, Gregory, I was thinking that we really need to go cautiously here. I mean, in business you gotta go slowly."

Gregory looked at her a moment. This was not the Wanda he was used to. Whereas she always seemed enthusiastic and full of life, now she seemed guarded, almost suspicious. "I agree, Wanda. I'm not trying to rush anything."

Wanda looked relieved. She didn't like having this kind of conversation with Gregory, but she was trusting Vinny's instincts more than her own. "Good. Now, what was the wonderful news you had?"

Gregory's shoulders sagged. His yearning to tell Wanda she was his half-sister had completely disappeared. "Oh, it can wait."

"But you seemed so excited when you got here. What is it?"

He looked at her. This beautiful young woman, pink hairbrush in hand, her luscious blonde hair cascading down around her shoulders, how could she be his half-sister? He glanced up at the house and at the pastures beyond, suddenly feeling very disoriented. *What am I doing here?*

"Gregory?" Wanda asked.

"This isn't a good time, Wanda. I do have news, but I'd rather share it with you later."

She was disappointed. "All right." But her mood brightened when the roar of an engine coming down the drive penetrated the air. "Vinny!" she shouted, and ran towards the car.

Gregory turned and saw Vinny pulling his Maserati to a stop. He got out and Wanda gave him a big hug, then hooked his arm and led him towards Gregory. "Hello, Vinny," Gregory said.

"Hiya," Vinny responded without enthusiasm. "You ready, babe?" he asked Wanda.

"Almost. I'm just finishing with my hair, but I'm all packed."

"Going someplace?" Gregory asked.

"Vinny is taking me to Bushkill Falls," Wanda gushed. "For the weekend."

Gregory was so startled all he could say was, "Oh."

"Hope you don't mind?" Vinny asked, his attempt at light-hearted humor failing to mask his sarcasm.

"Me?" was all the answer Gregory could muster.

"Of course he doesn't mind, silly," Wanda said. "You'll have to excuse us, please, Gregory."

"Sure, of course. I needed to be going anyway."

"Okay, bye. Come on, let's say goodbye to Mother," she said to Vinny, pulling him towards the house.

Gregory watched them go inside. *Vinny and my half-sister. That just can't be right. But what can I do about it?* He started back to his truck, passing Vinny's Maserati. *Guy's got some money, with a car like this. Just not enough, I guess.* The license plate with a Penn State logo caught his eye. Suddenly he stopped, looking at the plate more carefully. His lips move silently as he memorized the numbers. He ran to his truck, jumped in, grabbed pen and paper from the glove compartment, and wrote down the license plate numbers, then started the engine, and sped away.

Instead of turning left towards the Zook farm, Gregory turned right and headed for Doc Jenkins' place. After a while, he pulled into the driveway and parked, the usual cacophony of barking dogs greeting him. He found Doc Jenkins seated on a bench in his front yard.

"Hello, Gregory," he said. "Have a seat. You look tired."

Gregory thankfully took up the offer and sat down next to the good doctor. "Thanks."

"What brings you out this way?"

"Doing a little investigating and I thought you might help."

"Still trying to find your birth mother? Any luck?"

"Not really. But this is something else. I'm wondering if you can help me find the last name of somebody."

"Not sure I can help you there, Gregory," Doc said. "I'm not much in the last name department."

"But you know people who are." He pulled out the piece of paper he'd written on. "You have connections with the police. I remember when we had that trouble with Ivan's poisoning those horses, you were very friendly with the police. Right?"

"I may know a person or two. What do you need?"

"I need to know the name of the person who owns this car." Gregory handed Doc the slip of paper on which he'd written down Vinny's license number.

Doc Jenkins took the piece of paper. "Well, that shouldn't be too hard. Seems I just operated on Donald Simkins' Labrador last week. Also seems I only charged him half of my usual fees. Donny's a sergeant and he's got access to the DMV's computer. It shouldn't take him long to trace it. What's it about?"

"I'm not sure yet."

"You know, Gregory, all this investigating 'bout got you killed last time. You sure you want to be doing this?"

"I don't think this'll lead to much trouble, Doc. Nothing involving an insurance scam or anything like that. Just a little domestic matter, nothing to get all worked up over."

"If you say so." Doc folded the paper and put it in his pocket.

Gregory thanked him, got in his truck and hurried back to see Bo and, hopefully, Rebecca. Doc went inside to call Donald Simkins. Both of them had ignored an important fact: The major cause of violence in the United States was "a little domestic matter."

CHAPTER 15

"Ich bin meet," Hanna said, getting up from her chair and stretching her arms towards the ceiling. "So tired." She had to be careful not to knock over one of the nearby quilting frames that Lydie had gathered into her living room. "There's hardly room to stretch, Lydie. Why'd you have to cram us together so tight?"

"I told you, Hanna, we've got to make quilts for Rebecca as fast as we can. That agent of hers is getting impatient."

"I don't like these designs," Mabel said from behind her frame. "Saddles in all the corners and a horse blanket in the middle. Whoever heard of such a thing? Why can't Rebecca design traditional quilts?"

"Because that's not what the agent can sell," Lydie said. "And it's not what she wants to make, either."

"That girl is all *ferhoodled,*" Mabel replied. "She never should have bought that quilt shop, she should have married Jacob and helped him farm. Like you, Madie. Why couldn't she be sensible like you?"

Madie Lapp, the fourth woman who had answered Lydie King's call to come to a quilting bee in her home, looked up from the quilt she was working on. Her face seemed to be permanently stamped with a smile since she and Amos had been published at the last church service. "I told her not to let him go, Mrs. Zook," she said, "But she wouldn't listen."

"I didn't know what to say to Jacob's mother in church," Mabel continued. "I've never been so embarrassed in my life. And now Rebecca's invited Gregory to church again."

"She has?" Lydie inquired, straining to keep the delight out of her voice.

"Told me so last night," Mabel said. "Why is she so interested in having Gregory come to our church?"

"She likes him," Hanna said.

"How do you mean, Hanna?" Mabel asked.

"Same way Madie likes Amos," Hanna explained.

"What?" Mabel exclaimed. "It better not be the same."

"Why not?" asked Lydie.

"He's *English!*" Mabel said. "She is not marrying an Englisher!"

Lydie knew that Gregory wasn't really English. He'd been raised English, and everyone thought he was English, but his mother knew the truth: He was actually Amish. It was a truth she could never reveal. She might not have to, however, if Gregory converted to being Amish on his own. And marrying Rebecca might be a good way of persuading him to convert. To convert, and to live close to his mother for the rest of his life. "She's a grown-up woman, Mabel," Lydie said. "She can make her own choice."

"Whose side are you on?" Mabel asked.

"I didn't know there were sides."

"Well, there are," Mabel said. "I pray to God she's not going to follow her foolishness about Jacob with even more foolishness."

"He seems like a nice man," Madie offered.

"I like him," Hanna said, taking her seat and beginning to sew.

"Hanna!" Mabel said in exasperation. "Nothing good's happened ever since Gregory came here. Horses died, Ivan killed himself. I wish he'd find his birth mother and go home."

"If he finds her, he might stay here," Lydie said.

"What makes you think she's here?" Mabel asked.

Lydie quickly backtracked. "She's probably not here."

"She must be some kind of tramp," Madie said.

"Tramp?" Lydie asked, her voice rising slightly in unconscious self-defense. "Why do you call her that?"

"Sure," Mabel said. "Having a child when she wasn't married, then giving him up for adoption. What kind of woman would do that?"

"A bad one," Hanna said. "He'll never find her, though."

"What makes you say that?" Lydie asked, as calmly as she could. The conversation was making her uncomfortable.

"My six senses," Hanna said. "Even if he finds her, she wouldn't take him. She doesn't want him. If she'd wanted him, she never would have given him up."

"That's not true!" Lydie blurted out. All three women looked at her, startled by the passion in her voice.

"Do you know something, Lydie?" Mabel asked. "Do you know who Gregory's birth mother is?"

"Of course not," Lydie said. *God, forgive me for lying, but I just can't tell them.* "How would I know something like that?"

"I don't know," Mabel said. "You just seemed so sure about it."

"The only thing I'm sure about," Lydie said, recovering, "Is that if we don't get back to sewing, we're never going to finish these wall hangings for Rebecca. Have you finished making your wedding dress, Madie?" she continued, changing the subject.

"Oh, yes, otherwise I'd never have been able to come over and help out," Madie said. She turned to Mabel. "Don't worry, now that Johnny's back, maybe he'll court Rebecca."

"Johnny! He's even worse!" Mabel replied. "His father drinks, and his brothers and sisters have already left the church. Maybe it'd be best if she ended up an old maid."

"Us old maids have all the fun," Hanna said. "Men are just trouble anyway."

"Some of them are," Lydie agreed, remembering her past. "You're lucky to have children, Mabel," she said. *I have a child and I can't even acknowledge him.* "I wouldn't be too hard on Rebecca. Have you finished your canning, Hanna?" she asked, changing the subject again.

"Not yet. Got my beans done, but still have my 'maters to do. How about you?"

"Since I've been working on Rebecca's quilts, I've fallen behind. But now that you all have helped finish them, I think I can get to the canning soon. Thank you all again for doing this quilting." She spoke to Mabel. "Even if you don't like the designs."

"I guess they're not so bad," Mabel said, realizing that, all things considered, she was, indeed, lucky to have children — and to have such good ones, too. "If it makes Rebecca happy...."

"And when Goldfart sells them, she'll make lots of money," Hanna said.

Madie laughed, Lydie smiled, but Mabel hastened to correct her sister. "His name is Gold*farb*, Hanna! How many times do I have to tell you?"

"Forty-three!" Hanna said. This time even Mabel joined the laughter. She actually admired her sister for overcoming her disability and living her life with such good humor.

The conversation turned to other local matters — how Miriam Beiler had a successful season selling her vegetables at her farm stand, how Morris Hochstetler ought to pull his suspenders up, his pants were almost falling down — and the afternoon drifted into evening as the four friends continued to manifest one of the basic tenets of their faith: helping out others.

As the November sun sank slowly into the horizon, Rebecca hurried home. She'd had to wait patiently while Emily Miller had dawdled about the shop, looking at patches, chatting about her family's new mule, telling Rebecca about an auction she'd gone to in Brownsville and all the farm equipment that Samuel Fisher had purchased at a steal. Finally Emily had bought one skein of yarn, departed, and Rebecca had quickly locked up.

Normally, she would have taken her time walking home, since oncoming dusk was a favorite part of the day for her. In fact, if no one were around, when she got home she would often climb up the barn ladder to her special place and watch the sun go down until Hanna called the men into dinner. Since she'd opened her shop, her mother and Hanna had agreed that Rebecca could do most of the cleaning up after the meal, so she'd often used her precious few minutes to sit quietly. *Be still and know that I am God.* The way her life was going — ordering, purchasing, accounting, designing, gathering eggs, cleaning up — Rebecca valued her moments of stillness more than ever.

But today she was in a hurry, so the lush fields of rich, brown earth, the men and boys on horse-drawn wagons turning that earth, the young Amish children chasing each other in freshly-mown lawns didn't catch her eye as they usually did. Today she wasn't a young Amish woman coming home from work. Today she was a schoolteacher.

She smiled as she turned down the lane to her home. *Schoolteacher. I always wanted to be one.* Except she didn't have a class of twenty children, she had a class of one man. The thought of her upcoming lesson with Gregory hastened her pace even more.

When she reached the farm, she went to his cottage, as they'd agreed. They'd also agreed to sit outside. Both of them wanted the intimacy, and were simultaneously afraid of it, so finding a "safe" place to conduct their lesson had been easy. When she didn't see Gregory outside, Rebecca felt confused, and even a little sad. She had really looked forward to this lesson and now Gregory wasn't there. But his "Hello, Rebecca!" soon restored her spirits, as she turned and saw him descending the hill from the barn.

"Sorry, had to take care of Bo," he said, when he reached her.

"And how is my favorite horse?"

"Missing you, as a matter of fact. When are we going to go riding again?"

The reminder of the time she had ridden behind Gregory on Bo made her blush. That had been the time he had first kissed her. "I just don't seem to have any time, Gregory. I'm afraid you'll have to settle for Wanda."

Why did I say that? Rebecca chastised herself. But she knew why. Gregory always seemed to be going over to Wanda's, or talking about his business with Wanda, or talking about how Bo and Wanda's new horse, Wise Guy, got along so well together. Sometimes, when she lay in bed and thought about Gregory and whether they could possibly have a life together, Wanda's name would intrude. Or rather, Wanda's beautiful face and body would.

Gregory ignored her remark about Wanda. "I'm not giving up. I owe it to Bo. In fact, my plan is to borrow Wise Guy, put you on Bo, and give you a real riding lesson. Tit for tat: You teach me and I'll teach you. What do you say?"

"I say you'd best see how our lesson goes first."

"Shall we sit on the bench?" He indicated the small bench nestled under a beech tree.

"I think it'd be best if we faced each other."

"I'll get a chair, just a sec." Gregory disappeared into the cottage and emerged with a wooden kitchen chair, which he placed in front of the bench, and then sat on it. Rebecca sat on the bench.

"Maybe the best way to proceed is for me to teach you certain phrases, and then you can learn the words from that," Rebecca began. "We don't have books of grammar or anything, and I don't think it makes sense for me to teach you verbs and past and present tense and such not. Do you agree?"

"Shall I get a pad and write it down?"

"We don't have a written language. I wouldn't know how to spell the words."

"Okay, I'll learn it all aurally."

"Fine. Let's start with introducing ourselves. When you see me in the morning, you might say '*Guder Daag, Rebecca.*'"

"*Guder Daag, Rebecca,*" Gregory repeated. "What's that mean?"

"'Good morning.' We can learn 'afternoon' and 'evening' later, but it might be useful to know *Guti Nacht.* That means 'good night.'"

"Wait a minute," Gregory said. "'*Guder*' means 'good' in the morning and '*Guti*' means 'good' at night. Why is that?"

"I don't know," Rebecca answered. "English is just as confusing."

"I know. 'R-e-a-d' sometimes means present tense and sometimes means past tense."

Rebecca felt the need to take control. "Let's not stop to ask questions, let's just repeat things first, okay?"

"Whatever teacher wants!" Gregory smiled disarmingly, but Rebecca ignored it, determined to proceed.

"Now, I might ask, '*Was iss dei Naame?*'"

"And I'd answer 'Gregory,'" he said. "I've picked up a few things, living here. '*Was iss*' sounds like 'What is,' and 'Naame' sounds like 'name.' I figured *'dei'* didn't mean 'to die' in this context: 'What is DIE name?' wouldn't make much sense."

Rebecca laughed. "If you keep making jokes, we'll never get anywhere."

"Sorry, I'll be a good student from now on." Gregory sat up straight and gave Rebecca his strict attention. *"Was iss dei Naame?"*

"Not bad," she said.

"I'll need more encouragement than that!"

"You'll get it when you deserve it."

"I can tell you're going to be a strict teacher."

"Yah, ich bin. 'Yes, I am." She paused, collecting her thoughts. "Now, after we greet each other, we might ask 'How are you?' That would be *'Wie bischt du?'"*

"And I would answer 'I'm on top of the world!'" Gregory said. Having Rebecca teach him was making him almost giddy, impelling him to tease and act silly. But he could see that Rebecca was being very serious about teaching him. "I'm sorry, I don't mean to act foolish. What's the word for 'fool?'"

"We never say 'fool' or 'foolish.' I don't even know the word for it."

"You never say it? Why not?"

"The Bible tells us not to."

"What? Where?"

"Matthew 5: 22: 'Anyone who says 'you fool' will be subject to the fires of hell.'"

"Amazing. I had no idea the Bible said such a thing."

"It's talking about not being angry with your brother and not calling him names."

"I can see I'm going to learn a lot more than just language from you."

"Now, *'bruder'* is 'brother' and *'schweschder'* is 'sister.'"

Gregory said them. He did fine on pronouncing *'bruder,'* but his tongue got tied up when he tried the "schw" sound.

"That sound is hard in our language," Rebecca said. "It's spelled with a 'W,' but 'W' is pronounced as 'V.' *Schweschder,"* she said slowly.

He tried again, but it sounded like a fish burbling. Rebecca laughed. "Here, let me show you." She put her fingers on the outside of his mouth and pushed the sides more together. "'Schw'," she instructed.

Gregory didn't respond. The touch of her fingers on his face had sent a chill up his spine. He looked at her, deeply, then said, with her hands still on his face, "How do you say 'I want to kiss you?'"

Rebecca paused, but she didn't take her hands away from his face. She, too, looked deep into his eyes, and she was about to tell him how to say it when they both heard a voice that startled them.

"Gregory wants to kiss you, Becca!" Hanna said. She had come to find Rebecca to call her in to dinner. "Well, do it, do it!" she urged delightedly.

Rebecca immediately dropped her hand and they both stood up, separating as quickly as possible. "That's not the way to do it," Hanna instructed. "You have to come together, not go apart."

"Hanna, what do you want?" Rebecca managed to say, her face pink from embarrassment.

"I want Gregory to kiss you," Hanna said.

"Well, he's not going to," Rebecca said. "I was just teaching him to speak Pennsylvania Dutch."

"Teach him how to say 'I love you,'" she said. "*Ich liebe dich.*"

"I love you, too, Hanna," Gregory replied, hoping his lighthearted answer would diffuse the situation.

"Not me, Gregory, Rebecca," she said, pointing at her niece. "Say '*Ich liebe dich*' to her."

"Maybe some other time," he replied softly, and then quickly continued, "Thank you for the lesson, Rebecca. I learned a lot, and I look forward to our next one. Bye, Hanna." Gregory nodded and headed for his cottage.

As he retreated, he heard Hanna call after him. "'*Ich wil dich un bes geva.*' That's how you say it, Gregory. '*Ich wil dich un bes geva.*' 'I want to give you a kiss.'"

Once inside, Gregory leaned back against the door and closed his eyes, remembering how Rebecca had touched him. He slowly, lovingly placed his fingers on his face, as she had done, and whispered softly, over and over: *Ich wil dich un bes geva. Ich wil dich un bes geva.*

CHAPTER 16

As Gregory sped along in his pickup on Pennsylvania Route 22 out of Hershey, he hardly noticed the passing scenery. Much as he tried to keep his mind on the task at hand, his thoughts kept returning to Rebecca and yesterday's lesson. *"Guder daag, Rebecca,"* he said out loud, practicing the phrase for the hundredth time, relishing the sound of the language that had become so special to him.

He had roused himself early that morning just so he could go outside his cottage and say *"Guder daag"* to Rebecca, as she was gathering eggs. She had replied, *"Guder Daag, Gregory. Wie bischt du?"* Then he'd paused: He never had learned how to answer that question; they had been distracted by the discussion about the book of Matthew and its prohibition of the word "fool." So he had replied, making it up as best he could, *"Ich bischt* great*!"* Rebecca had laughed, teaching him *"Ich schpiel gut."* *"Ich schpiel gut,"* Gregory had repeated.

When she'd turned to go, Gregory had stopped her. "Wait. Aren't you going to say 'Goodbye,' 'Have a great day,' something?"

"We don't really say that."

"Really? Why not?"

"I don't know. When we're finished with a conversation, we usually just leave. Sometimes we don't even say "goodbye.""

"You Amish are so rude! I've got to teach you some manners. Repeat after me: 'Have a great day!'"

"I'm beginning to regret that we don't have a word for 'fool,'" Rebecca had teased back. Then she had looked him and said, with utmost warmth, "Have a great day, Gregory."

The look she had given him, the depth of feeling she had put into those simple words, had stunned Gregory so much that he had not immediately replied. When Rebecca had turned and headed for the house, he'd found his voice and had shouted, "You, too, Rebecca!"

"You, too, Rebecca," he said again, as he motored along. Then he said softy, *"Ich liebe dich.* And I hope you 'liebe' me back!" He smiled. There was something about loving this simple, Amish woman that made the playfulness in him come bubbling to the surface.

He gripped the steering wheel more tightly, forcing himself to concentrate on the task at hand. When Doc Jenkins had called him that morning, he'd rushed right over. "Bandini," Doc had said, handing him a piece of paper. Gregory had thanked him, taken the paper, gone immediately to the library, where he'd Googled "Vincent Bandini." He was disappointed when he got no results, but not really surprised. He'd already decided what he must do next: follow the one clue he had, which was that Vinny Bandini had played football at Penn State University.

Outside Lewistown, Gregory swung north onto Route 322. This part of the drive promised to be more beautiful, since it passed by the Laurel Creek Reservoir and through Rothrock State Forest. Gregory relaxed and slowed his speed. He scrunched his body around, trying to get comfortable. *Been a long time since I've traveled this far. Five months since I left home. How my life has changed! No movies, no television, no phone calls, no going out for dinner, no visiting relatives.* How had he become so Amish-like without even noticing it? He must have been longing for something simpler.

He passed a billboard that advertised "Days Past Carriage Rides." There was a picture of an Amish buggy pulled by a black horse. "Experience the simple joys of Amish life! You'll never forget it!" the sign promised. Gregory frowned. So many people were trying to exploit the Amish way of life these days. He noticed the tourist buses on their way to Lancaster, dozens of them. He knew about the "Amish Experience" farmland tours and the one-room schoolhouse tour that promised a certified guide who would "unravel the riddles of Amish life." And, though he'd never watched them, he also knew there were several television shows about the Amish. *They don't even know what real Amish are like. They're just trying to make money because the Amish are so different from the rest of America. Why can't they leave us alone!* Gregory's eyes widened in surprise. "'Us,' I thought 'us!'" His frown turned into a smile. He was truly beginning to think of himself as part of the Amish community. Maybe someday it would be true.

He arrived in State College mid-afternoon. After asking around, he found the alumni office, parked his truck in Visitor Parking, and proceeded upstairs. Opening the half-glass door to the Office of Alumni Affairs, he approached a desk behind which a petite, redheaded young woman was clicking away on her computer keys. "Excuse me," he said. "My name is Gregory Pinckney and I am trying to track down a former student. His name is Vincent Bandini."

The redhead looked up. "Are you an alumnus?"

"No, ma'am."

"We don't give out that information to just anyone," she said crisply.

Gregory wasn't surprised, but he wasn't going to give up so easily. "I understand," he said. "But I don't want any other information except to know whether he went here. I don't need his address or phone or anything, just to confirm he attended Penn State."

"Might I ask, why?" She gazed at him critically.

Gregory decided to tell her. After all, there was nothing underhanded in his quest to find out more about Vinny Bandini. "My half-sister, Wanda Heminger, is dating Vinny. It might be serious. But we don't know much about him, so I drove up here to find out anything about his past. I don't want my half-sister marrying somebody she shouldn't."

The young woman's gaze immediately softened. "That's so good of you. I had an older brother, but he was killed in a car accident. I know he would have looked after me the way you're doing for Wanda. Just a minute." She turned away from Gregory and clicked vigorously on her computer keys. "Yes, here he is. He did go here."

"Thank you. I'm so sorry about your brother."

"Thank you. You take care of your half-sister."

"I will." Gregory started to leave, then stopped. "May I ask you something? Is there a special bar where most Penn State alumni hang out, where the players go after the season, where really die-hard fans are likely to go?"

"Oh, yes, that's easy. It's the Arena, on Martin Street."

"Thanks!" Gregory hurried out the office door and moved quickly down the stairs, thinking fast. *Vinny is telling the truth about having gone here, but I know he's lying about something. What?*

His next stop was Beaver Stadium. As he parked his truck, he could hear the faint sound of a whistle and the thump of shoulder pads banging into each other. The team was practicing for its home game against the Indiana Hoosiers that Saturday. He looked up at the massive structure of concrete and steel that towered over him. He imagined the stands filled with over 100,000 people, all screaming. The bands from both teams would be blaring out fight songs. *So much noise!* He shook his head, as if to clear it of the imagined sounds. *Our lives are so full of noise!*

He approached one of the gates. A guard, sitting on a stool, rose to block his way. "Is it possible to watch?" Gregory asked.

"Absolutely not," the guard said firmly.

"Well, is there a records room inside, a place with pictures of all the teams, maybe something about the players?"

"Not in here. You might try the All Sports Museum."

"Thanks." Gregory took a shot. The guard looked to be in his fifties; he might have been there a while. "Did you ever know a Vinny Bandini who played here?"

"Nope."

"Let me ask you something. Is there some guy who's been around a long time, loves Penn State to death, and knows just about everything there is to know about the teams, past and present?"

"Sure. He's a legend. Name's Johnny Caskill, but everybody calls him Smudge."

"That's an odd nickname."

"Got a birthmark on his forehead, looks like an ink smudge."

"Let me guess," said Gregory. "I can probably find Smudge at the Arena."

"You can definitely find him there," the guard replied. "Opens and closes the place."

"Thanks." The guard nodded and returned to his stool, as Gregory made his way back to his vehicle. He decided to forego a visit to the Sports Museum. *I need personal information. I need Smudge.*

Ten minutes later, he walked into the Arena Bar and Grill. It was already filling up with the Happy Hour crowd. The stereo was playing some rap song, the bass pulsing so loud he could feel the vibrations in the floor. Dozens of undergraduates were sitting at tall tables, at the bar, or standing, most of them drinking beer, a few holding ice-filled glasses of liquor. It was shockingly loud for Gregory. He had been living in a world full of silence for a long time now, and the noise almost disoriented him. *How can people relate in this racket?* Then he remembered. It wasn't so long ago that he, too, had frequented such places while in law school at the University of South Carolina. A sense of relief washed over him. *I'm glad I don't want to do that anymore.*

He was going to ask the bartender if Johnny Caskill was here, but as he walked towards the bar, he noticed an interior poolroom, where an older man was shooting pool by himself. He wore dirty khakis, a blue-and-white striped shirt, and had a Penn State cap perched on his head. *Gotta be Smudge.* Noticing a beer mug on the pool table, Gregory went to the bar and shouted at the bartender, "What's Smudge's drink?"

"Rolling Rock."

"Draw me one."

"Only one?"

Gregory paused. He hadn't had a beer in almost half a year. He hadn't had any alcohol. Another fact to put into his growing "I've-changed-without-realizing-it" column. But he also realized it would help if he were as sociable as possible with Smudge. "Yeah, make it two."

When the bartender had filled two Rolling Rock mugs, Gregory carried them into the poolroom, where the noise was low enough to allow for ordinary conversation. He set one beer down next to the one already resting on the side of the pool table. Smudge looked up. He hadn't shaved in a few days. Sure enough, there was a birthmark the size of a fifty-cent piece in the upper left corner of his forehead, looking exactly like an ink spot in a Rorschach test. "For me?" he asked in a voice raspy from a lifetime of smoking cigarettes.

Gregory nodded. "My pleasure."

"Wanna play?"

"Sure," Gregory answered. His father had taught him how to play pool, and he'd spent enough hours in his fraternity poolroom to feel that he wouldn't embarrass himself too much.

"I'll break, if that's all right," Smudge said. "Eight ball's the game." He put the cue ball at the head of the table, chalked up his stick, leaned down and slowly pulled the cue stick back and forth one, two, three times, then struck the ball with a strong, straight stroke. The white ball blasted into the triangle of solids and stripes, the number nine ball caroming into a side pocket. "Stripes," Smudge announced.

He then proceeded to put on the most dazzling display of pool shooting Gregory had ever witnessed. "Thirteen, side." Cue back and through, thirteen ball in the side pocket. "Ten, corner." Thwack! and the ten ball zipped seamlessly into the corner pocket. "Fifteen...." "Twelve...." "Fourteen...." Gregory could only stand and admire such artistry as each ball disappeared into the designated pocket. For his final shot, Smudge's target eleven ball was blocked by one of Gregory's solids, so he jumped the cue ball over Gregory's, knocked the eleven on the side, and it squirted into a corner pocket. Cleaning up with the eight ball was a simple matter of an easy hit into a nearby pocket. "Another?" Smudge asked.

"Glad we weren't playing for money," Gregory said.

"We could," Smudge answered, smiling a gap-toothed smile.

"No, thanks. If you don't mind, I'll just take a moment to drink my beer."

"Good idea." Smudge picked up his mug. "Cheers."

"Cheers," Gregory said. He drank. The cold, hoppy taste felt odd in his mouth. But, after the long, hot drive, it tasted good.

"You a stranger here?" Smudge asked. Gregory nodded. "What brings you?"

"Actually, you do."

"Huh?"

"Well, not actually you, but your knowledge. I'm trying to find out information about a former football player named Vinny Bandini."

"Vinny the Snake?"

"The snake?"

"That's what we called him."

"He good at slithering through the line or something?"

"You kidding? Vinny was slow as a bus. I didn't give him the nickname, but I think they called him that because he was always snaking his buddies' dates. Carla put a stop to that, though."

"Carla?"

"Yeah, Carla Mancuso. What a knockout. Vinny met her his senior year. She was a freshman, but she didn't look that young, you know what I mean?" Smudge winked at Gregory and took a big gulp of beer.

"So Carla stopped Vinny from playing around, huh?" Gregory sipped his own beer.

"More the other way around," Smudge said, with a laugh. "Carla was, let's say, popular. After graduation, Vinny went off to work somewhere, but he was back here every chance he got, pestering Carla to marry him. Finally she did."

Gregory almost spat out his beer. *Vinny was married?* His head was spinning. "Are they still married?"

"Far as I know. Carla's not the kind of girl you want to divorce, you know what I mean?" He winked again.

Gregory took a long drink from his mug, trying to collect his thoughts. If Vinny was married, why was he acting like he wanted to marry Wanda? He couldn't do it legally. Was he planning on living with two wives, neither of them knowing about the other one? But why? Why not divorce Carla and marry Wanda, if she's the person he wanted to be married to? Unless there was some reason he couldn't divorce Carla. So why was Vinny taking Wanda for a weekend at Bushkill Falls, if he wasn't working up towards asking her to marry him?

"Another game?" Smudge asked, polishing off the last of his beer.

"No, thanks, gotta get going."

"Vinny the Snake...." Smudge mused. "I kinda miss him."

"Good player?"

"Hah! Wasn't even on the varsity. But those were good betting years, you know what I mean?" Smudge racked the balls, and then chalked up the cue stick to play another game by himself.

"Not really."

"Let's just say betting the point spread always seemed to pay off, almost like some people knew how Penn State was going to play that day. Some people including me," he said, and laughed, then coughed his smoker's cough.

"And you think Vinny had something to do with that?" Gregory asked, still trying to make sense of it all.

"I didn't say nothin'!" Smudged vowed earnestly. "Far as I'm concerned, you and me ain't never met!" He turned back to the pool table and blasted the cue ball into the rack of balls, scattering them and, of course, making one.

"Well, thanks," Gregory said. As he left the room, Smudge was once again running the table.

Gregory got into his pickup and pointed it towards Honey Brook and home. *Home!* His first real foray into the non-Amish world, that "other" world he had left behind, had exhausted him. The speeding cars; the huge stadium; the dark bar, with its incessant chattering and extremely loud music, and, mostly, the astounding news he had just heard and the extremely troubling questions it engendered.

As he drove long, Gregory pondered them. *Should I tell Wanda about Vinny and Carla? Should I confront Vinny first? Maybe there's an explanation. Maybe he's no longer married. Doc Jenkins can help me answer that. If he's still married, then he's just pretending to want to marry Wanda. But why pretend?*

When he finally tumbled into bed later that night, the questions were still rattling around his brain. His trip to Penn State had been worth it, he knew that. But when he finally drifted off to sleep, he didn't know a single answer to all the questions it had raised.

CHAPTER 17

Vinny was praying. At least, that's what it looked like he was doing. His eyes were closed, his hands were folded together before him, and he was kneeling in the pew at Our Mother of the Immaculate Conception church while the priest continued saying the Mass. But Vinny wasn't praying. Instead of his mind being focused on things of the spirit, it was whirring with thoughts about how to accomplish the most important thing in his life right now: getting Wanda to accept his wedding proposal. Then he would have to get her to go to Vegas and marry him. And all before Christmas at the latest, if he was going to set up the joint bank account and transfer the money to Mancuso, all in time for the January 1 deadline. That gave him a little more than a month.

The weekend at Bushkill Falls had gone splendidly. Walking hand in hand. Romantic dinners. Kissing in the soft moonlight, while tumbling water playing a soothing melody in the background. It had been hard to part with Wanda at night, but he knew she'd appreciate his not trying to take things too far. He was playing the part of the consummate gentleman very well, considering he'd had such little practice. And now it was time for the *coup de grace.*

He smiled, remembering his conversation with Wanda earlier that morning, when he'd called to ask if she would like to attend Mass with him that afternoon. She had been surprised. "Mass?" she questioned.

"Yeah," Vinny had answered. Then he'd remembered how he'd cautioned himself to use only good English and good grammar, so he'd repeated, "Yes. Falling in love with you has made me start thinking about my own life, my own upbringing, in case, you know, we was — " he corrected himself — "we were to have children or something. I was remembering how my mother, may she rest in peace, would always take me to Mass. I was raised a good Catholic boy, Wanda, but, somehow, I slipped away from the church without even knowing it."

"I know, Vinny. I have, too."

Great, she's on my side. "I want to get back to the good things in life, the wholesome things, the important things. If you and I are gonna — going to — get married, I want us to start going to church again. I'm not saying you have to become Catholic, you know — *Watch the "you knows"!* — "we can decide that later, but I just have this strong urge to go to church with you. Would you, please?"

"Vinny, that is so sweet!" Wanda had gushed. "Of course, I'd love to go to church with you. Thank you for asking."

So there they were, kneeling in the church, while the priest concluded the Mass. Vinny had been surprised. Hearing the familiar words of the Gospel, reciting the familiar responses, had had a soothing effect on him. The beautiful stained-glass windows, the sun slanting through them and coloring the inside of the church, were truly inspirational. The vast interior of the massive building had somehow worked its magic, just as it had done when he was a boy, reminding him of the awesomeness of God. Incredible as it seemed, as the service had proceeded, he had actually begun to feel glad that he was in church again.

He glanced sideways at Wanda. She truly was beautiful, praying there with her eyes closed, her hair neatly pinned, the striking lines of her cheekbones sculpting her face, the fullness of her lips mumbling the prayer along with the priest. For a moment, Vinny wondered if he actually could marry Wanda, if they could escape to some far away country, raise goats or something and forget about all the hassle of living in America. *Yeah, right. And Uncle Joey would send us a Christmas card. Only it might explode in my face.*

"May the blessing of God Almighty, the Father, Son, and Holy Spirit be with you, now and forever more. Amen." The priest spread his arms wide in the embrace of the Benediction.

"Amen," Vinny and Wanda said together, then rose and left the church in silence.

Outside, Vinny proceeded with his plan. "Wasn't it wonderful?" he asked.

"It really was," Wanda said sincerely. "I'm so glad you asked me."

"Ever been to a Catholic service?"

"No. I was raised a Methodist, but, like I said, I haven't been to church in a long time."

"Maybe we can go again some time?"

"I'd like that, Vinny, I really would." Wanda gave him warm smile.

Vinny smiled back. "Good." *Now for part two.* "Take a walk? They got some beautiful grounds here."

"Love to."

He took her arm and guided her towards a path that led behind the church. It wandered through some small pine trees. He took Wanda's hand in his as they meandered among the hydrangea, some blue with blossoms even this late in the autumn, and the carefully cultivated pachysandra that ran along the path. "Nice and cool in here, isn't it?" he asked.

"I like it."

Normally, alone with a beautiful girl in the woods, Vinny would have tried to put the moves on her. But this was about more than stealing a kiss or two; this was business, serious business. "Wanda, I'd like to tell you a little about myself. I mean, we had such a fabulous time at Bushkill Falls, and it's no secret I'm really falling for you, and so I just want you to know a little more about me, in case, you know...." He looked at Wanda, and she smiled back at him. Yes, she knew. "Well, I was an only child and, like I said, raised Catholic."

"Where?"

"Hoboken." It had actually been in Jersey City, but Vinny didn't want anyone knowing much about his past if he could help it. "My father was a plumber and my mother was a schoolteacher." The first part was true, but he elevated his mother from a stay-at-home mom to impress Wanda. "Taught second grade. She really loved little kids."

"I do, too, Vinny," Wanda said, and gave his hand a squeeze.

A squeeze? Okay, good, this is going good. "Yeah? That's great!" He took a moment to think. He hadn't really been planning on making his mother a schoolteacher, but, now that he had, he decided to go with it. "She used to teach me grammar, corrected me all the time. She always said, "If you can't talk right, you can't do right." *Hey, that's not bad, whatever the heck it means!* "I kind of got away from it for a while, but I want to get my good grammar back. Matter of fact, I'm thinking of going back to school." *Whoa, where did that come from?*

"Really? In what?"

Good question. I hated school! Let's see.... "Everything. I mean, I gotta take it all, I never did get my high school diploma."

"Then how did you get into Penn State?" Wanda asked.

Stupdido! Watch what you're saying! "Oh, I got some kind of special dispensation, because of the football and all. I'll tell you about it some time."

"I'd like to hear it."

So would I! "Anyway, that's not the point. The point is … the point is...." *What is the point? Oh, yeah, my mom.* "The point is, my mother made me promise her something." They had reached a small, curved cement bench just off the path. "Mind if we sit?"

"Sure." Wanda sat down and crossed her legs prettily. Vinny sat next to her, then decided that was too close; he wouldn't be able to concentrate on his story with her so near and smelling so sweet, so he stood back up.

"This is kind of hard, Wanda, but I want you to know. My mama, may she rest in peace, made me promise that I would get married by my thirtieth birthday. Of course, she won't be here to see it...." Vinny took out a handkerchief and dabbed at his eyes.

"Why not?" Wanda asked, concerned.

"The cancer," Vinny said, willing his voice to be as hoarse as possible. "The cancer," he said again, whispering.

Wanda sprang to her feet. "Oh, Vinny, I'm so sorry!" She hugged him hard. "So, so sorry. She died?"

Vinny managed to nod. Wanda held him for a moment. He pretended to make a great effort to get a hold of himself. "I'm all right," he whispered. "Please, sit down and let me finish."

Wanda returned to her seat on the bench. "You see, Wanda, my thirtieth birthday is next month, December 15th. I know this sounds ridiculous, but my mother really impressed upon me not to wait too late to get married. She was afraid if I kept playing around, I never would do it. And she didn't want me to be too old to enjoy fatherhood. So she picked that deadline." *Time for the final flourish.* Vinny dropped to one knee. "Wanda, would you do me the honor of becoming my wife? I promise to love you for the rest of my life. Please, Wanda, say 'yes.' For my mother. And for me." He looked at her and willed his eyes to burn with all the passion he could manage.

Wanda got up and moved away from him. *She's not gonna do it. And I thought I gave a good performance!* Vinny forced himself to stay still. Finally, she slowly turned to face him. "Vinny," she said, "You were so good to me at Bushkill Falls. You treated me with such respect, you were never pushy, always asked me what I wanted to do, didn't just tell me what you'd already decided we should do. If I had a husband who would treat me that way, I don't know what could go wrong with our marriage. I would be honored to become Mrs. Vincent Magnini."

For a moment, Vinny looked confused, the title sounding strange to him. He almost corrected her. Then he remembered that "Magnini" was the name Wanda knew him by. He quickly recovered and took Wanda in his arms. "Thank you, Wanda, thank you! This is for you." He pulled a jeweler's case from his pocket and opened it. A diamond ring glistened in the sunlight.

"Vinny, it's beautiful!"

"Try it on." He slipped the ring onto her finger and she held it up to admire it.

"It's so beautiful!" She threw her arms around him and he kissed her. The kiss felt so wonderful that, for a moment, Vinny was confused as to whether he was enjoying kissing her because he really loved her or because he was relieved to know he was finally going to get his hands on her money.

"I was thinking we might get married in Las Vegas," he said.

"Las Vegas?" Wanda asked.

"I've got a lot of friends there, and since you don't seem to have that many here, I thought you wouldn't mind. We'd fly your mom out, of course."

"I never considered marrying in Las Vegas," Wanda said uncertainly.

Vinny acted quickly. He didn't want anything to disturb this moment. "We can talk about details later, babe." He had an inspiration. "Hold my hand," he said. He took her hand and stood by her side. "Now look up." They both looked to the skies. "Mama," he said, "She said 'yes'!"

Later that night, after Vinny had taken Wanda home and they had told Liz, who seemed very happy about it, he went to his favorite bar to celebrate. He was into his third martini when his cell phone rang. "Hello," he answered. The voice on the other end gave him pause, as always.

"Vinny," Joey Mancuso said.

"Uncle Joey!" Vinny replied. He decided to share the news with his uncle right away. "I proposed to Wanda and she said 'yes.' Isn't that good news?"

"Maybe," Mancuso said. "But I got news, too."

"You do?" His throat tightened. Mancuso's news had a way of never being good.

"Got a call from a friend of mine at Penn State. Seems a guy named Gregory was up there asking about you. You know a Gregory?"

"Yeah, he's a friend of Wanda's."

"I hope he's a friend of yours, too. 'Cause you know what Gregory learned about you, Vinny?"

"No, Uncle Joey." Vinny prepared himself for the worst.

"He found out you was already married to Carla. And I'm wondering: What if this Gregory fella tells Wanda you're already married, what happens to your wedding plans then?"

The line clicked dead. Vinny stared at his cell phone, stunned. He put it back into his pocket. *Gregory knows?* He cursed under his breath. *Everything's perfect, except for that.* He thought hard for a minute, then clenched his teeth and pursed his lips. *There's only one thing that happens to guys who know too much.*

CHAPTER 18

The earth splattered out from under the hooves of Bojangles as he galloped down the deserted lane. Gregory leaned forward, urging his horse faster and faster. He loved the rush of wind in his face, the hard bouncing of his body in the saddle, as Bo pounded over the earth. When he reached the end of the lane, where it curved towards the nearby farm, he yanked on the reins, turned Bo around, and started him back again.

Gregory had been racing up and down the lane for nearly an hour, trying to clear his head. Since he'd returned from Penn State, he had been trying to decide what to do about Wanda and Vinny. He was proud of himself for not having given in to his first impulse, which was to drive straight to Wanda's house and tell her what he'd learned. It had cost him a sleepless night, endlessly considering the consequences of telling her. If she didn't believe him, how would he prove it? What if she got mad at him for investigating Vinny? Would it help if he told her he was her half-brother or would that just confuse matters?

When first light had come, he couldn't stand it anymore and had gone to the barn, saddled up Bo, and begun riding him as hard as he could, trying to forget the questions in the pounding thrill of a muscled horse speeding beneath him.

He couldn't go to Cedar Ridge Farm, where there would have been plenty of pasture to ride over, so he'd had to settle for this dusty lane he'd discovered on one of his walks about the countryside. He longed to turn off and ride over the adjacent fields, but, even though most were now bare of crops, he knew the Amish farmers wouldn't appreciate his turning up their soil. So up and down the lane he flew.

When he reached the other end of the lane, Gregory reined in Bo, jumped off, and led him to the trickle of a nearby creek. *"Crick," Rebecca calls it.* Ah, yes, Rebecca! When would they have time for another lesson? When would they have time for something beside lessons? At least he would see her when he went with the family to church tomorrow.

Gregory looked at his horse, who had his mouth in the creek, slurping water. "Tired you out, didn't I, boy?" He gave Bo's side an affectionate pat. "Sorry. We'll walk home from here."

Heading home, Gregory felt better. If he confided in Rebecca, she would help him know what to do. *But maybe I'll wait to tell her that Wanda and I are related. One thing at a time. The thing to solve now is getting Wanda to break off her relationship with Vinny.* As he turned towards the barn, he saw something that took his breath away. Parked near the barn was a silver Mercedes. Gregory recognized it right away.

How did they find me? Gregory had written his parents from time to time over the past few months, just to let them know he was all right, but he had purposefully not told them where he was. He'd put his cellphone in a drawer and had let the battery run down. But, somehow, now they were here.

"Hello, son!" Gregory turned at the sound of his father's voice booming at him from the lane to the farmhouse. He looked the same. Broad shoulders, a full face beginning to get a little jowly, and hair so bright it had earned him the nickname he'd had all his life. Yes, "Red" Pinckney was an impressive-looking man, standing there in crisply-creased, tan slacks, white button-down shirt, and designer loafers, looking exactly like the supremely successful lawyer he was.

"Gregory!" his mother shouted and rushed towards him. She had let her blond hair grow since he'd last seen her, but otherwise she looked the same, too. Body well-toned from workouts, bright red nail polish complimenting equally bright red lipstick, Versace dress and shoes, looking every bit the doyenne of Charleston society. "I've missed you!" she said, giving him a strong embrace. "Let me look at you." She pulled back. "At least you look like you've been eating well, but those jeans could use a wash."

"What are you doing here?" Gregory asked.

"I came to see my son, if you don't mind," his mother said with a smile. "Although I had a hard enough time finding him."

"How did you?"

"Bit of detective work," his father said, joining them. "Tracked down the social worker who had worked with your birth mother. Apparently you had done the same thing. She shared with us the news that your mother had been Amish from Pennsylvania. Your mother noticed that you had taken the baby quilt your mother — I mean, your real mother — had made for you."

"I'm his real mother," Meredith Pinckney interrupted. "I raised him."

"Yes, yes, let's not get into that now," Red said dismissively. "But Pennsylvania's a large place," he continued, returning to his narrative. "So then I had a bright idea. I Googled you. And you know what turned up?"

"That you were involved in some sort of insurance scam!" his mother exclaimed. "And a suicide! We read about it in the Lancaster papers. Are you all right?""

"I'm fine, Mama."

"But what happened?"

"It's a long story. I'll tell you sometime. But, what are you doing here?" he asked again.

"She told you, we came to see you," his father replied.

"Are you staying?"

"No, no, got too much work to do," Red said. "Gotta get back to Carolina. But it's not that long a drive, so I decided to take a few days off and see if we could find you. And we did. You're kind of famous around these parts."

Gregory remembered the newspaper articles at the time of the police investigation. Ivan's poisoning the horses and his suicide, if that's what it was, and this newcomer at the center of it — all of it had caused quite a stir at the time.

"We booked a room at the Holiday Inn," Meredith said. "Not really what I'm used to, but at least it's clean. And guess what? Your landlords have invited us to come to supper tonight. Isn't that lovely?"

"The Zooks?" Gregory asked, surprised. "You've met them?"

"We met two old ladies. They said the men were in the fields, and there's a daughter at a quilt shop. When we told them who we were and why we were here, they insisted that we come share a meal with them. Isn't that nice?"

"The Amish are very generous," Gregory said. *A meal with the Zooks and my parents?* The thought made him uneasy.

"Well," his father said, "What shall we do until suppertime?" He and Meredith looked expectantly at Gregory. "You have anything you have to do, son?"

Tell my half-sister the man who is courting her is an adulterer. He sighed, knowing he wasn't going to make any progress on solving that problem while his parents were in town. "No, Daddy, I'm free. But I don't really know what to suggest. There's not a lot to do around here."

"Would you mind if I used your bathroom?" his mother asked.

"No, Mama, I don't mind, but you might. It's an outhouse."

"An outhouse!" his mother cried. "You mean, all these months you've been using…?" She paused. "I don't suppose they have one at the main house either."

"Actually, they do, they just never got around to upgrading the cottage."

"Meredith," Red began, "I don't think we want to borrow their bathroom. Why don't we hop in the car and find us a nice restaurant, grab a bite to eat, then we can figure out what we want to do the rest of the afternoon?" He didn't wait for answer, but turned and headed towards the Mercedes. Gregory knew there was no point in offering another opinion, so he took his mother's arm and they followed.

During lunch, Gregory told them how he had become involved in solving the horse insurance scam. He decided not to tell them about Rebecca. He knew that they would not think highly of his involvement with an Amish woman. Besides, what exactly *was* his involvement? When they asked what he'd been up to all these months, he realized the answer was "not much." Yet, somehow, his life had never seemed richer. It was as if, by getting rid of so much in his life — television, the computer, restaurants, athletic events, studying for the bar — he had somehow made his life fuller. Enjoying the pleasures of a simple meal, watching the sky fill up with stars, riding Bojangles around the countryside, delighting in the smell of the earth, the sight of waving grain, the clip-clop of horses, the laughter of children — by actually noticing where he was and what he was feeling instead of just rushing through the day, Gregory had turned what looked on the outside like a "not much" existence into what felt on the inside like a "so much" one. He didn't share this feeling with his parents, however. He wasn't even sure he knew how to articulate what had happened to his life in the past few months. He only knew he was grateful for it.

They spent the afternoon driving around the beautiful countryside. When his mother pointed at Amish in their buggies, or Amish following horses pulling ploughs in their fields, or Amish women in their coverings, or Amish children in their tiny straw hats and white aprons, Gregory realized how these sights were no longer unusual to him. They were just part of the way he lived now. And when he'd asked about life back home, and his mother had told him about her ladies' luncheons and his father had told him about his golf game, it confirmed in him the feeling that he much preferred the way he lived now to the life he'd left behind. He only hoped his parents wouldn't try to make him come home. He had a different home now.

A trip to the outlet mall helped fill in the hours. Meredith bought a new dress for the dinner that night, even though Gregory tried to persuade her not to. His father bought a bottle of Scotch, even though Gregory told him the Amish don't drink. He tried to think of something to bring to the Zooks as a gift for the supper, but all he could come up with was a blue candle that smelled of apples.

The meal began inauspiciously enough. When Gregory and his parents entered the warm, cozy farmhouse, chowchow, pepper cabbage, and a serving dish of cut celery and carrots were already laid out. Mabel had brought out her finest china and silverware for the occasion, and Hanna had ironed a white tablecloth to perfection. "What a lovely table!" Meredith exclaimed.

"Thank you," Mabel said.

"My father carved it," Hanna said. "Aren't the legs pretty?"

"I meant the setting," Meredith replied uncertainly.

"I ironed the tablecloth," Hanna said proudly. "Cut the celery and carrots, too."

"Mrs. Pinckney doesn't care what you did, Hanna," Mabel said.

"How do you know?" She turned to Meredith. "Do you care?"

"Well, I...."

"Mama, Daddy, you've met Mrs. Zook and Hanna," Gregory quickly interrupted. "This is Mr. Zook."

"Please, call me Elam," he said, shaking Red's and Meredith's hands.

"That's a unique name," Red offered.

"Not up here."

"I'm Gregory Pinckney. Most folks call me Red. This is my wife, Meredith."

"How do you do?" Elam said. "This is my son, Henry." Henry shook hands with Red and Meredith. "And this is my daughter, Rebecca."

"You're the one who owns the quilt shop," Meredith said. "We wanted to stop by, but Gregory thought you'd be too busy."

"I'm sorry you didn't," Rebecca replied, eying Gregory. He gave her a small smile. Until he had decided how much to tell his parents about Rebecca, he wanted to keep them apart. "Maybe next week."

"Oh, we'll have to be heading back on Monday," Red said. "Just came up to see how Gregory's doing."

"Step into the living room," Elam said, gesturing to his right. The Pinckneys and Gregory walked farther into the house.

Meredith looked around and noticed she was the only woman. "Aren't the others coming?" she asked.

"The women stay in the kitchen until the meal is ready to be served," Elam explained.

"Oh," Meredith said. Gregory could tell she didn't approve, but she didn't say anything.

"Good idea!' Red said heartedly. "Women leaving the kitchen was the worst thing that ever happened to marriage."

Gregory tried to cover up. "Daddy's joking," he said.

"The hell I am!" Red responded. Gregory cringed. The Amish didn't swear.

"Have a seat, Meredith," Elam said, and she sat in the armchair he'd indicated.

"Thank you, Elam," she said. "I like that name very much. Where's it come from?"

"I'm named after my grandfather. But it's from the Bible. Elam was the son of Shem, who was a son of Noah's. I guess that makes Noah the grandfather of Elam."

"Imagine that!" Meredith said. "I never think about Noah having children or grandchildren. But I guess somebody had to propagate the race after the flood."

"Saw you working the field today, Elam," Red said. "You think it's more expensive to keep horses than to own a tractor?"

"No matter. I can't own a tractor, and I don't want to."

"Who says and why not?" Red asked.

"The Ordnung says."

"What's that?"

"The Ordnung is a set of rules the Amish live by, Daddy," Gregory interjected. "They have no central church, every local church has its own set of rules, but some common rules have been handed down for centuries."

"As a lawyer, I'm very interested in rules. Where can I get my hands on this Ordnung."

"You can't," Henry said. "It's not written down."

"How do you know what the rules are?" Red persisted.

"We just know them," Henry answered. "Sort of the way you English learn grammar growing up, we learn the Ordnung. It's just passed down."

"Well, I like a rule I can read," Red said.

"That's the lawyer in you!" Gregory said lightly.

"Speaking of which, I hear you've been doing a bit of lawyering," Red said. "Mabel tells me you're helping Elam with the easement of his farm for the Lancaster Farmland Trust. Glad to hear all that law school wasn't a complete waste of time and money."

Gregory proceeded cautiously. He was glad to be helping Elam, but he didn't want his father to think he was seriously considering becoming a lawyer. "I've helped him with a little of the paper work. We're getting an appraisal to see what the development rights are worth, so Elam can get a tax deduction."

"You sure you want to do this?" Red asked Elam. "I've seen your property. Might be worth a lot of money to a developer. I know a few."

"He's sure," Henry said firmly.

"Elam is deeding the land over to Henry," Gregory explained. "Henry loves farming."

"And I'm tired of it," Elam said. "I'm going to open a leather shop,"

"So it's a win-win," Gregory said. "It's really a win-win-win, because there won't be any more cookie-cutter houses built, at least not on this Amish farmland. It will remain as beautiful and as productive as it is now, forever!"

"Dinner is served," Rebecca said, poking her head out from the kitchen.

Elam led the way to the table and placed himself at the head. Meredith had followed Gregory to his side. "Why don't you sit over there," Gregory said.

"I want to sit with you," his mother replied.

"The Amish have the men on one side, the women on the other," Gregory explained.

"That Ordnung thing?" Meredith said a little sarcastically. Then she remembered her manners and added, "I'd love to sit with the women," and moved to the other side of the table and sat down.

Hanna, Mabel, and Rebecca began bringing in the food. Beef roast, mashed potatoes, egg noodles with brown butter on top, gravy, succotash, cranberry and orange Jello, and warm bread. Soon the table was so full of plates, serving dishes, and bowls that there was hardly any room left. "My goodness!" Meredith exclaimed. "This is enough to feed an army."

"We like to eat," Hanna said, taking her seat.

"They need to eat," Gregory opined. "They work so hard, six days a week. I don't think I've ever seen a fat Amish person."

"I'm plump," said Hanna.

"Because you love your ice cream," Rebecca said.

"I like ice cream, too, Hanna," Meredith said. "What's your favorite flavor?" But there was no answer. Looking around, Meredith could see that the Zook family had all bowed their heads. She looked at Gregory and he motioned for her to bow her head in prayer. She complied, waiting for someone to say a prayer. No one did. Finally, as if by silent cue, Elam raised his head and the rest of his family did likewise, followed by Gregory, Meredith, and Red.

Elam cut the roast as, one by one, people passed their plates to him. As soon as Meredith's plate was returned to her, Hanna said, "Have some potatoes, I mashed 'em myself," and she dumped a large spoonful onto Meredith's plate.

"Not so much — " Meredith tried to stop her, but it was too late.

"They're good for you," Hanna said. "Put some meat on your bones."

"Maybe she doesn't want meat on her bones," Mabel said.

"She ought to, she's too skinny," Hanna declared. "Have some succotash." She placed it in front of Meredith. "You can serve yourself." She watched carefully as Meredith took a small spoonful. "How come you eat so little?"

"*Schtup sei blowa*," Mabel said.

Ich bin sei net un blowa," Hanna answered, thrusting her face towards Meredith. "Am I bothering you?" Her goofy smile was inches from Meredith's face.

Somewhat flustered, Meredith managed, "Why, no, I…."

"Please pass the bread," Gregory interrupted, hoping to steer the conversation away from Hanna and Mabel. He glanced at his mother, who began picking uncomfortably at her food. "How was work today?" he asked Rebecca, hoping to find an ally in keeping the conversation flowing, but away from his mother's eating habits.

"Fine," she said. "Lydie dropped off the wall hangings she and the women made for me. I am so grateful for your help," she said to Mabel and Hanna.

"Rebecca's an artist," Gregory said proudly to his mother and father.

"Not really," Rebecca demurred.

"Amish don't have artists," Mabel declared.

"Why not?" asked Red.

"She means the Amish don't like to draw attention to themselves. They think it's prideful, and pride is a sin," Gregory said.

"Is that in your Ordnung?" Red asked.

"Yes, it is," Elam said. "Rebecca makes quilts that are a little different from the usual Amish quilt. She has a gift, from God, and she wants to share it with other people, but she's trying to do it within the rules of the Ordnung. It's not easy to figure out how to do that, is it, daughter?"

Rebecca gave her father a warm smile, grateful that he sympathized with her struggle. "No, Dat, is isn't."

"Well, we don't have to call her anything. Just let her do what she does," Henry chimed in. "No one's complained yet." Rebecca shot her brother a smile.

"And people like 'em," Hanna said. "We took a trip to New York and went to a gallery and a man bought one of Becca's quilts right there, paid her a thousand dollars for it. That's real money. And another man wants to help her sell some more, that's why we were making them for her. He presents her."

"Represents her," Gregory said. "He's her agent."

"Got a funny name," Hanna began.

Mabel rushed to stop her. "Hanna — !"

"Goldfart," Hanna finished.

Red laughed. "Might have a hard time selling quilts with an agent named that!"

"It's Goldfarb," Rebecca explained. "Sometimes my aunt likes to say things she knows will draw attention to herself."

"Yep, I'm an artist!" Hanna said. The whole table laughed, including Hanna. Gregory breathed a sigh of relief, hoping things might go a little more smoothly now.

For a while, no one spoke, everyone concentrating on eating. "This is delicious," Meredith said finally. "What do you call it?"

"Chowchow," Mabel answered.

"What's in it?"

"Green beans, yellow beans, kidney beans, yellow beans, firm green tomatoes, onions, cabbage, celery, cauliflower, sugar, and salt."

"Oh, my," said Meredith. "Quite the concoction!"

"Everything but the kitchen sink," Red said.

"Why would we put the kitchen sink in chowchow?" Hanna asked.

"That's just an expression," Gregory explained. "When you have a whole list of things and it's a long one, people sometimes say you've got everything but the kitchen sink."

"Why pick on the sink?" Hanna asked. "I like sinks. Spend lots of time at 'em. I like kitchens, too. I wouldn't throw in anything from the kitchen. I'd say, 'everything but the living room sofa.' I don't like sofas."

Gregory opened his mouth to respond, but realized he had absolutely nothing to say to such a statement.

"'Scuse me a minute, I need some air," Red said, getting up. "I'll just step out on your porch for a minute, if you don't mind." Not waiting for an answer, he left the table.

"Daddy!" Gregory called after him. He turned to the others. "I'll just see if he's all right," he said, and followed his father onto the side porch, making sure to close the door behind him.

Red was finishing a long pull from a silver flask. "I needed that," he said, and held out the flask to Gregory.

"No, thanks. Daddy," he said, keeping his voice low, "The Amish don't drink."

"Well, I do. Especially after a meal like that. That's the plainest food I've ever eaten."

"They don't spice their food much."

"You really like these people?" Red asked, taking another sip of Scotch.

"Yes, Daddy, I really do."

"Looks like a boring life to me. Why don't you come on home, son? You don't have to be a lawyer if you don't want to, but it's a good life down there. You can join the club, we can play some golf, go fishing, eat some *good* food. Whattaya say?"

"I like it here."

"Well, you ain't got my blood, that's for sure," Red said pointedly, reminding Gregory of his parentage.

"Daddy, can I ask you something? When you worked for the University of South Carolina on their NCAA committee, did you ever hear of any scandal involving Penn State?"

"What years are we talking about?"

"Let's see … Vinny looks to be about thirty years old…."

"Vinny?"

"Vinny Bandini. Ever hear of him."

"Nope."

"How about a guy named Mancuso?"

"Mancuso? What's his first name?"

"Don't know."

Red thought for a moment. "Mancuso … Mancuso…. Seems to me…. Yeah, that's right! There was some kind of gambling scandal connected to a Mancuso and Penn State. Football team. It never made the papers. All of a sudden, the investigation just stopped. Wouldn't be surprised if the Mafia wasn't involved."

"That sounds about right."

"What's it to you, son?"

"Nothing, Daddy, just doing a little investigating for a friend of mine."

"Now you be careful, Gregory. You go investigating the Mafia, you might step on the wrong toes. Your friend got some gambling debts?"

"No, nothing like that."

"Good. Don't ever get in debt to a mobster. They always get paid back."

"I won't — That's it, that's it!" Gregory suddenly shouted. "It's a pay back!"

"What are you talking about?"

"Yes, yes...!" Gregory continued, thinking out loud. "Ivan owed somebody half a million dollars. What if Vinny was collecting the debt for Mancuso? Mancuso wouldn't like it that Ivan died, and he'd make Vinny pay up 'cause it was Vinny's job to collect from Ivan!"

"What kind of gibberish are you talking about? Who owes what to who, and why?"

"That insurance scam I was investigating, Daddy. The man who killed himself, Ivan Heminger, owed someone half a million dollars. I was trying to figure out who, and you just helped me do it. Thank you!"

"You're welcome, but I still don't know what the heck you're talking about."

"You don't need to. Just know that you've maybe helped save my — " Gregory paused. He was about to say "my half-sister," and that really would have sent the conversation off into a direction he didn't want. "Nothing, Daddy. You just helped me figure how to help a friend of mine, that's all. Come on, let's go back inside, we've been out here a while."

Gregory headed for the door. "Just a minute," Red said. He took one more gulp of whiskey, and then pocketed the half-pint in his coat pocket. "Okay, ready for the Amish."

Gregory grimaced, then led the way back into the dining room. Hearing his mother say, "I just love those Amish television shows, don't you?" he grimaced again.

"They don't have a television, Mama," Gregory said.

She continued, "Is there really an Amish mafia?"

"Funny, we were just talking about the Mafia," Red said. Gregory shot him a pleading look, and, for once, Red understood and said no more.

"We don't know anything about that, Mrs. Pinckney," Elam replied calmly. "I suspect whoever writes those things is just making it up."

"What about 'Breaking Amish?'" Meredith persisted. "That's reality TV. It's these ex-Amish teenagers and all their adventures. I think their whole point is, the Amish are like everybody else. Do you think that's true, Gregory?"

All eyes turned towards Gregory. "Mama, I haven't met a lot of Amish. But I do know that the Zook family, and most of the Amish I have met, are different from the people I knew back home. They have a deep faith — "

"We go to church," his mother interrupted.

"Yes, Mama, I know you do." Gregory realized that he wasn't going to be able to explain why he felt the Amish were different. He didn't care to try. He felt they were and that was good enough for him. "I don't think I can explain it to you, Mama," he finally said.

Sensing his distress, Rebecca said, "I'll clear the dishes, if everybody's finished eating."

"I'll bring in dessert," Hanna said happily. "There's shoofly pie and red velvet cake and ice cream!"

"May I help?" asked Meredith.

"No, you're the guest," Mabel said, "Please don't get up." She, Hanna, and Rebecca rose and began carrying off plates and bringing on clean ones. Gregory had to fight his own impulse to help. It felt strange to be sitting there with the men while the women did all the work. It felt old-fashioned, as if the women's liberation movement had never happened. For the Amish, it seemed, it hadn't.

Something about that thought made Gregory uncomfortable. His discomfort lasted all through dessert, through the thank you's to the Zooks and the good-byes to his parents. It even colored his "goodnight" to Rebecca. How he longed to talk to her about this feeling, but he couldn't. And that made him even more uncomfortable.

Only when he was finally in bed and thinking about the evening's meal did he begin to understand what he was feeling. The supper with the Zooks had shown him, in a way he hadn't understood before, just how different his family was from Rebecca's. No television, no telephones, no drinking — he'd always thought those were surface things, but what if they signaled something greater? The role of women and the role of men — he'd always thought it would be easy to adapt to Amish ways, but what if it weren't? Seeing his family eating with the Zooks brought home to him in a very personal way the real differences in the two cultures, Amish and English. What he was really asking himself was: *Will it make a difference for Rebecca and me? Will being raised under the rules of the Ordnung be so different from being raised under the rules of the English that our relationship will be impossible?* That was the question that kept him tossing and turning the whole night through.

CHAPTER 19

Rebecca glanced at her watch. The Sunday service had been going on for two and a half hours. *Only a half-hour to go. Don't know why I'm so anxious for church to be over. Usually I love it.* She glanced across the bench inside the King's farmhouse. There sat the answer to her question: Johnny Schmucker, seated in one row, and Gregory in the row behind him.

She thought back to the way Johnny had greeted her before church, the huge smile he had given her, the way he had taken her hand in his and held it for a long time. All this in front of Gregory. Although she had been afraid to look at Gregory, she could sense his eyes burning right through the back of her head. *Is he jealous of Johnny?* The thought had brought a small smile to her lips. At one point, he might have had good cause to be jealous. Then Johnny had left, pursuing his dream of playing professional baseball. Now he was back, complicating Rebecca's life.

Rebecca shifted in her seat. Thoughts of Johnny always excited her in some way. He was so good-looking, with his blond hair and blue eyes, and so light-hearted and happy-go-lucky. And he was a wonderful kisser. The "stirring," Madie had called it, asking if Rebecca had felt a kind of electrical jolt when Johnny kissed her. She had!

She didn't feel a jolt when Gregory kissed her. It felt more like a thick quilt wrapped tightly around her entire body, heating her up from head to toe. *Ach, what am I doing, thinking of kissing in the middle of church!*

She concentrated on the sermon Omar King was giving. He had taken his lesson from Romans 12, verses 1-8. "Do not be conformed to this world," Paul had written to the Romans. That idea was basic to the Amish faith, why the Amish removed themselves from the world around them, their nonconforming life requiring abstinence from drinking, dancing, movies, television, cars, tractors — the list was a long one. But that wasn't the part of Romans that Rebecca liked. As she listened, Omar quoted it now: "Having g-g-gifts that differ according to the g-g-grace given to us, let us use them." He went on to finish the quotation about using gifts in prophecy, teaching, serving, generosity, and other things. But Rebecca focused on the idea she found crucial: "Let us use them." *If God has given me the gift to be able to create something that is pleasing to others, then doesn't He want me to use that gift? That's what Gregory says I should do.*

Thinking of Gregory reminded her of his parents. How strange they had seemed to her — well, not strange, maybe, but certainly different. Mrs. Pinckney, in her designer clothes, sitting next to her mam, in her plain ones. Mr. Pinckney, sneaking out to have a drink — she had smelled liquor on his breath later. Did Gregory like to drink? Would he resent her if he had to give it up to be with her?

Even though she'd promised Gregory to bring him to church this morning, she had asked if he wouldn't have rather gone to church with his parents. He'd actually laughed when she'd said that, explaining that his parents hadn't been to church in years. Although Rebecca knew lots of people didn't go to church, she still found it hard to imagine a life without coming together in community to worship God. Left unspoken was the idea that Gregory probably hadn't been to church much himself. Now here he was in an Amish church. Rebecca sighed. It was too confusing. And a little frightening, to think how different her life had been from Gregory's. *Are we too different from each other to ever have a life together?* She offered a silent prayer. *God, don't let that be true. But Thy will be done, not mine.*

On the other side of the room, Gregory was having his own problems paying attention to the service. Sitting for two-and-a-half hours listening to a language he didn't understand was exhausting. Every once in a while, he heard a word Rebecca had taught him or he had heard in conversation. He was a good linguist, and it helped that he had studied German in college, so sometimes he could puzzle out the meaning of a sentence, but basically, he had to content himself with enjoying the rhythms of the Amish language.

He'd enjoyed singing the hymns. He soon picked up the idea of listening to one man sing a phrase, then joining the congregation in response. He had the hymnal, the *Ausbund*, in hand, so he could follow the words, though there were no musical notes printed. Apparently, the Amish passed these hymns down through the generations. And the length of each hymn. The first one had lasted twenty minutes! Gregory kept waiting and waiting for some sign that the hymn was finished, but the congregants kept on singing, kept on stretching out the words in that chant-like rhythm, which must have been what music had sounded like in the sixteenth century. Singing the hymns made Gregory feel like he was part of something very old, as if he were singing with thousands of Christians who had preceded him down through the centuries.

He raised his eyes and saw the back of Johnny Schmucker in the row in front of him. He hadn't seen him since Johnny had canoed Rebecca down the crick that Sunday. *Has she seen him? I haven't been with her that much. Johnny could have come by the shop plenty of times and I wouldn't have known. But she loves me!* Gregory was wise enough to know that love is a fickle thing. And a powerful one. Had Rebecca been overwhelmed by Johnny? They had certainly acted very friendly toward each other before church that morning.

"Let us p-p-pray," Omar intoned. Gregory bowed his head, vowing to make an extra effort to concentrate on the service and not on the young woman praying across the aisle, who was making the same vow about him.

A half hour later, church had finished and Gregory was sitting outside at a table with the other men, while the women served. Pumpkins lay scattered about the yard, and the air was as crisp and cool as spring water. Across from him, Johnny was talking to Henry. "This *schnitz* pie is delicious."

"It's Rebecca's specialty."

"She served me a double helping," Johnny said. "I complimented her on her fine cooking. She'll make somebody a wonderful wife. Maybe I'll be the lucky man."

"Maybe you will," Henry said.

Over my dead body, Gregory thought.

Johnny took another bite. "This is so good, I might have to go propose to her right now!" The men at the table laughed — everyone but Gregory. "After all, how could she resist such a good-looking man?"

"And one so modest, too," Henry joked. *He is good-looking, I gotta admit*, Gregory thought. He took another bite of Rebecca's pie. It didn't taste very good, with Johnny across the table, bragging about himself. He pushed his plate away.

"Not hungry?" Henry asked.

"I'll eat it, if you don't want it," Johnny offered.

Gregory pulled his plate back and took a huge bite. "No, thanks," he said, finding it impossible to keep a sharp tone out of his voice.

"Hey, Henry," Johnny said. "How'd you like to play some basketball this afternoon?"

"Just the two of us?"

"We might be able to find some other players. Don't want too many, your barn's not that big."

"I'll play," Gregory said suddenly, a touch of aggression in his voice.

"Didn't know you played, Gregory," Henry said. "We could've been shooting hoops all summer."

"I'm not saying I'm any good, but I'll do my best." Actually, Gregory had been an all-star in high school. That had been a long time ago, but he figured he could hold his own against Amish men — and against one Amish man in particular.

"Let's get Amos to be the fourth," Johnny suggested, "Then Madie can come and she and Rebecca can watch us play, be sort of like cheerleaders. With Rebecca cheering me on, I'll beat the heck out of all of you!"

"You and whose army?" Henry shot back. "If Amos plays, how will we divide up?"

"I'll play with you," Gregory said quickly to Henry. *I don't want to be on Johnny's side, I want to play against him.*

"I don't know," Henry began, "Amos is pretty good. And Johnny's really good."

"Heck, it's just a game," Gregory said nonchalantly.

"I'll go get Amos," Johnny said, rising from the table. "And tell Rebecca, too." He picked up his cup and plate and walked to the end of the table, where he leaned down and spoke to Amos. After a moment, he straightened, gave a thumbs-up sign, and walked briskly towards Rebecca, throwing his paper plate and cup in the large garbage can on the way.

Gregory watched him speak to Rebecca. She looked his way and he smiled. Then she turned back to Johnny and spoke to him. Johnny happily touched her lightly on her arm in acknowledgement, shouted to the others, "See you at the barn!" and jogged towards his horse and buggy.

Bring it on! Gregory thought. The mere thought of Johnny and Rebecca together angered him on some level, made him want to beat Johnny. Not literally, of course. Beating him in a basketball game would be a good outlet for the aggressive feelings he was suddenly having. *I'm ready!* He gathered up his plate and cup, threw them in the garbage, and went to say his thanks to Lydie. Rebecca joined him.

"I really enjoyed the service," Gregory said. "Please tell your husband thank you."

"Did you understand any of it?" Lydie asked.

"Not a lot. Rebecca's been teaching me some Pennsylvania Dutch, but I don't know much yet."

"He's a good student," Rebecca chimed in.

"I don't doubt it," Lydie said. "I hear you've been learning important words like 'love' and 'kiss.'" Rebecca blushed deeply. "I'm just teasing you. Hanna told me."

"My aunt's got a big mouth sometimes," Rebecca said.

Lydie turned suddenly serious. "I'm glad you're learning those words," she said. "You two would make a wonderful couple." Then she whispered, almost conspiratorially. "And don't think you couldn't get married because Gregory's not Amish. That may not be the obstacle you think."

Rebecca and Gregory didn't know what to say. Why was Lydie King encouraging their romance? And what did she mean about Gregory's being English not posing a problem? Gregory spoke. "All right, Mrs. King.... Well, thank you again. I really enjoyed your lovely home."

"I thought we agreed you'd call me 'Lydie,'" she replied.

"Yes, thank you, Lydie," Rebecca said.

"Thank you, Lydie," Gregory echoed. And they both scurried away, each independently trying to puzzle out Lydie King's strange behavior.

Swoosh! The basketball ripped through the cords. *Nothing but net*, Gregory thought. *Haven't lost my touch completely.* He dribbled a few times, and then launched another shot. This one banged off the rim and into a corner of the barn. *Maybe I have.*

He, Johnny, Rebecca, Amos, and Madie were on the second floor of the Zook barn. Bales of hay were stacked high, but half the floor had been left empty. Once they'd swept away some scattered hay, it made for a pretty good basketball court. There was a large door rolled open underneath the basket.

Henry led Gregory to the edge of the open hayloft door. "Once, I was just goofing off by myself up here," he said. "I must have been about twelve or thirteen. I'd left the door open. It was hot and I needed some air. That was fine, as long as I was just throwing up jump shots. Then I decided to do some layups. The basket sticks out a little, you can see." Gregory looked up. The rim stuck out from the wall some three to four feet. "I guess I got a little too into my fantasy. You know how you do, being the announcer and doing the moves at the same time." Henry went into an announcer-like voice. "Zook has the ball. The clock is winding down. He fakes left, spins right, he's got a clear shot to the basket! He's in the air — " Henry laughed. "I was in the air all right. In my enthusiasm, I'd run too far past the basket and launched myself through the open door."

"What?" Gregory gasped.

"Idiot!" shouted Amos.

"Dumb move of the century!" shouted Johnny. They both laughed loudly.

"It was stupid, all right. Thank the Lord my dat had left a wagon full of hay right under the door. I landed soft as a baby in a box of blankets. Not even a scratch. But from then on — " He stopped and went to the door. "I make darn sure this door is closed before I play any basketball up here." He yanked the handle and the massive door rolled to its locking mechanism and clanged shut. "Now we're safe," he declared.

"The cheerleaders are ready, when are you going to start?" Madie yelled. She and Rebecca stood on one side of the court.

"Let's hear a cheer, then," Amos called back.

"A-M-O-S, go Amos!" shouted Madie.

"That's more like it," Amos said, smiling.

"How about you, Rebecca?" Johnny asked.

Rebecca looked at him, then at Gregory. She didn't want to hurt anyone's feelings, so she yelled, "Go team!"

"Which team?" Gregory asked. *Are you going to pull for Johnny or for me?*

"Both teams," Rebecca responded.

"All right, that's enough cheering," Henry said sarcastically. "The noise is hurting my ears. Who gets the ball first?"

"Let them have it," Gregory answered. *Let's see what kind of player Johnny is.*

"Okay," Henry said. "Remember, after a missed basket, you've got to take the ball back behind the line before you can shoot. If you make the shot, you get to keep the ball and shoot again. Here we go."

He flipped the ball to Johnny, and Gregory came out to guard him. For a long moment, they looked at one another, staring each other down. Then Johnny passed to Amos. Two dribbles, then Amos passed it back to Johnny, who launched a jump shot over Gregory that swished through. Johnny gave Gregory a big smile. "Nice shot," Gregory said, but there was very little kindness in his voice.

Amos took the ball behind the line, passed to Johnny, who dribbled fast to the corner, turned, and shot. *Swish!* Another basket. And another big smile at Gregory. Gregory didn't bother complimenting Johnny, he just set himself for the next play with a determined look on his face. *Just wait 'til we get the ball.*

This time it was Amos who drove the basket, then pulled up for a short jumper over Henry. Another basket.

"Yay, Amos, yay, Amos, yay, yay, Amos!" Madie shouted, jumping into the air in her best imitation of a cheerleader.

"Go team!" Rebecca shouted. When Gregory shot her a look, she almost felt like explaining, "I'm just being nice," but held her tongue. *What's happening with Gregory?* she wondered.

"We'd better miss one, Amos," Johnny called. "Don't want to embarrass these guys."

"Very funny," Gregory said. But he began to worry that maybe they might be embarrassed. Johnny and Amos were pretty good.

"We forgot to say what we're playing to," Amos said.

"How 'bout to fifty?" Henry asked.

"That's not much," Johnny said. "It's already six to nothing."

"Fifty's fine with me," Amos said.

"Fine," Gregory agreed, hardly taking his eyes off Johnny.

Amos again drove the corner and fired a jumper, but this time he missed and Henry grabbed the rebound, dribbled behind the line, and then passed to Gregory. Gregory dribbled the ball patiently while Johnny guarded him. *My time now.* He shot, but the ball clanked off the front of the rim into Amos' hands. *A little rusty. If I don't get my stroke back soon, this really could be embarrassing.*

Gregory stole a glance at Rebecca. She looked worried — at least he convinced himself that's what her look signaled. He needed to know that she really wanted him to win, not Johnny. But she seemed determined to be fair and cheer for them both. This only made Gregory determined to try harder.

When Johnny attempted the same drive to the corner he'd beaten Gregory with before, he anticipated, slapped the ball as Johnny ran past, and stole it from him. He quickly retrieved it, and, since no shot had been attempted, he didn't have to take the ball behind the line, but drove to the basket for an easy layup. *Finally!*

"Go team!" Rebecca shouted. Gregory looked at her and she gave him a big smile. *That's better*, he thought.

The game settled down into a rhythm, each team scoring some and missing some. After another fifteen minutes, the score was thirty to twenty, in favor of Johnny's team. Johnny had the ball. Instead of driving to the corner, he drove straight at the basket. Gregory was with him, step for step. Johnny leapt in the air, Gregory going up beside him. Johnny leaned away from the basket and tried to flip it over Gregory's outstretched hand. Gregory batted it away, but in so doing, his body crashed into Johnny's and they both crumpled to the floor. "Oh!" Rebecca cried and ran towards them, Madie and Henry and Amos gathering around as well.

Slowly, Gregory struggled to his feet. He noticed Rebecca's anxious look change into a smile. He looked down at Johnny, still lying on the floor. *I didn't really mean to hurt him.* Johnny lay there for a long moment, but then he opened his eyes. "Nice block," he said. Gregory stuck out his hand and helped him to his feet. He felt relieved. Something about Rebecca's reaction convinced him that he was the one she was really pulling for to win.

From then on, Gregory played with an increased intensity, driving the basket, blocking shots, finding Henry with an expert pass underneath the basket. On some level, he knew he was trying too hard. *I'm like the high school star wanting my girlfriend to give me a big hug after the game and tell me how much she loves me.* But he couldn't help himself. In that tiny basketball court on the second floor of the Zook barn, all the primordial urges of the caveman claiming his woman surged through his body. He wanted to win. He wanted to beat Johnny. He wanted to show Rebecca that he was the man for her, that he was a winner, that she should be with him for the rest of her life, not with Johnny.

The gap closed. Thirty-eight, thirty. Forty-three, forty. And, finally, forty-eight, forty-eight. Tied. "Next basket wins," Henry called out. Johnny was holding the ball at the top of the key. He smiled at Gregory. Gregory crouched, watching Johnny's eyes. He dribbled to his left, but Gregory was right there with him. He spun to his right. Gregory slid right, blocking his path. Stymied, Johnny pulled up for a jumper. Gregory leaped up and stuck a hand in his face. The ball clanked off the rim. Henry gathered it in and fired it to Gregory, who had broken free. Gregory didn't hesitate, but shot the ball as soon as it hit his hands. It missed. Amos caught the rebound and threw it towards Johnny, but Henry stepped in the way, deflecting the ball into Gregory's hands. Now it was their turn to try to win the game.

Gregory got set, dribbling deliberately. Johnny stepped in front to guard him. They looked at each other, Johnny crouched, arms outstretched, Gregory dribbling, dribbling, dribbling. A dart to the right — Johnny was there. A feint left — Johnny was there, too. Then Gregory remembered a move he had perfected in high school but hadn't tried since. *Why not?* He started right, then dribbled the ball between his legs to the left. The surprise move gave him the margin he needed to race to the basket for a layup; Johnny lunged from behind to block the shot, but too late. The ball banked through the basket for the victory.

"Whoo-oo!" Henry shouted, running over to slap hands with Gregory.

"Yay! Yay!" Rebecca shouted, jumping in the air. Gregory looked at her and gave her a huge smile. Embarrassed by her enthusiasm, she turned to Amos and Johnny. "You guys played great."

"Thanks," Johnny said. "I guess we know which team you were pulling for now," he added, but with a smile on his face. Rebecca blushed.

"Good game, Gregory," Amos congratulated him.

"Thanks. You played great."

"You were wonderful," Madie said, snaking an arm around Amos.

Gregory looked at Rebecca. He wished she could put her arm around him, but he knew this wasn't the time or place. "Great game, Johnny," he said.

"Really enjoyed it," Johnny answered. "Let's do it again some time. Seems like you might be around for a while." He winked at Rebecca, and then stuck out his hand, and he and Gregory shook. "Well, I've gotta be getting home."

"Us, too," Amos said, walking towards the stairs with Madie.

"See you at supper," Henry said to Rebecca. "Can you join us, Gregory?"

"I'd love to," Gregory answered.

"Okay, teammate," Henry said; he gave Gregory a smile, and followed Amos, Madie, and Johnny down the stairs.

Gregory suddenly found himself alone with Rebecca. The warm, fading sunlight came through a small open window high in the barn. After the noise of the game, a quiet settled over them.

"You really did play great," Rebecca said.

"Thanks. It's funny, I wanted so bad to win. It was like I was trying to show off for you or something, trying to impress you. I feel a little silly about it."

"Don't. I kind of liked it, pulling for you, but not telling anybody I was. It made me realize...." She let the thought die.

"What?"

For an answer, Rebecca said, "I want to show you something. Follow me."

She went to the far side of the barn and began climbing the ladder nailed into the wall. Gregory followed her up. When she reached the top of the ladder, she stepped onto a thick beam that spanned the upper reaches of the barn. "What are you doing?" Gregory called.

"You'll see."

"Isn't it dangerous?"

"Just step onto this large beam and hold on to that smaller beam above your head. This used to be a kind of third floor in the barn, 'til Dat took it out." Gregory stepped onto the beam and reached up to steady himself with the smaller beam. "Now, just these last two steps in the wall...." She showed him a small ladder that led up to a tiny platform nestled under the highest window in the barn. "I had Henry build me that platform."

"Why?"

"You'll see. I've never had more than one person there, but I think we'll fit." She began to climb the ladder. When she'd settled herself on the platform, she called down to Gregory. "Come on up."

He climbed the tiny ladder and hoisted himself onto the platform underneath the window. It was so small that he found himself squeezed against Rebecca. How he'd longed to be close to her, and now he was.

"Look," she said, and pointed out the window.

Gregory gazed out at the countryside below him. The setting sun bathed it in a luminous glow, a soft yellow sheen shimmering over the fields. The rows of ploughed field corn alternated in contrast to the green strips of alfalfa. Black-and-white cows stood lazily along the crick or rested in the shade of trees. White farmhouses and barns sat solidly, anchors to the incredible beauty of the Amish countryside. "Wow," he said, and then, again, "Wow."

"This is my special place," she said. "I come here to be alone, when I need to think things through, when I want to feel closer to God."

"I can see why. The view is beautiful."

"I saw you here," she said.

"Huh?"

"Yes. About a month ago. I was praying about what to do about Jacob, whether to marry him or not. I asked God for a sign. When I opened my eyes, I saw you on Bojangles, far in the distance. It looked like you waved to me."

"I remember," said Gregory, his voice lowering in intimacy. "I remember it well. I was on the way to Wanda's, and I stopped and turned and looked back at the farm. I thought of you. And I blew you a kiss." He put his hand to his lips and blew her a kiss.

"That's what you were doing!" Rebecca said happily.

"Yes. And if I'd been close to you, like now, instead of that kiss having to travel over all that distance, it could reach you like this." He brought his face next to hers and kissed her. She responded, placing her hand on his back. He drew her closer, the kiss deepening, growing in pleasure, warmth, and love. They both relaxed into the natural ecstasy of the moment. It was a kiss they had been waiting a long time to experience.

"I wanted to share this place with you," she whispered into his ear. "So it could be special for you, too."

"It is special to me," he whispered back. "And so are you. I love you, Rebecca."

They kissed again. Rebecca had never felt so blessed. "This must be what it feels like when angels kiss," she thought happily, swooning in the warmth of loving and being loved.

CHAPTER 20

Rain. It had started last night after Rebecca had said goodnight to Gregory and gone to bed. She had found it soothing, the rhythmic drumming of the water on the farmhouse's tin roof, lulling her into the sweetest of dreams, the pitter-patter echoing the love-soaked beating of her own heart. She'd carried out her morning chores in a kind of daze, hardly noticing the rain as she'd gathered her eggs. Every now and then she would touch her lips with her fingers, gently rubbing them, remembering the feel of Gregory's lips, full upon her own.

On her walk to work, she had noticed the gullies beginning to spill over and the water rushing down street curbs into the drain grates. At least once a year Lancaster County experienced a torrential rainstorm, one that caused the cricks to overflow, sometimes even forcing traffic to be diverted due to high water. *Probably keep the customers away, but I don't mind not being busy today. Give me lots of time to remember yesterday.*

"It's raining cats and dogs," Lydia said, looking out the shop window. She had come to help Rebecca pack up the ten wall hangings and send them to Mr. Goldfarb. Lydia had very much enjoyed stitching the majority of the quilts herself. It was pretty well acknowledged by all the women in Honey Brook that she had the most beautiful stitching around. And distinctive: Anyone who knew her could always tell if a quilt had been stitched by Lydia. The stitches were meticulously even and tight, her knotting of the threads never showed, and the knots were always secure. "You must have gotten really wet walking to work, Rebecca."

"I didn't mind."

"Mind on other things?" Lydia asked, with a small smile.

Does she know about Gregory and me? How could she? "Some of the time," Rebecca answered vaguely. Her answer was honest, as long as "some of the time" meant about ninety per cent of it. "Thank you for helping me package my quilts," she said, folding them and placing them inside a large cardboard box.

"They turned out beautifully, Rebecca. I'm sure Mr. Goldfarb will be happy with them. Now you can relax a little."

"I certainly hope so."

"Maybe you can have some more language lessons with Gregory," Lydie said, placing another quilt in the box. "Tell me, what do you know about Gregory?"

"Well, just that he's from South Carolina, he studied to be a lawyer, but he didn't like it, and he came up here to look for his birth mother."

"Has he had any luck?"

"I don't think so," Rebecca answered. "He said one woman threw him out of her house. I guess asking someone if she'd had a child out of wedlock is kind of a sensitive question."

How Lydia longed to answer that question! But she couldn't, not without bringing shame to herself and embarrassment to her husband, Omar. The best she could do was to pursue her plan to keep Gregory close by helping him to marry Rebecca. "Yes, I could see that. Does he know who his father is?"

"He thinks it might have been Ivan Heminger."

"Ivan Heminger!" Lydie exclaimed, with as much feigned surprise as she could muster.

"Gregory isn't exactly thrilled to think Ivan might have been his father, since apparently he tried to kill Gregory. And he did kill all those horses."

"He was an evil man," Lydie said, with firm conviction.

"The night he was almost killed, Gregory remembers a woman's voice calling him 'son.' He's sure that woman was his mother, and he thinks she might have saved his life somehow."

Right on both counts, Lydie thought. "Isn't that something!" she said. "To think, his mother might be right here. How did he find the woman who threw him out?"

"He researched Ivan's youth, and it turns out this woman had dated him when they were teenagers. He did get an idea, though," Rebecca continued. "He saw a young Amish girl working as a housekeeper in the woman's house, and Gregory thinks maybe Ivan had impregnated an Amish girl who might have worked for his parents. That seems possible, doesn't it?"

Lydie, shaken, busied herself with closing the cardboard box's lids. *All too possible! But there's no way to know I was the one who worked for Ivan.* "Doesn't seem very possible to me," she finally said. "I wouldn't spend too much time on that approach. There, they're all packed. Have you got any tape?"

"Right here." Rebecca went behind the counter and retrieved the packaging tape. Together, she and Lydie sealed up the box. "I'll get his card and address it." Rebecca returned to the counter, opened a drawer, took out Mr. Goldfarb's card, grabbed a pen, and carefully inscribed the address on the cardboard box. When she had finished, she and Lydie stepped back and looked at the package.

"Congratulations, Rebecca, you did it!" Lydia said. "I'll put it in my buggy and take it to the post office. But not today. Can you believe all this rain? The cricks will overflow for sure, if this keeps up."

"Will you be able to drive your buggy home all right? How's your horse deal with rain?"

"Oh, I'll be fine. But maybe I'll stay here until you close and give you a ride home. You'll be soaked, if you walk."

"I've got my slicker, I'll be fine," Rebecca answered. "Please, don't stay here on my account." The phone rang. "Excuse me." Rebecca answered the phone. "Rebecca's Quilts."

"Rebecca, it's Steven Goldfarb."

"Oh, hello, Mr. Goldfarb. You'll be happy to know that I have just this minute finished packaging the wall hangings. I'll mail them tomorrow. I hope your client will be pleased."

"I'm sure he will be. Rebecca, I have some wonderful news. Now pay close attention. This will require some serious thinking on your part, but I hope you'll see what a fine opportunity this is."

"Opportunity?"

"A friend of mine teaches at the Ringling College of Art and Design. You know where that is, don't you?"

"No, Mr. Goldfarb, I don't."

"It's in Sarasota, Florida. I believe you told me there's an Amish community there. Pine … something."

"Pinecraft. Amish and Mennonite. Why are you asking about Pinecraft?"

"That's all part of the plan. Now listen carefully." Goldfarb paused for a minute. "I have arranged for you to teach a course on quilt making at the college."

"Teach?"

"Yes, teach. But that's only part of the proposition. While there, you will also have an art show."

"Art show?" Rebecca was confused.

"Yes, Rebecca. You're an artist, remember?" Hearing nothing, Goldfarb continued. "No one teaches quilting at the college. My friend was very excited to be able to offer such a course. And he knows the perfect gallery for your work. I'm glad you haven't sent me the wall hangings yet. I talked to the client, and he's agreed to wait. You can take those quilts to Florida with you for your show. And while you're there, you can make more quilts. The teaching shouldn't take up that much of your time."

Seeing the hint of desperation around her eyes, Lydie asked, "Are you all right?" Rebecca nodded dumbly, but she felt anything but all right.

"Rebecca, are you there?" Goldfarb asked.

"Mr. Goldfarb," she began, "I don't understand. Are you suggesting that I go live in Florida and teach?"

"Only for eight weeks," he answered. "It's a special extension course they've agreed to offer."

"But I don't know how to teach," she protested.

"There's nothing to it, Rebecca. There won't be a curriculum or anything. You just show the students how to quilt and help them do it. It's more of a workshop than a course. And you won't have to give them a grade. They'll be taking your course for extra credit."

The more he talks, the crazier it sounds. "I don't know, Mr. Goldfarb. It's kind of a lot to ask. Move to Florida, teach a course. I don't know what to say."

"I understand you must think about it, Rebecca. But remember this: They will pay you for teaching. Four thousand dollars for the eight weeks. Plus, I bet you can get commissions to do more quilts from the people who come to your show. I'm trying to get your name out. I'm trying to brand you."

Like some steer? Rebecca looked up to see that Lydie was holding a glass of water out to her. She drank it gratefully.

"Rebecca, you don't have to decide anything right now," Goldfarb went on more calmly, realizing his excitement had only heightened Rebecca's anxiety. "The semester doesn't start until after the holidays, so you won't miss Christmas with your family. Why don't you talk it over with them? Let's say we'll talk again in a couple of weeks, is that all right?"

"I guess so," Rebecca answered uncertainly. Her voice was weak and shaky.

"Fine, fine. Just don't bother mailing me those wall hangings until you decide. But think about it hard, Rebecca. This could be a big step forward in your career. I'll call in two weeks, but you call me before if you know what your answer is. I hope it's yes, Rebecca. Speaking as your agent, I definitely advise you to take advantage of this opportunity. Good bye."

"Good bye, Mr. Goldfarb." She heard the click of the receiver on his end and slowly placed her own receiver back in its cradle. One word kept ringing in her ear. Career. *If this is what a career feels like, I'm not sure I want one.*

"More water?" Lydie asked.

"No, thank you."

"Do you want to tell me what that was all about? It seemed to upset you."

"It was Mr. Goldfarb. He told me he wants me to go teach at the Ringling College of Art and Design in Sarasota after the New Year. And to have an art show of my quilts."

"Rebecca, that's wonder — " Lydie stopped, remembering how distressed Rebecca seemed. "That could be a wonderful opportunity, but you don't have to do it if you don't want to."

"That's what he called it. An 'opportunity.' To 'brand' me. Do I need to be branded, Lydie?"

"That's probably just an agent's way of talking. I wouldn't worry about the words. And I wouldn't worry about not having taught before. I taught school for several years, and the idea of it is much scarier than the reality. You know what you should do?"

"What?" Rebecca asked. She truly wanted someone to tell her what to do.

"Ask Gregory what he thinks."

Gregory! Yes! He's English, he's been in the world, he'll have good advice. And he cares about me, he showed that yesterday. I need him. "Lydie, that's a really good idea. I can talk to him tonight."

"Why wait? This is obviously bothering you a great deal. You need to deal with it now, or, at least, begin to deal with it. I think you should borrow my buggy and go see Gregory right this minute."

"Your buggy?"

"Of course. You don't think I'd let you go out in this awful weather on foot. Do you know where he is right now?"

"He said he was going to Wanda's to talk about their business. I don't know if the rain kept him home or not."

"Knowing Gregory, I doubt it. Start with Cedar Ridge Farm, and, if he's not there, find him at your farm." Without waiting for an answer, Lydie went to take Rebecca's slicker from the rack and brought it to her. "My buggy's tied up out back."

"But the shop?" Rebecca questioned.

"I'll stay here until you get back. But take your time. I've got nothing to do today, and I doubt we'll be very busy here."

Rebecca put on her slicker. "Are you sure, Lydie?"

"I'm glad to do it, Rebecca. Nothing would make me happier than to see you and Gregory — " She stopped herself. "Than to see you make the right decision on this important matter. I know Gregory will have some good advice. Now, get going before it rains even harder."

With that, she went to the back door and held it open. Ducking her head into the rain, Rebecca untied Lydie's horse, climbed into the buggy, and rode away, the rain pounding down relentlessly.

As Rebecca was driving towards Wanda's house, Gregory was nearing the Heminger Stables himself, riding through the rain on Bojangles. His yellow slicker wasn't protecting him much, but he'd made up his mind that today he was going to tell Wanda that he was her half brother. He was tired of carrying his secret around. *It's time to move on.*

He had decided to tell her about Vinny another day. First he'd let her get used to the idea that they were related, let her come to trust him more, then he'd tell her. He wished he had written proof about Vinny. He planned to try to obtain a copy of the wedding license, but he wasn't sure how to go about getting it. If he couldn't find any written proof, she'd just have to trust him. That's why he had to tell her this first.

Arriving at the stable, Gregory led Bo inside. "Sorry about this rain, boy. I know it wasn't much fun." He found some food and poured it into a trough. "Snack on that. This won't take long. I want to get back to a warm, dry place as much as you do." He patted his horse on his flank and left the barn.

Mounting the stairs to the veranda, he heard the TV blaring from inside the house. *Liz. I don't want her around when I break the news.* He rang the doorbell. *Wanda will just have to come out here.*

Wanda answered the door. "Gregory! What in the world brings you out in this weather?"

"Something I've needed to tell you for a while."

"If it's about our business, surely it can wait."

"It's not, and it can't."

"Come on in, then," Wanda said, standing back and holding the door open. The TV blared more loudly.

"I wonder if we could talk out here."

"In the rain?"

"It's dry on the porch. It won't take long."

"Okay. I can't wait to hear what's so important." She stepped inside, threw a sweater around her shoulders, and joined Gregory on the veranda, closing the door behind her.

"Let's sit over here," Gregory said, moving towards the table.

He pulled a chair out for Wanda. "Thank you, kind sir," she said, flashing him her dazzling smile with its perfect, white teeth. Gregory sat down opposite her. "What's up?"

Now that the moment had finally arrived, Gregory realized he had no idea how to proceed. He decided the evidence would give him greater courage, so he pulled the test results out of his pocket. "What's that?" she asked.

Gregory took a deep breath. There was really nothing to do but begin. "Wanda, I have some terribly important news to share with you. It's shocking news in many ways, but I hope you'll think it's good news."

"You're scaring me," she said, sitting up straighter.

"It's nothing to be afraid of. It's about Ivan."

"Daddy? What about him?"

"These papers — " Gregory tapped them on the table. "Are the results of DNA testing I ordered, concerning my blood." He paused. "And yours."

"Mine?" she asked. "Why are you testing my blood?

"To see if we are related." *Here goes.* "And it turns out, we are."

Wanda's face wrinkled in incomprehension. "What in the world are you talking about? What do you mean, we're related? How could we possibly be related?"

"Through your father. It turns out, he's also my father." Gregory looked at her, his body tensing in anticipation of her reply. Despite what he had told himself, he realized now, at the moment of truth, he had no idea how Wanda would take the news.

She gasped. "What?" Her face contorted even more. "Are you serious? I don't understand, Gregory."

"It's simple, really," he explained. "I am adopted. My birth mother, whoever she is, came from around these parts. Apparently she and your father had relations. I don't know how else to explain these DNA results."

"How did you get my DNA?"

"I apologize for that part, Wanda. I got it from the lip of a container of sweet tea you drank once when you were thirsty, after a ride on Bo. I guess it was kind of sneaky of me, but I just had to know. "

"So you sent our DNA somewhere to be tested?"

"The DNA Testing Center of America. They're very reputable."

Wanda rose and walked to the edge of the veranda. She peered out at the rain. Gregory stood up, waiting for her to speak. "I just can't believe it...." She heaved a deep sigh. "Did Daddy know?"

"I never told you this, but right here on this porch, Ivan called me his son."

"He did?"

"Yes. And I needed to find out if he was telling the truth."

Finally, she turned to face him. "Are you really my half-brother?"

"I'm pretty sure I am."

"It's kind of incredible."

"I'm as amazed as you are."

"I guess you and I are thinking of starting what might be called a 'family business,' then?" She smiled.

Gregory, relieved at her attempt at humor, gave a short laugh. "Yes, I guess it is."

"Well, then, come here, 'family.'" She opened her arms. Gregory walked into them and they embraced warmly, tightly, and for a long time, each privately enjoying the knowledge of a long-lost family tie.

Behind them, in the half circle of the driveway, a black buggy had come to a halt. Even through the rain, Rebecca saw clearly Wanda's invitation to an embrace, and Gregory's enthusiastic acceptance. She didn't know it was a family embrace. She only knew that last night Gregory had kissed her passionately, told her she was special, and now he was wrapped in Wanda's arms. With a sharp yank on the reins, she drove the buggy away as fast as she could.

CHAPTER 21

Rebecca gasped in anguish as she whipped the reins up and down, up and down, urging the horse onward, desperate to get away. *How could you do this, Gregory, how could you?* Tears welled in her eyes, as the sense of betrayal sank deeper into her heart. *After last night! Why?*

She could hardly see, so she let the horse guide the way. It turned onto the main road, galloping along the side. Cars sped past, blaring their horns, spitting rain against the buggy. Rebecca hardly noticed. She was crying harder now, sobs escaping her breast. The horse turned down a lane — the lane to Rebecca's farm, though she didn't notice. All she could do was whip the reins as hard as she could, urging the horse on to somewhere, anywhere, as long as it was away from Gregory.

Suddenly, the horse reared, stopping the buggy. The crick on her farm, the small crick that fed into the larger crick, was now a raging torrent. Rebecca leaned out the buggy's window. The rain slammed into her face, pricking her with its hard drops. She shielded her eyes. *The farmhouse! Home! I need to be home!* She withdrew inside the buggy, picked up the reins, and whipped them hard. The horse wouldn't budge. She leaned out the window again. "Move!" she shouted. *"Gay gal!"* she screamed. *"Gay!"*

She whipped the reins again. The horse made a few tentative steps into the raging stream, the water rushing past its legs, almost reaching its underbelly. "Hee-ahh!" Rebecca screamed as loud as she could and whipped the horse ferociously. The horse leapt forward, but the water was too strong. It knocked him sideways into the raging current, his fall pulling the buggy over. The door sprang open when it hit the water, flinging Rebecca into the crick.

The water sucked her under but, in an instant, she was propelled to the top again. She gasped for air, then was tumbled forward, the swollen crick bouncing her against one bank, then the other. She found her head above water and gratefully sucked in a breath. "Help!" she yelled, but the sound hardly carried over the chaotic noise of the rushing water. "Help!" she tried to call again, but water splashed into her open mouth, choking her, and then she was swept under again, the water pummeling her along, mercilessly, until she reached the end of the smaller crick and was thrust into the thundering waters of the main crick, now swollen to the top of its banks.

Rebecca felt something bump into her. She reached desperately for it. A log! She grabbed it with her other hand and hung on. Her face was half in the water, half out, the current pulling her rapidly along, but now she had a life raft of sorts. *I can't swim! I've got to hold onto this log and pray! Dear God* — she tried, but a whirlpool spun her around and her prayer was lost in the rush of fear that engulfed her.

But God heard her prayer. At least, that's the way she would remember it later. For who was standing in the yard of his cottage but Gregory? After his reunion with Wanda, they had decided that they would meet the next day and talk about the future. So he had hurried home, making Bojangles gallop all the way. "I want a shower, Bo!" he'd yelled at his horse through the rain. "I want to stand naked in God's great Universe, nothing but me, and Him, and Nature, and sing His praises for the incredible world he has given me!" Despite the rain, his joy was boundless. He'd had that wonderful night with Rebecca, and now he had a half-sister to love as well.

He had put up Bo and was about to strip off his shirt when he saw something passing by in the crick at the edge of his yard. It looked like a log, but it also looked like something was clinging to it. Gregory ran a few yards closer to the raging crick, straining to see through the rain. *It's a person! Somebody's holding onto that log!*

He wasted no time, but immediately started running alongside the crick. If he'd jumped in right away, it would have been impossible to catch up to the log. *I've got to get ahead of it! I've got to get in and hope the log comes towards me.* Then he realized what happened to the water. *The fork! If they're pulled to the right fork, they'll be flowing away from me and I'll never catch them. To the left, God, make them go to the left!*

With that prayer on his lips, he stopped running alongside the crick and began cutting across the field, on a diagonal towards the left fork. The field was completely soaked, the earth seeming to grab at his ankles to pull him down. He slipped once and sprawled across the ground, mud streaking his face, matting his hair, and soiling his clothes, but he immediately jumped up and resumed the chase. *What if I'm chasing nothing? I can't even see the log anymore!*

He was running fast now, covering great gobs of earth with each strong stride, running with desperate purpose. The left fork loomed ahead; he could see it. Then another terrifying thought struck him. *The dam! I've got to get to it before it goes over the dam! It'll be like a waterfall now!* He reached the edge of the crick and looked upstream. The rain poured against his face. He shielded his eyes. *I can't see! Everything's bobbing up and down.* He put his other hand up for more protection. *Yes! There it is, I'm sure of it!* He looked harder. *There it is, there it is! It went down the left fork!*

He ran alongside the crick towards the dam. He could hear the water pouring over the dam, loud and ominous. It had become a raging waterfall. Gregory stopped by the water's edge. He couldn't jump in too soon or he would be swept along in front of the log. He had to time it perfectly, entering the water, swimming against it with all his might, losing a little ground to the oncoming log, but not enough so he couldn't catch it. He wasn't worried about drowning himself. He was an excellent swimmer, all-state in his college days. But he was worried about mistiming his leap.

The log bobbed into sight, the person still clinging with both hands. He could see that it was a woman, her blue dress billowing out behind her. He took a deep breath, stripped off his shirt and shoes — and dove.

The water was surprisingly cold. He came to the surface, already swimming against the current. He was managing to hold his own, not being swept too quickly toward the dam. Fortunately, the crick narrowed a little at just this point. The person-draped log was being forced in his direction. *Come on, come on!* He stroked and kicked. The log spun around, moving away from him. *No, come back here!* Gregory put his head in the water so he could swim harder for a few strokes. When he looked up again, the log was just ahead of him. He took another stroke and reached out with his other hand. But the log spun away. It was moving past him! He lunged, throwing his body out of the water as high as he could, stretching both arms out, desperately grabbing for something, anything! His right hand felt cloth and he clutched it. *The dress!* "Hold on!" he shouted. "Don't let go! You've got to hold onto the log!" He grabbed more of the dress with his other hand, and pulled himself slowly up the material, hand over hand, until he grasped the body.

The woman let go of the log. *What are you doing, no!* Her weight began to drag him down. Remembering his Red Cross swimming classes, Gregory immediately stuck one arm under her chin and began swimming backwards towards the bank. But the current was pulling them both downstream. He could hear the noise of the dam-waterfall growing closer. *At least she's not fighting me.* The woman's body had gone limp in his arms. He looked over his shoulder. The bank was closer. But so was the dam. "God, help me!" he prayed out loud.

Then he saw it. A tree near the bank had branches hanging over the crick. *I can do it!* He gave three final, forceful kicks and lunged for a branch, catching it in his left hand. For a moment, he just hung on, catching his breath, letting the water rush past him and his now-saved passenger. Gradually, his breath slowed. He put his legs down. He could feel the bank underneath his feet. The slope wasn't very steep. Carefully, painstakingly, he began to inch his way towards land, pulling himself up the branch with one hand, moving him and his cargo up the bank with his feet. When he had reached the top of the bank, he noticed gratefully that the water was calmer — still rushing, but not with overwhelming force. He heaved the now-limp body halfway up the bank, ducked under the water, got as much purchase as he could with his feet, then sprang up, pushing the body over the top of the bank. Then, using the branch, he hauled himself up to safety as well.

Breathing heavily, he looked down to see whom he had saved. "Rebecca!" he shouted. "Oh, my God, Rebecca!" He reached behind her shoulders and pulled her into a sitting position. "Are you all right? Rebecca!"

Slowly she opened her eyes. "What happened?" she asked in a shaky voice. "I fell into the crick...."

"Yes. Thank God I saw you."

Then she noticed. "Gregory!"

"Yes! Oh, Rebecca!" And he tried to hug her to him.

Rebecca shoved him violently. "Get away from me!" she cried.

"What — ?"

"I said get away!" she shouted. She pushed herself away from him and scrambled to her feet. When she wobbled a little, Gregory reached to try to steady her, but she slapped his hand away. "Don't touch me!"

"Rebecca, what's wrong?"

"What's wrong? What's wrong?" she shouted again. "You're a liar, that's what's wrong!"

"A liar? What do you mean?"

"I mean you and Wanda! I saw you! I saw you this afternoon, kissing her and hugging her!"

"Kissing her and hugging...?"

"How could you do that to me, Gregory? After what we'd shared on Sunday! After you'd kissed me and told me you loved me!" She started to cry.

Gregory wanted to hold her, but he knew he couldn't, not yet. Instead, he forced himself to speak calmly. "Rebecca, you must listen to me. You must give me a chance to explain."

"How can you explain that?" she asked between tears.

"I can, but you must listen to me. Please." He waited a minute for her to speak, but she was focused on trying to control her tears. Seeing her crying like that tore his heart in two, but he knew he had to get her to believe him before he could console her. "Rebecca," he said solemnly, "I was hugging and kissing Wanda because I had just told her that she is my half-sister." He paused to let that knowledge sink in.

Rebecca found that absurd. "Please don't make it worse by lying some more," she said bitterly.

"I am not lying, Rebecca. Look at me," he said. "Won't you please look at me?" Rebecca slowly raised her eyes to meet his. "I know it sounds ridiculous, but it's true. You know I thought Ivan was my father. Well, I managed to get a saliva sample from Wanda, and I sent it away for DNA testing, along with my own sample. You know what DNA is, right?" She nodded. "Well, the results came back: Wanda is my half-sister. Ivan is the father of both of us."

Rebecca stared at Gregory. "How?"

"Ivan must have conceived a child with my birth mother when they were both young. She went to South Carolina to have the baby. I am that baby." He looked at her. "I have the DNA results back in my cottage. I can show them to you." He dared to take a step closer to her. "But I would rather you believed me just because I told you it's true."

Rebecca hesitated. Gregory's voice — soft and gentle, yet firm — calmed her. She looked deep into his eyes. He held her gaze steadily. "Wanda and I hugged in the happy knowledge that we were basically brother and sister. The love I feel for her is completely different from the love I have for you. Everything I said yesterday is true. If anything, knowing how close I came to losing you in that water has made you even more precious to me now."

Relief flooded Rebecca's heart and soul. *He's telling the truth. He still loves me.* "Oh, Gregory!" she said. She took a step towards him, but the physical and emotional strain of the last half-hour finally took their toll, and she collapsed towards the ground.

He caught her before she hit the earth and swooped her into his arms. "Come, my precious one. Let me take you home and take care of you. Forever."

She put her arms around him and nestled her face into his neck. The rain, which she had forgotten about in the depths of her despair, once again splattered her body, but she didn't care. She felt his strong arms around her, as she relaxed into his sure gait — safe, warm, and loved.

CHAPTER 22

Vinny sat in his Maserati at the top of the long driveway that led down to Cedar Ridge Farm's stable, smoking a cigarette. He didn't like smoking much anymore — he'd quit several years ago — but sometimes he found it helped him to think, to focus, to marshal his mental faculties, and he needed to be very clear-headed and focused today. *At least it's stopped raining.* Having to do what he had to do in the rain would have been harder. But it was good that the cricks and rivers were still high. *That'll help hide the evidence longer. With any luck, the evidence will be hidden forever.*

Vinny wasn't counting on luck, however. He was counting on meticulous planning. In his business, it was best to plan and to plan well.

He rolled down his window, flipped the cigarette out, and then went over his plan one more time. The hardest part had been to figure out how to get Gregory alone, and where. Gregory liked to ride his horse. He could maybe have followed him and taken care of things that way, but that would have been too risky. Somebody might have seen him. And it would have been too easy for Gregory to get away. He needed him in a confined space. Wanda and Gregory were planning a business partnership. He'd use Wanda to get Gregory to come to her house.

How to actually do it had stumped him for a while. He didn't want to shoot Gregory or stab him. If his body were ever found, it would be best if it looked like an accident. Like he had hit his head and drowned. But Vinny wasn't planning on Gregory's body ever being discovered. He'd make sure it was tied to enough weight to stay on the bottom of the river for a long time. They didn't call them concrete shoes for nothing.

Gregory's horse was another problem. He knew Gregory usually rode over to Wanda's. What to do with the horse? He'd considered overdosing it with a drug, like Ivan had tried to do. But he didn't have any drugs and, if he went to somebody to get some, that somebody could always talk and that talk could lead to Vinny. Best to keep this a one-man show. He'd just untie the horse, slap it on the rear, and hope it went home. The horse really wasn't a problem. Gregory rode the horse to Wanda's, then Gregory disappeared. Simple as that.

He drummed his fingers on the steering wheel and rolled down the other window. It was a warm day, humid after all the rain of the day before. He checked his watch. It was twelve-fifteen, time to leave. He'd go to Wanda, have her write the note, change what she'd written, deliver it, call up Wanda, get her to go look at the wedding dress with her mom, call later and say he'd been held up, Liz would want to do some shopping for sure, he'd do the dirty, meet up with them, go back, wait for Gregory, Gregory wouldn't show, end of story.

He started the engine and went down the driveway. He wasn't going to enjoy this. But he'd enjoy having to tell Mancuso he couldn't repay the debt even less. Getting Wanda's money was the only way, to get it he had to marry her, and to marry her he had to make sure Gregory didn't tell her he was already married. It'd already been four days since Mancuso had told him Gregory had been asking about him. Vinny had worried every day that Gregory would come to see Wanda; that's why he'd spent the whole weekend at Cedar Ridge Farm with her. He wanted to be there if Gregory dropped by. Gregory hadn't come, and when it had started raining, he had gone home. But he couldn't be always watching the farm. No, he had to make sure Gregory never gave Wanda the news. Never.

He eased his car around the circle in front of the house and parked. He didn't want to bother with Liz, so he honked the horn. As soon as Wanda appeared in the doorway, he called, "Come on out, babe. I've got great news!"

She ran down the stairs as he got out of his car. "What is it, Vinny?"

"I met this guy at the racetrack and I was telling him about t that business you and Gregory are starting and he got really excited. The guy owns lots of horses. He's looking for a place to stable 'em. I'm thinking, he could stable 'em here. The guy's got a ton of money, Wanda, a ton! I'm betting he could help you and Gregory with your business, get you started off in a big way."

"I don't understand, Vinny. You warned me to go slow."

"That was before I found this guy. If somebody else is putting up a lot of the cash, you don't need to worry about Gregory putting in any. And as the main investors, you and Donny — that's his name — you and Donny could keep an eye on Gregory, make sure he behaves. He's probably a good guy; I was just a little concerned about his lack of business experience. You like him, don't you?"

"Of course! He's my — " She paused. *Maybe this isn't the time to tell Vinny about Gregory and me.*

"Your what?"

"My neighbor, and he's always been real nice to me."

"Good. Now, Donny's going away on business tonight, so I told him to come by here at five. Strike while the iron is hot, right?"

"I've got to tell Gregory. He doesn't have a phone, so I'll drive over."

"No need. I'll tell him, I'm heading that direction anyway. Just write him a note, will you? I can drop it off, if he's not there. Just a minute." Vinny leaned in his open car window, opened the glove compartment, and took out a small pad and a pencil. "Here you go."

"Okay." Wanda took the pad and pencil and bent down to write on the hood of the Maserati.

"Don't tell him what it's about, just tell him you've got a big surprise for him about your business and to be here at five o'clock."

Wanda wrote quickly, and then handed the note and pencil to Vinny. He glanced at it and smiled. *Perfect.* "Okay, I'll get it to him, and see you here at five." He gave her a quick kiss, jumped in his car, and sped off. Looking in the rearview mirror, he saw her wave goodbye.

He had no intention of taking the note to Gregory. Instead, a few minutes later he parked his car across the street from Rebecca's quilt shop. He sat behind the wheel, debating whether he should take the note inside himself. Deciding Gregory might have spoken to Rebecca about him, Vinny decided he'd best find another way to get the note to Rebecca, and thence to Gregory. But first, he had to make an important change.

Unfolding the note, Vinny once again took out the pencil. Laying the note on the passenger seat, he gently rubbed out the "5" Wanda had written and carefully wrote in "3" in its place. He looked at the note. The pencil lead had erased completely, and now it looked as if Wanda had invited Gregory over to see her at 3 pm, not 5 pm. Vinny checked his watch again. It was almost 1 pm. That was plenty of time to get rid of Wanda and her mom, sneak onto the property, and be there to welcome Gregory with — well, not with "open arms." More like with clenched fist. He chuckled to himself, confident in his plan's ultimate success.

Vinny re-folded the note and looked about him, focusing on the other side of the street. Plenty of people were passing by on the sidewalk, but most of them were older. He wanted a young person, preferably a boy. It was a school day and not too many children were about. He finally spotted an Amish boy about ten years old. *Not in school 'cause he's helping with the farm. Good.* He got out of his car, walked quickly up the street, and then crossed to the other side. When the boy approached him, he said with some urgency, "Excuse me, but could you do me a big favor."

As expected of a people raised to be kind and considerate, the boy stopped. "If I can."

"I'm supposed to deliver this note to the lady in the quilt shop you just passed, but I'm really pressed for time. Would you mind taking it in for me? I'd be glad to pay you." Vinny knew the boy would never accept payment, but he thought it would make his appeal appear more legitimate.

"That's all right, sir, I don't mind. And there's no need to pay me."

"Thank you so much. Tell the lady to please read the note so she'll know what to do. She must read it, all right?"

"I'll tell her."

With a nod, he handed the boy the note, turned and walked briskly back across the street, seemingly in a hurry. But instead of returning to his car, he walked in the opposite direction, went down a side street, then circled back until he had a view of the doorway to the quilt shop from a lane across from it.

He watched as the boy entered the shop. After a few minutes, the he left and continued down the street. Vinny waited for Rebecca to appear. *Come on, come on, take him the note!* Three o'clock wasn't that close, maybe she would wait a while before contacting Gregory. *Come on!* Finally, a woman emerged from the shop, got into a buggy tied to a nearby post, and drove away in the direction of the Zook farm. He watched her move out of sight. She looked older than Vinny thought Rebecca would be, but, with her covering, he couldn't really tell, so he assumed it was Rebecca. *She's got plenty of time to get him the note, he'll have plenty of time to get to Cedar Ridge Farm by 3 o'clock, and I'll have plenty of time to be there waiting for him.* With a satisfied smile, Vinny proceeded back onto the street, got into his Maserati, and drove away.

For what seemed like the umpteenth time that day, Gregory walked out of his cottage, stared up at the Zook farmhouse, and started pacing around his yard. Rebecca wasn't in the quilt shop; she was home, recovering from her near-drowning yesterday. Gregory had carried her to her house and had delivered her into the care of her mother and aunt. That had been more than twenty-four hours ago. He longed to see her, but he knew that he'd just have to wait until she recovered. As best he could, he contented himself with knowing she was in good hands. *Someday I'll be the one taking care of her* was the only thought that gave him peace, as he kept up his lonely vigil from the cottage yard.

When he could force his thoughts away from Rebecca, he thought about Wanda. And Vinny. To get a copy of the marriage license from the state's vital statistics office he'd need the date of the marriage, the full name of the husband and wife, and, the reason the record was needed. "To save my half-sister from a swindler" was not likely to be a reason the state would look kindly upon. Even assuming he could get the required information, he'd have to write a letter requesting a copy of the license, and it could take months for the state to respond. *Wanda's just going to have to trust me, and we're going to have to find a way to prove it together.* Gregory paused, remembering all the detective work he had done to discover who had tried to kill Bojangles. Now he was at it again. But he had to do it for Wanda.

"Gregory!" A female voice called to him from the other side of the cottage. For a moment, he thought it might be Rebecca. "Gregory!" the voice cried again, but he could tell it was an older woman's voice, not Rebecca's.

He went around the cottage and was surprised to see Lydie standing beside her buggy. Even though the sun had come out that morning, the buggy still looked a little wet. After he had delivered Rebecca to her house, Gregory had gone to where she'd told him the buggy had capsized. The horse had righted itself and was standing near the crick. Gregory had driven the buggy to the quilt shop, explained to Lydie what had happened, then had returned to his cottage and fallen into a deep sleep. Lydie had promised to open the shop for Rebecca the next day, so why was she standing here now?

"Hello, Lydie. Is something the matter?"

"No, the shop's fine. How is Rebecca?"

"I haven't seen her today. Mabel and Hanna are looking after her. She's not injured. I think they just want to make sure she gets plenty of rest and good food."

"She'll be good as new by tomorrow. It's so lucky you happened to see her."

"I thank God for that."

"Surely He had a hand in it."

"If it's not about the shop, what brings you out here in the middle of the day?"

"Somebody brought me a note for you." She handed it to him. "It's from Wanda, about a meeting today at three." He read it quickly. "Forgive me, but my instructions were to be sure to read it. I think the person wanted me to know I should get it to you right away."

"The person?"

"Actually, it was an Amish boy," Lydie said, "Delivering the note on behalf of someone else."

"Wanda? Why didn't she just bring it to me here?"

"I don't think it was Wanda. The boy said a man gave it to him."

"Did he say what he looked like?"

"He wasn't very good at describing him. And I didn't want to press him, make him think there was something wrong."

"It's kind of curious," Gregory said, looking at the note again.

"I thought so, too."

"Maybe the man has something to do with this meeting. Wanda calls it a 'big surprise,' says it's important. I guess I'll find out all about it at three. Thanks for bringing this by."

"Glad to be of help." She took a moment to look at Gregory. *Something doesn't seem right about this.* "Goodbye," she said, returned to her buggy, and drove away.

"'Bye, Lydie."

He went inside his cottage and made lunch. After eating it, he still had time until three o'clock, so he decided to go for a long ride on Bojangles. After almost a half-hour riding through the countryside, it was close enough to three that he rode over the ridge to Wanda's farm. He dismounted and left Bojangles untied outside the barn. "Don't go anywhere," he commanded. He knew he wouldn't. Bo had been there so often, he was comfortable waiting for Gregory. And there was plenty of grass to keep him occupied.

As he walked towards the house, Gregory paused. *That's funny, where's Wanda's car?* He looked around. *And the man we're meeting, wouldn't he have driven a car here?* He checked his watch. *Two fifty-eight.* With a shrug, he walked on, climbed the stairs to the veranda, and rang the doorbell. No answer, so he rang it again. "Wanda? Hello?" He could hear the dim noise of the TV. "Liz?" he called, opening the door. "Anybody home?"

No answer. *Maybe I've got the wrong day....* He closed the door and was about to go home, when a worry made him stop. *Maybe something's wrong. I'd better go see.*

He went through the door into the hallway. Looking to his left, he noticed no one was in the front room. He walked down the hall. The TV sound was coming from a room on his right. The door was closed. He knocked. "Wanda...? Liz...? It's me, Gregory." Getting no response, he opened the door. The TV was in the corner but no one was watching it. *Might as well turn it off.*

He walked towards the TV. The door closed behind him and Gregory turned around. "Vinny!"

"Hello, Gregory," Vinny replied evenly. He was wearing a black shirt, stretched tightly over his muscular body, and dark slacks. Gregory noticed how well-built he was. "Surprised to see me?" His tone was light, almost friendly.

"Yes, I am. Where's Wanda?"

"I sent her and her mom on a little errand. They'll be back for the five o'clock meeting, but I'm afraid I'll have to tell 'em it was cancelled."

"Five? The meeting's at three."

"That's one of the meetings. The important one."

"What are you doing here?"

"I'm the 'surprise' that Wanda mentioned in her note."

"You know about that?" Gregory muscles tensed.

"Know about it? I had her write it."

"Why?"

"So you and I could have a little meeting, private-like."

"What do you want to meet about?" Gregory asked. He hadn't moved since Vinny had appeared, and neither had Vinny.

"About what you were doing at Penn State, asking questions about me. I'm curious, Gregory: What'd you find out?"

Gregory shifted his weight. He quickly glanced around the room. There was a window to the outside, but it was closed. *Locked, no doubt.* There was the door. *He didn't lock it, that's good.* There was a small bookshelf, a chair or two, a small sofa in front of the TV, which was mounted on top of a stand with rollers, and the TV, which was still on, tuned to some talk show. "I didn't find out much," Gregory stalled. "You're a pretty mysterious guy."

"I have a feeling you found out a lot," Vinny said. "You might even say, you found out too much."

Gregory realized there was no use pretending. "Well, Vinny, I did find out something interesting. That you are married. Which makes me wonder why you're dating Wanda. My guess is, to get at her inheritance by marrying her. And I wouldn't be surprised if a man named Mancuso is involved." Gregory tried to keep his voice calm and steady, but he could feel perspiration building under his arms.

"I think that definitely qualifies as too much. 'Cause what you found out, Wanda don't need to know, you get my drift?" He took a step forward and Gregory raised his hands halfway to his side. "Getting ready to fight me, Gregory? I don't think that'll turn out too good." Vinny smiled steadily at Gregory.

"What are you planning to do?" Gregory asked, his voice rising.

"Silence you," Vinny responded, his voice changing to a cold hardness. He reached behind his back and withdrew a gun from his belt. Gregory tensed. "Oh, don't worry, I ain't gonna shoot you, Gregory. Too easy to trace. I'm gonna knock you out — " he flipped the gun so he was holding it butt handle out — "and then, you're gonna take a little trip to the bottom of the river. A river cruise, you might call it. Only you've only got a one-way ticket." He took a step towards Gregory, raising the gun.

Gregory sprang behind the TV and rolled it towards Vinny. He dodged, the TV striking him innocuously in the leg, but distracting him enough that Gregory had time to fling the five or six books that were sitting on top of the bookshelf at Vinny, who had to raise his arms to duck. Gregory immediately grabbed the entire bookshelf, lifting it with all his strength, and pushed it at Vinny. It crashed into him, staggering him backwards, far enough away from the door that Gregory had a clear path to it. "Come back here!" Vinny shouted as Gregory yanked open the door and fled the room.

He ran as fast as he could down the hallway, hearing Vinny's footsteps behind him. *Don't let him shoot! Don't let him shoot!* But Vinny was not going to risk a gunshot in the middle of the afternoon with no alibi to his whereabouts, if they ever traced the bullet.

Gregory took the stairs three at a time and sprinted across the driveway towards the barn. "Bo!" he shouted. "Here, boy!" Bojangles turned his head and took a few steps towards Gregory.

Seeing his direction, Vinny ran down the stairs and around the house, where he had hidden his Maserati. He jumped behind the wheel, ignited the engine, and drove into the driveway just in time to see Gregory gallop off on Bojangles. *He's headed home, I know it! Where else would he think is safe?* Vinny gunned the engine and sped up the driveway, racing as fast as he could to the Zook farm. *He may beat me there, but then where's he going to go?*

When Vinny had disappeared, a third party joined the race. The barn doors were flung open and a horse and buggy took off over the pasture, the driver urging the horse at breakneck speed after Gregory and Bojangles.

"Hee-yaiii, Bo, come on, come on!" Gregory and Bo raced over the fields towards the Zook farmhouse. He didn't know where else to go. The farm meant safety to him, and safety was what he needed now. But when he came over the last rise and looked down at the farmhouse, he realized he couldn't go there and endanger everyone's life. There was no phone to call from, so what would they do? A quick glance around revealed that Elam and Henry were nowhere to be seen. *Probably out plowing, or gone to town, who knows? I need to think, but to do that, I've got to hide. But where?* He stared at the farm. *Come on, think! Think!* And then he had it. He dug his heels into Bo. "Let's go, boy, let's go!"

Gregory raced down the ridge toward the barn. *Bo, what am I going to do about Bo? I can't just leave him in the barn, Vinny'll know I'm here.* On an impulse, he continued past the barn and raced to the edge of the large crick. The waters had retreated to nearer their normal height. He jumped off Bo, yanked off the saddle, blanket, and bridle, then took Bo's face in his hands. "Remember that time I rode into the surf on your back? Remember how you loved to swim? You've got to swim, Bo, you understand? Just cross the river or go somewhere, but don't come back to me. DO NOT COME BACK TO ME, BO!" With that, he led him into the water, slapped his rump hard with his hand, and yelled, "Swim, Bo, swim!" To his great relief, Bo moved forward into the water, and, as Gregory turned to run back to the barn, he saw his horse moving slowly but comfortably down the crick.

Gregory ran past his cottage and into the barn. Once inside, however, he had no idea what to do. *Vinny's not sure I came to the farm, but it's the logical first choice.* He looked around. A few bales of straw piled against one wall, an old wagon wheel leaning against another, some farm implements hanging on a third. A *hoe against a gun? I don't think so.* He saw an old barrel and thought about trying to squeeze inside, but he didn't like the idea of being trapped. His best hope was for Vinny not to find him. *I just need time!*

He climbed the ladder to the second floor. Hay bales on half the floor and the other half cleared for basketball. *Nowhere to hide here.* He looked overhead at the beams, and then he had it. He raced for the far wall and began climbing the ladder nailed into it. Up and up he scrambled, as fast as he could, until he'd reached the little platform where he and Rebecca had spent those precious moments. *Her special place. I hope it's special for me.* Once there, he drew his feet underneath him and lay down, so no part of his body would show to anyone looking up.

As Gregory nestled in, Vinny was just turning down the lane that wound past the Zook farmhouse. He slowed his vehicle to avoid running off the road, but there was no way to avoid going past the farmhouse. *They'll just have to be busy and I'll just have to hurry.* He noticed that the lane went downhill towards the crick and then rose just a little towards the barn. He cut the engine to avoid further sound. *Maybe they won't have noticed me.* He realized he wasn't thinking too clearly, didn't really have a plan, except: *I gotta get to him before anybody else!*

The car cruised to a stop some twenty yards short of the barn. Vinny stepped out and looked around. No one. Looking towards the fields, he didn't see anybody either. With a final glance at the farmhouse, he walked towards the barn. He was calmer now, sensing he was closing in on his prey. *Where else would he go on his horse?* Gregory could have gone anywhere, but Vinny had spent a lifetime observing the actions of people under stress, and he knew that the first instinct was always "home," some place that represented safety and security. *If he's not here, then we'll figure out what to do next. He can't hide forever. I'll keep a sharp eye on Wanda, and if he tries to contact her....*

He glanced at the stable, stopped and listened. No sound. *Where's his horse?* He went to the stable and slowly opened the door. Empty. The mules were out in the fields with Henry and Elam. He closed the door. He walked the small distance to the barn, slid open the door, and stepped inside. *If he's here, this is the place to hide.* He smiled. *Or try to.*

He looked around in the complete stillness of the inside of the barn. Slowly he walked along the wall that had the barrel and bales, pushing the bales aside with his foot, tilting the barrel to make sure no one was inside. Satisfied that Gregory was not hiding on the ground floor, he made his way to the ladder and climbed to the second floor. He noticed the hoop at one end, the wide door opened beneath it, the bales pushed against the wall. A few strands of straw lay scattered across the floor, but most of it had been swept to the sides by a broom. "Gregory!" he called out. "I know you're in here." He said it more to amuse himself than anything, but sometimes a sudden shout might flush a bird. Or a man. The only answer was silence. He walked the length of the floor and leaned out the open barn door. Still no one about. *Maybe they've gone somewhere.* Looking again around the room, he satisfied himself that there was no place to hide. *Guess he ain't here.*

He turned to leave, crossing the floor to descend the ladder. Just as he was about to step down, he looked at the wall. Something about the straw there.... It was disturbed, scattered about, as if somebody.... He noticed the ladder nailed to the wall, then looked above him at the beams crisscrossing the ceiling. The ladder seemed to lead to nowhere, so why was it there? He stepped away from the wall a little and looked up again. *Probably there was another floor or something at some time, or they used it to hang the tobacco. Who knows?* He was about to go back downstairs when a tiny platform high up near the ceiling, underneath a small window, caught his eye. He stopped and looked at it hard. *Could a person fit on that?* He considered the climb. And the time: He'd been there a while, someone was bound to be back soon. Why bother? But then he remembered why: If Gregory was hiding there and he left him, and Gregory told Wanda about Carla and blew Vinny's chances to use Wanda's money to repay Mancuso, Mancuso would be upset. And an upset Mancuso might mean a dead Vinny. He went to the ladder and began climbing it.

Below him, a figure sneaked into the barn, watched Vinny's ascent up the ladder, and quietly crossed the floor to the foot of the ladder nailed into the wall. With Vinny focused on reaching the beam high above him, the unnoticed figure began climbing the ladder to the second floor, careful not to make a sound.

On the platform, Gregory heard Vinny coming, rung by rung. He knew he couldn't stay there, and he knew he couldn't consider the situation lying down. He sat up quickly. Hearing the noise, Vinny looked up. A large smile broadened his face. "Why, hello, Gregory," he said steadily. "Fancy meeting you here. I'm afraid your little bird's nest is about to be disturbed." He began climbing again.

Gregory dangled his feet over the edge of the platform, looking around for a way to escape. The ladder was the only way up ... or down. Vinny was only fifteen yards away now. He had to do something. *I'm not staying here like a trapped animal.* But if he wasn't staying, then he had to leave, and the only way to leave was to jump. He considered the beams beneath him. The closest one was very broad. He knew he didn't have the agility to land on the beam and stay, but if he could get his feet on the beam just long enough to throw himself at the next beam over....

He jumped. As he'd hoped, his feet hit the beam but, not intending to land, Gregory needed just enough purchase to spring towards the other beam. He grabbed it with his hands, immediately hoisting himself up until he was seated on the beam. Vinny turned and looked. "Well, well, well," he said, "the bird's done flown the coop. But now where's it going?" And he slowly began to make his way back down the ladder towards Gregory.

Gregory began making his way across the beam as fast as he could. He wasn't sure what he'd do once he reached the other wall; he just wanted to get as far away from Vinny as possible. Vinny, having reached the beam, sat down and began moving himself towards Gregory. The wall was just ahead. Soon Gregory would have to make a decision about his next move. He didn't like the options, because there was only really one: jump again. But this time there would be no beam to hang onto. This time he would have to jump to the floor, some thirty feet below him.

He glanced over his shoulder. Vinny was concentrating on making his way across the beam as fast as he could: hands grasp the beam in front, pull himself forward. Repeat. Gregory looked down. He saw the open hayloft door underneath the basketball net. *Gotta make sure I don't stumble through the door, it's a thirty-foot drop.* He reached the end of the beam and stood as quickly as he could, steadying himself with a hand against the barn wall. He legs quivered a little as he stood, getting his balance. *God, help me to land safe. Deliver me.* Hearing Vinny's heavy breathing a few yards behind him, Gregory leapt as gently as he could towards the floor beneath him.

It wasn't gently enough. When his feet banged into the floor, he was thrown off-balance to his right. His head crashed into the stone wall, and Gregory slumped to the floor, unconscious.

From his perch on the beam, Vinny looked down at the body lying listless on the floor beneath. He waited a minute to see if Gregory moved. When he didn't, Vinny whispered, "Guess my little bird has taken his last flight." He began scooting backwards across the beam: hands near his thighs, push backwards. Repeat. At the other wall, he grasped the ladder, slowly turned himself around, and climbed down. He regarded Gregory unconscious on the floor. *Thanks for making my job easier, pal.* He slowly moved towards his target.

Suddenly, someone stepped in his way, startling him. "Who are you?"

"Someone here to stop you from what you're planning on doing."

Vinny squinted. He didn't recognize the person. "What have you got to do with all this?"

"Plenty. I don't know why you're after my boy, I just know you're not going to get him."

Vinny was confused. "Your boy? Who are you, Mrs. Zook? You're too old to be Rebecca."

"Never mind who I am. Why don't you just get out of here?"

Vinny noticed the push broom the woman was holding and gave a short laugh. "How're you going to make me? With a broom?" he asked scornfully.

"A broom was good enough for Ivan."

"Ivan?" Vinny asked, confused. "You knew Ivan?"

"Intimately, I'm sorry to say."

Vinny considered. *If she knew Ivan, she might know about the money. Gregory might have told her. Who the heck is she? Whoever she is, she's now gotta be part of the solution.* "Look, lady, I don't know who you are, but if you know what's good for you, you'll get out of here as quick as you can. This ain't none of your business."

"That's where you're wrong. It's very much my business."

"Have it your way," Vinny said, and stepped aggressively towards her, fists raised.

She immediately swung the broom at his head, forcing him to duck, then

moved to her right, away from Gregory's body. She didn't want to trip on him.

"You're pretty strong, swinging a broom like that," Vinny said. "But it's still just a broom."

He charged at her full speed, intending to tackle her. She dropped to the floor farther to her right, avoiding the charge and aiming the broom at his feet, thrusting it between his legs. She held on with all her might, so that it wouldn't wrench out of her hands. Vinny tripped, stumbled, and plunged through the open hayloft door, screaming as he fell. Then there was silence.

She got up and went to the barn door. Looking down, she saw Vinny sprawled motionless on the earth. He had hit hard, she could tell that. She wasn't sure from that distance whether he was dead or not, but she didn't care. All she cared about was lying a few feet away.

She bent and touched Gregory's cheek. It was warm. Gently, she probed his head. There was a small bump, but she knew he would be all right. He would come to, look down to find Vinny, not understand what had happened, but let the law deal with Vinny. He had been trying to harm Gregory, perhaps murder him. She didn't understand the situation, but she had complete faith that Gregory did. *He'll know what to do. What's important is, he's safe.*

She looked about her. Draped carelessly over a straw bale was an old horse blanket. She went over, picked it up, snapped it two times to shake out the dust, then brought it to Gregory. He was beginning to stir, his eyes trying to open. She didn't want to be there when he woke up, so she tucked the blanket over him, lovingly stroked his hair, then kissed him on the cheek. "I love you, son," she said, then quickly rose, hurried from the barn, got into her buggy, and drove away. Once again, Lydie King had saved her son's life.

CHAPTER 23

It was the strangest meal she had ever had with her family, Rebecca thought. Everyone went through the motions — "Please pass the chowchow, Mam," "Hanna, these potatoes are delicious!" — but they all were thinking about the envelope that rested against the glass door of the breakfront in the living room. The envelope from the Lancaster Farmland Trust.

Rebecca had picked up the mail on her way home from work and had delivered the envelope to Elam. He had turned it over in his hand, carefully, the way one might handle a baby chick. "Must be the appraisal figure," he'd said, as casually as possible, as if an appraisal of their seventy-seven acres multiplied by $1500 an acre wouldn't suddenly make them very rich. Not that money mattered to them that much. But a great deal of money has a way of changing one's perspective on things, if one isn't careful.

That is why, when the final prayer had silently been prayed and all the dishes had been put away, Elam had asked them to assemble in the living room, where he had solemnly retrieved the envelope and now stood holding it, addressing them all.

"Gregory told me I'd be receiving the appraisal of the value of the development rights for our farm soon, so I'm sure this is it." He paused and looked around the room. "This may mean that we'll be coming into a fair amount of money. The Trust will pay a proportion of this appraisal, which might be $1500 an acre. That's the reason I put off opening this envelope until now, because that could add up to a tidy sum." He put the envelope in his pocket.

"Before I open it, I want to remind us what our faith says about money." He took the Bible off the nearby desk and opened it to one of the marked pages. "Hebrews 13:5: 'Keep your lives free from the love of money and be content with what you have.'" Elam looked around the room. Rebecca, Mabel, and Henry were sitting upright in their chairs. Even Hanna, occupying her favorite rocker, was not rocking but listening intently. He turned to another page and read. "No one can serve two masters. Either he will hate the one and love the other, or he will be devoted to the one and despise the other. You cannot serve both God and Mammon. Matthew." Elam selected the next passage. "And this from Ecclesiastes: 'Whoever loves money never has enough; whoever loves wealth is never satisfied with his income.' Finally, this from Timothy, a verse I know you all know well: 'For the love of money is a root of all kinds of evil. Some people, eager for money, have wandered from the faith and pierced themselves with many griefs.'"

He took the envelope out of his pocket. They all were silent, waiting for him. "We will not let this money lead us from the faith, will we?" He paused, waiting. One by one, his children, wife, and his wife's sister shook their heads. "Good," he said, and opened the envelope. He read the letter carefully, then reported. "The development rights to our farm are $150,000. The Lancaster Farmland Trust will give us a proportion of those rights: $90,000."

Rebecca gasped. Mabel's eyes widened in surprise. Henry broke into a big smile. Hanna asked, "Elam, would that be enough money for me finally get that swing for the porch?" Everybody laughed. "Yes, Hanna," Elam said, "I believe we might just have enough for that swing." He walked to his wife and laid his hand on Mabel's shoulder. "And maybe you'd like a new sewing machine, one that can do fancy stitches, eh?" Mabel smiled and put her hand on top of his. Rebecca smiled, too. It wasn't often she saw her parents sharing a moment of quiet love.

"How 'bout me, Dat?" Henry asked. "We could use a new mule. Ol' Sally's getting kinda slow."

"A new mule is an excellent idea, son. After all, this is going to be your farm, soon's I get my leather shop built."

"You might want to hire yourself a man to help out," Hanna said. "Once Elam goes, it'll be just you, Henry."

"Yes," Elam said, "There'll be lots of changes around here, but we've got time, we don't have to figure all that out yet." He turned to his daughter. "And how about you, Rebecca. Anything you'd like, now that we might have a little extra money?"

"Yes, Dat, there might be. I've been pondering something Mr. Goldfarb wants me to do, and I might could use a little support cash, if I decide to do it."

"That's fine, daughter, just let me know. Now, isn't there someone else who ought to know what's in this letter?"

Gregory! Rebecca thought. *In all this anticipation, I've completely forgotten about him!* The thought of Gregory, and how he had escaped Vinny, produced a tinge of fear. Even though he was all right, the thought of how Vinny had tried to kill him still disturbed Rebecca. For the last two days she had tried to stay with Gregory as much as possible. She'd even asked Lydie to manage the shop. "Yes, Dat, there is someone who ought to know."

"Why don't you go down and tell him the good news?"

Rebecca rose from her chair, walked swiftly out the front door, and hurried towards the cottage. When she got there, she saw a note Gregory had pinned to the door: "Gone to see Wanda. Back soon. G." She was disappointed, but she knew he had an important conversation to have with Wanda, so she sat on the bench outside the cottage and settled down to wait.

Large chunks of earth flew in the air as Bojangles and Wise Guy pounded through the pastures at Cedar Ridge Farm. Gregory and Wanda had been galloping for at least half an hour, and, although their horses showed signs of tiring, Wanda relentlessly urged Wise Guy on, Gregory doing his best to keep up, content to let her ride as long and as hard as she needed.

It had been his idea for them to ride before they talked. For almost two days his brain had been ceaselessly churning through the innumerable questions surrounding Vinny and his attempt to murder him. When he had regained consciousness in the barn, Rebecca had been there. She reported that the EMS squad had already taken Vinny to Lancaster General Hospital. "He's alive," she'd said, "But he has broken a lot of bones and maybe even his back."

When Gregory had tried to explain what had happened, she'd shushed him. So he had lapsed back into semi-consciousness, and the next thing he knew he'd awakened in his bed, with Rebecca spoon-feeding him some of Anna's egg noodle soup. She had assured him that Henry had gone to inform Wanda, so Gregory had given himself a day to recover and a day for Wanda to visit Vinny in the hospital, if she liked, then he had saddled up Bo and ridden over to tell his half-sister all he knew.

He looked ahead of him at Wanda's strong back riding high in the saddle. Her blond hair whipped behind her in the wind. Finally he saw her shoulders relax and, as Wise Guy slowed to a walk and then came to a stop, Gregory pulled up beside her. Seeing her tear-stained face, with more tears brimming in her eyes, he stretched out a hand, she took it, and together they rode slowly back to the stable.

Once there, Gregory hopped off Bojangles, then lifted Wanda down from Wise Guy. She drew herself into his arms and he held her there, feeling her choking sobs in his chest, until she was finally quiet. "Let's sit on the veranda," he said. In silence, they took off the saddles, blankets, and bridles, led the horses through the gate to the pasture, then walked to the porch and sat down.

Gregory waited for Wanda to begin. Finally she said softly, "I'm sorry, I don't seem to be able to stop crying."

"There's a lot to cry about."

"I just don't understand."

"I know. It's kind of unbelievable."

"When I asked Henry to tell me why Vinny was in your barn, he said he didn't know. Vinny is still sedated in the hospital. They say his back is broken. So you have to explain it to me, Gregory. You have to tell me everything."

"I'll try, Wanda, but I don't know everything myself." Gregory took a deep breath. He had no idea whether Wanda would believe him or not. All he could do was tell her what he knew and hope she did. "Vinny was in the barn because he was trying to kill me," he said simply.

"What?" Wanda jumped up from her chair. "That's impossible!" Gregory held her gaze and said nothing. After a long pause, she sat back down. "Isn't it?"

"I wish it were, Wanda, believe me, I wish it were," Gregory said earnestly.

"But why?"

"This is even harder to believe, but I think it's because he thought I was going to break up his plans to marry you."

"Why would you want to do that, Gregory?" Wanda asked, a hint of accusation in her voice.

Gregory raised his eyes briefly to Heaven. *This is it.* He lowered them to look steadily into Wanda's. "Because Vinny is already married."

"That's not true!" Wanda shouted, rising again. "If he's already married, why is he asking me to marry him?"

The answer to that would hurt Wanda the most, Gregory knew, but what could he do? She had to know everything; then she could decide what to believe and what not to believe. "For your money."

"That's ridiculous! He doesn't need my money, he's got plenty of money."

"Not enough."

"Enough for what?" she asked angrily.

"Enough to satisfy the debt your father was trying to pay off with his insurance scam. Five hundred thousand dollars."

Something about that amount struck Wanda. She thought back to the day at the racetrack. "Five hundred thousand dollars, perfect!" Vinny had exclaimed. *So this is what he meant by "perfect."* She slowly resumed her seat. "Go on, Gregory. Tell me all you know."

"I know Vinny's last name is Bandini, not Magnini, like he told you. I know he's married to Carla Mancuso Bandini. I have reason to believe that when Vinny was at Penn State, he helped Carla's uncle, Joey Mancuso, win some large bets regarding the Penn State football team, and my guess is that Vinny went to work for Mancuso and that's when he met your father. I mean," Gregory corrected himself, "Our father."

"But why would Vinny be responsible for our father's debt?"

"From the little I know about how mobsters work, I'd say it's because Mancuso *said* he was responsible. Since Ivan was dead and Vinny had failed to collect, he simply made the debt Vinny's."

Wanda was silent for a moment, trying to make sense of it all. "Is that why he wanted to get married in Las Vegas?" she finally asked.

"I didn't know that."

"There are plenty of lowlifes in Vegas," she continued. "They could help Vinny arrange a wedding — a fake wedding." As the pieces began falling into place, she spoke more rapidly. "And once we were married — or, rather, once I *thought* we were married — Vinny could easily get to my money through a joint bank account."

"Something like that, I guess."

"The scum!" Wanda shouted. Gregory could hear the hurt through her anger. "The dirty scum...." Her voice trailed away in anguish.

Gregory looked at his half-sister. A few days ago she had been happily contemplating her marriage. "I'm sorry, Wanda," he said. "I am so very sorry."

For a long while, neither spoke. All was still around them. Finally, Wanda asked, "Have you told the police?"

"No."

"Why not?"

"First of all, it would be just Vinny's word against mine, and his motive would be hard to prove. But, mainly, because of you. You deserve the chance to talk to Vinny yourself. After that, we can decide what to do. I'm not doing anything unless we do it together."

"Thank you," Wanda whispered gratefully. She closed her eyes. "I'm tired."

"Go lie down. I'll feed Wise Guy something before I ride home. And, Wanda, promise me you'll contact me if you need anything, anything at all, okay?

She opened her eyes. "Okay," she replied, managing a small smile. She stood up, and Gregory stood, too. "I've barely had time to think about the fact that you and I are related," she said.

"There'll be plenty of time for that."

"Or our business."

"Plenty of time for that, too."

"Plenty of time...." Wanda mused thoughtfully. "Daddy's death.... Vinny's betrayal.... Plenty of time, that's what I'm going to need...."

"You've got it. And remember: I'm not going anywhere."

"Good."

Gregory pulled her into his arms and gave her a brotherly hug. *She believes me.* They separated. She smiled wanly and went inside the house. He descended the stairs, fed Wise Guy some grain, re-saddled Bojangles, and rode back to the Zook farm and his next conversation about the incredible events of the past few days.

Rebecca ran to him when he rode up. He swung his leg over Bo's neck, hopped to the ground, and handed Rebecca the reins. "Hello, Bo, you beautiful thing," Rebecca said, stroking Bo's face.

"Hey, save some of that praise for his owner," Gregory said, taking off the saddle.

"I might, if his owner would stop trying to get himself killed."

"I was just trying to find out who Vinny is." He took the saddle and hung it over a fence rail.

"You found out, all right," Rebecca said, reprovingly.

"I wanted to protect Wanda," Gregory protested.

Rebecca slipped off the bridle and hung it on the side of the barn. "That was good of you, Gregory. Just promise me you won't put yourself in danger anymore." She tenderly brushed some strands of hair back behind his ear. "How is your head?"

"Pretty good, considering."

She touched it. "Still a little lump, but nothing serious." She looked at him. "I still don't understand all this, Gregory. Except that I almost lost you."

He took her hand in his. "You'll never lose me," he promised, looking intently into her gray-green eyes, noticing the freckle. What some might see as an imperfection, Gregory saw as God's way of marking Rebecca's beauty as uniquely her own.

"I'll lose you if you don't stop chasing after people who are trying to do you harm," she admonished. "First Ivan, now Vinny. Who's next?"

"How about you?" he teased.

"Me?"

"I'll chase after you, and you'll harm me a lot, if you won't let me catch you."

"Oh, you!" she exclaimed, playfully bopping him on the head. When she saw him wince, she realized she'd hit his lump. "I'm sorry!"

"See there, harming me already."

"Will you be serious for a minute, Gregory?"

"All right, I will. It's just, knowing you feel about me the same way I feel about you makes me sort of light-headed. Shall we sit or walk?"

"Let's walk."

Gregory took her hand and they set off across the fields. "Did you tell Wanda?" Gregory nodded. "How did she take it?"

"Pretty well, considering. I think she believes me about Vinny."

"You were so lucky, Gregory."

"I still don't know what happened. I remember jumping to the floor, then I guess I hit my head and was knocked out. When I came to, there was a blanket over me, just like at Ivan's shed. And I'm sure I heard that same voice calling me 'son.' Could it be my birth mother?"

"It makes sense. But how is it that she's always there when you need her?"

"My guardian angel."

"Mothers are good at that."

"It might mean she's nearby, maybe that she even knows I'm here," Gregory said excitedly. "I wish she'd identify herself."

"Give her time, and maybe she will. Or maybe God will lead you to her. For now, just be grateful somebody was there to save you. I know I am."

They walked in silence for a while. The sun was very warm for November. Some of the fields of corn were plowed and planted with next year's crop; others still had scraggly stalks and neglected ears scattered about. Rebecca picked up a stalk and dragged it along beside her, thinking. She knew she needed to talk to Gregory about Mr. Goldfarb's offer, but she didn't want to. So many difficult things had happened lately — her near-drowning, Gregory's near-murder. She felt overwhelmed. But she had to know what Gregory thought about the offer.

"Gregory," she began, "I need to talk to you about something." She withdrew her hand from his. Sensing it was something serious, he stopped. "No, I want to keep walking." She tossed the stalk aside and they walked slowly on. They had headed, without intending to, towards the dam, and she could hear the faint rumble of water rolling over it.

"Mr. Goldfarb called me last week with an 'offer,' he called it." He waited for her to explain. "He said I could teach a course in quilting — "

"Rebecca, that's wonderful — "

"Let me explain." She took a deep breath and started again. "The course would be at a college in Florida." Gregory's eyes widened, but he didn't say anything. "It wouldn't start until sometime after Christmas, and it would last for eight weeks. Mr. Goldfarb said I could have an art show of my work while I was there. He's trying to 'brand me,' whatever that means." She paused.

Gregory waited, but when she didn't go on, he said, "Is that all?"

"Just that I'd make a lot of money, but that's not what's important."

"What is?"

"My family. The fact that I've never taught before. The fact that Florida is so far away." She looked directly at him. "And you."

He smiled. "Rebecca, I understand that this would be a big commitment, and a big change in your life. But, to give you my honest opinion: I think it is a fantastic offer. You know how I've always encouraged you to be an artist. You know how talented I think you are. But I know you've struggled about how to balance your Amish faith with the talent you feel burning inside you. Maybe this is another sign from God, maybe He's giving you this chance to explore your talent, explore the outside world, find out what others think about your art, maybe learn a new profession like teaching, and figure out just how to balance your art with your faith."

"But I'm not an art — "

Gregory quickly put a finger on her lips. "Yes, you are. And you know it." He looked at her with great purpose. "Don't you?"

She looked back at him. What she saw in his eyes settled her soul. *He loves me. He wants what's best for me.* She slowly smiled, a smile so full of confidence and love, it felt like every pore in her body was vibrating with joy. "I do know it," she said. "I do."

He swept her into his arms and kissed her. She closed her eyes and fell into his embrace, letting herself go, drowning in the warm and wonderful feeling of loving and being loved. She felt his arms, strong around her back, his lips full on hers, the scent of his hair, smelling faintly of autumn leaves. She felt his being meld with her own. She felt whole.

When they broke apart, Gregory said, "Look," and pointed. Rebecca saw that they had arrived at the crick's edge, near the dam where Gregory had rescued her. "Did you ever think how miraculous it was that your body was swept down this fork instead of the other one? If you'd gone the other way, I wouldn't have been able to save you."

"Mam always cautioned me about going down this fork. She always said it was too dangerous. Better to take the safer fork to the right."

"Maybe God's trying to talk to you, Rebecca. Maybe He's telling you not to take the safe fork, but to take the riskier one. Maybe He's saying, 'Go ahead, be an artist, take the left fork. I'll protect you.'"

She looked at him, grateful for his wisdom. "Maybe He is."

"You ever hear of Yogi Berra?"

"Wasn't he a baseball player or something? Johnny used to talk about him."

"Yeah, he was. And he said: 'When you come to a fork in the road, take it!'"

"What?" Rebecca exclaimed, laughing. "That's silly! That doesn't tell you which fork to take."

"Nope. That's your job: when you come to a fork in the crick, take it!"

Rebecca laughed again, and Gregory joined her. He grabbed both her hands and began swinging her around and around, both of them whirling on the bank of the crick like a couple of children, their peals of joyful laughter echoing off the water, up into the heavens, and far, far beyond.

THE END
of
FORK IN THE CRICK

AUTHOR'S NOTE

Growing up in Greenville, SC in the 1950's, I confess I had never heard of the Amish. After an education in the northeast, I had heard about them, but knew nothing about them or their faith or culture. Imagine my surprise, then, to end up married to a woman raised in her grandparents gross-daddy house on their Amish farm near Lancaster, PA, a woman who would be the first in her family to be educated past the eighth grade. My delighted surprise, I hasten to add. For I soon came to admire the Amish for their simple ways, their profound faith, their love of the land, and their deep sense of community.

Some time ago my wife's cousin, Howard, came up with the idea of my writing an Amish novel. The novel began as an attempt to tell a funny story about the challenges my wife, Reba, experienced marrying outside her faith, especially from members of her own family. She, her cousin, and I had many story conferences, and the more we talked, the more the novel changed from being a series of humorous family anecdotes into a real Amish romance, one overlaid with mystery and attempted murder. As I know from a lifetime of writing for the theatre, the final work is often a far cry from the initial idea, but never have I been more surprised to find out that I am the author of not only one, but two Amish romances, with a third on the way, to complete my *Rebecca's Amish Romance* trilogy. I decided to write a novel and I ended up writing three!

I couldn't have done it alone, of course, so thanks are due. To Howard, for the inspiration and detailed notes, especially concerning the Mafia storyline. To Reba's family, Mabel, Anna, and Lydia, for answering my endless queries about Amish life in general and their own Amish experiences in particular. To my sister-in-law and author, Diana Martin, who provided invaluable advice about plotline and character. To members of my immediate family —Mary Wyche, Frank, and Ben -- and my friend Elizabeth Neely for reading the early drafts and giving valuable feedback. And last, but far from least, to my wonderful wife, Reba, for helping me not only with storyline but with all the intricacies of Amish life, from what to call their bonnets to how to harvest tobacco, and myriad details in between.

And to Rebecca, Gregory, and all my other characters for coming to life and surprising me in such delightful and intriguing ways!

If you enjoyed my story, remember that Chickadee Prince Books, the publisher who brought this to you, is a small independent artists' collective press devoted only to quality work, and it needs your word of mouth to survive. Please tell a friend and write a review on Amazon and Goodreads of this book or other CPB books.

Granville Wyche Burgess
November 2017

OTHER BOOKS FROM CHICKADEE PRINCE THAT YOU WILL ENJOY

The Inevitable Witness by Ed Rucker
The *Bobby Earl* Series, #1 - ISBN: 978-0991327478

"A Los Angeles lawyer defends a professional safecracker accused of murder in Rucker's debut legal thriller.... Earl's a shrewd, worthy protagonist, surrounded by exceptional characters, including reliable investigator Manny Munoz and second-chair district attorney Samantha Price. This novel certainly doesn't skimp on twisty plot turns, but retains an understated, authentic approach to the law."
— *Kirkus Reviews*

Bobby Earl is the guy you call when it's time to fix bayonets and go to trial. But when he's tapped to defend a notorious safecracker arrested for killing a decorated LAPD officer, Earl's own life is suddenly in danger, and Earl must dive into LA's dangerous underworld, and battle a court system in which the news media and politics corrupt the wheels of justice.

*

There's More Than One Way Home by Donna Levin
ISBN: 9780991327461

"A witty, modern voice delivers a captivating tale about a mysterious death."
— *Kirkus Reviews*

Anna Kagen seems to have it all: She's young, beautiful, and married wealthy, prominent man. But within the walls of her San Francisco mansion spends her time dodging her husband's barbs and hunting down potential fri for her son, Jack, a 10-year-old on the autistic spectrum.

That old life suddenly seems idyllic when, on a school field trip, she make small error in judgment that sets in motion a chain of events that leads to an boy's death. Suddenly Jack is a suspect, her husband's career is in jeopardy Anna has to choose between loyalty to her son ... and what may be her chance at happiness.

www.ingramcontent.com/pod-product-compliance
Lightning Source LLC
Chambersburg PA
CBHW070952120726
47910CB00004B/1209